PSYCHO HATE

N.O. ONE

PSYCHO HATE

ISBN-13: 978-1-917471-12-1

DEDICATION

For the badass bitches who straighten their own crown,

you're never alone.

We've got your back <3

To those of you fierce enough to bow at the feet of your

queens...we see you.

Warning / Foreword

We love that you've picked up our books! But please, take the warning here seriously if you in any way shape or form have triggers of any kind. This trilogy deals with a variety of subjects, sexual assault, lots of violence, death, characters you may not agree with...

We try to deal with some of the sensitive subjects in a way that isn't completely on page, but we can't guarantee that they won't affect you in some way if they are triggers for you.

If by any chance you have a specific thing you need to know about, feel free to drop us a message on social media, email us, or visit our website—details for these at the end of the book.

If you're the person who likes to check the number of times certain words appear in a book before you read it, here's a helpful word count:

Fuck - 668

Dick - 44

Cock - 37

Cunt - 17

Pussy - 38

For those still with us... ;)

The characters in this series will do what they need to do to get to their end goals. Please don't go into this trilogy thinking that these characters are morally gray because, at times, they are downright abysmal.

Remember, this is fiction!

So, as usual, strap in and strap on.

The main male character can be seen first off *8 years ago* in The Escort Series, but we have made sure this trilogy can be read without having to read anything else first.

Lastly, we hope you enjoy Aleko!

GLOSSARY

Sons Of Khaos

President/Prez: Griffin Michaels

Vice President/VP: Hoops (Leo Clarke)

Sergeant At Arms/Sgt at Arms: Shade (Slate Carter)

Road Captain: Crow (Lucas Minecast)

Secretary: Sledge (Rainer West)

Treasurer: Bear (Brock Levine)

Enforcer: Psycho (Aleko Kastellanos)

Members: Grinder (Diego Russet)

Boner (Felix Gray)

Axle (Rafael Rodriguez)

Diablo (Holden Diaz)

Prospects: Python (Flint McKenna)

Bash (Sebastian Flores)

Toxic Rebels

President: Isaac/Zac Moore

Vice President: Jake Wilson

Sergeant At Arms: Cameron Matthews

Road Captain: Booker (Benjamin Stripley)

Secretary: Jah-jah (Elijah Mountbatten)

Treasurer: Goblin (Graham Whitley)

Enforcer: Brick Earhart

CHAPTER ONE
ALEKO

"Fucking take it. Spread your legs wider and take my dick like a good girl." Motherfucker, this tight little pussy is squeezing my cock so hard I'm afraid I'll pass the fuck out. As soon as I saw her in the crowd, I knew she'd be the perfect after-race treat and, holy shit, I was not wrong.

"Is that all you've got?"

I pause at her words, the combined throb of my dick and her cunt a reminder that we're both getting some hardcore pleasure out of this outdoor, nowhere-near-private tryst.

With my hands firmly wrapped around her hot-pink and light-blue pigtails while I fuck her from behind, I lean in and growl, "You want me to hurt you?"

"I want you to give me everything you've got."

Fucking Christ. Everything I've got? For a brief moment, I wonder if I've already fucked this girl, if maybe she's one of the Khaos Khunts and I'm too drunk from winning my first race in months to remember her. Nah, can't be. A man doesn't forget a pussy capable of choking his dick like this.

"Hmmm, hold on, Cherry Pie, and don't cry your little heart out when you feel my pounding every time you try to sit down." Not giving her time to respond, I press the side of her face into the bed of some dude's huge pickup, holding her down as I slam my hips against her perfect little ass over and over again.

Sweat beads at my brow, my breathing matching the rhythm of my fucks as I slip my hand between the truck and her mound, searching out her swollen clit.

Ah, there it is. I'm a betting man and I'd put my favorite possession on the line and say this girl is about to blow into the warm night surrounded by at least two hundred people just a few yards away.

"Fuck, don't stop. Don't fucking stop." This crazy girl swings her arm back, her fingers latching onto my arm and her nails digging into my skin like she's aiming to make me bleed. Fuck, I want her to make me bleed. In fact, I'm looking forward to seeing her marks on me in the morning when I fuck her all over again.

I grin. Women who demand an orgasm are so fucking sexy. Like, yeah, baby, expect that I'll make you come.

No way am I stopping, my dick would fucking revolt anyway, but the thought never crossed my mind. Why would it? She's hot and tight and her juices are coating my cock, making the friction in her pussy this side of perfect. The only thing better than what's happening right now would be exactly this, but without a condom.

Leaning forward, just a little closer to this fucking beauty, her cherry scent invades my senses once more. It's my favorite flavor, which is another reason I know I haven't fucked her in the past. I'd know a cherry-flavored pussy anywhere. Reaching into my back pocket, I pull out a lollipop, but just before I pop one in my mouth, a better idea comes to me.

A little pinch to her clit followed by a hard thrust is all she needs before her stomach muscles tense and her hips seek out my dick, urging me to push deeper, harder, to give her everything I've got. Just as she begins to come undone, I pull out, replacing myself with the lollipop as I slide the sugary stick along her slit and scoop up her cum. As soon as I pop the sucker in my mouth, my dick pushes back inside her, earning me the most delicious cry from her pretty mouth.

That's right, babydoll, own it.

"Hold on tight, I don't want to give you a concussion." It would be a shame for her to forget this epic fuck in the middle of nowhere. With my hips finding the perfect rhythm against her tight ass, I grit my teeth against the stick of the candy and try my best to hold back my orgasm. Except her taste is invading my senses, my mouth, my nostrils, my entire fucking body.

"Less talking, more thrusting." With breaths shallow and a voice strained from her impending orgasm, I grin at the back of her head and, despite the weed hitting my brain just right, I rear my hips back and pummel her cunt like I want to punish its existence.

Revving engines, huge speakers belting out hard-core bass sounds, and people laughing and screaming all fade away around me until all I can hear is the wet slapping of skin on skin. My groin to her ass. Her hand to the bed of the truck as she searches out something, anything, to hold herself down. We're frantic, our rhythm desperate and our bodies taking control of this entire fucking situation.

When she fights against my hold, I move my hand and plant it on her other hip, accelerating my movements until she rears back and releases a cry of pure bliss into the muggy, North Carolina night.

That sound ends me.

With one final thrust, I move my hand to her shoulder and grunt my pleasure inside her. My dick spurts out jet after jet of cum into the latex as I lean back down closer to her neck and inhale her scent.

Fuck me. I can't stop coming. Between my win in the street race, the celebratory joint, and this girl?

Best night ever.

Once I feel like my knees can hold me steady, I circle the base of my cock and hold the condom down while I pull out. My little Cherry Pie lies there for a second longer and I'm guessing she's trying to regain consciousness from this monumental fuck.

Stepping back, I tie the end of the rubber and look around for a trash can somewhere. Fuck, the nearest one isn't that far away but it's in the middle of a group of racers talking shit.

"Don't move," I tell my little conquest, seriously contemplating taking her back to my suite inside our clubhouse and going for round two or ten. Reaching around, I suck on my lollipop then turn my girl's head around, fingers digging into her cheeks so her lips part like the Red Sea. "Taste yourself, you're fucking addictive." She doesn't know this yet but me sharing my sweets with anyone is a rarity, so when I place the cherry lollipop on her tongue, the sight makes me hard all over again.

Satisfied, I grin, releasing her cheeks when her eyes regain their focus and her mouth wraps around the sugary treat. It's time to get rid of this condom so I can get back to all the things I still want to do to her.

With my leathers pushed down to the middle of my thighs, I spend a good minute pulling them up while I calculate how long it'll take me to run to the container and throw this thing out.

Holding my pants up, I trot over to get rid of my condom, nodding at the racers who, with a quick look up and down my disheveled state know exactly what I'm up to just a few yards aways. Then, I button up my leathers and with a hopeful grin on my face, quickly make my way back to the pink-and-blue-haired chick.

By the time I reach her, she's dressed and walking away in the opposite direction, waving a hand over her shoulder and calling out, "Thanks for the birthday present. Enjoy the rest of your night."

I'm stunned, standing there like a fucking tool watching her jog away with her pigtails bouncing up and down on her shoulders. Being high does not help my reflexes. In fact, it takes my brain a few precious seconds to realize the girl that's got my dick hard all over again is going in the wrong direction.

And by wrong, I mean, not in *my* direction, the lollipop I gave her high above her head like she's waving a thanks for sharing.

What the fuck just happened?

Shaking my head, I follow her, but she's soon engulfed in the crowd. Girl wasn't all that tall so now she's practically invisible. My fingers on the top of my scalp, I drag my nails across my short, black hair from front to back then pull my hoodie up to cover my head.

She's gone and now I'm pissed off.

"Dude, where you going, man?" I whip around at the familiar voice of my chosen brother and frown.

"Did you see where the chick I just fucked ran off to?"

Bear throws his head back and barks out a laugh that can probably be heard clear across the Atlantic to my Greek motherland.

"Are you fucking with me right now? If you can't keep up with your Khunts, I sure as fuck can't." Then he slaps me on the shoulder, nearly causing me to lose my footing. I'm a big guy but Bear is fucking huge, which explains his club name.

"She's not a Khunt, she was…" I trail off, trying to figure out if I imagined her colored pigtails and heavy makeup, which was almost theatrical, as if she was playing Mardi Gras in June. "She smelled like cherries." Even to myself, I sound confused, not quite sure if the information I'm giving is even useful.

"Here." Bear hands me another one of my lollipops and grins like a fucking sociopath. "This will keep you busy until you find another pussy to sink your dick into." Bear is very choosy about the women he fucks, which somehow gives him the moral high ground to bust my balls about my revolving door policy. If it's clean, there's no reason to deprive myself of a good pounding.

Without even thinking, I take the sucker and rip off the paper before popping it into my mouth and murmuring a thanks. Then I walk away, still in search of my trophy fuck.

An hour later, the party's over, the racers are gone and we're back at the compound where all the Khunts await with open pussies and eager mouths.

My nightly ritual with my bikes is nothing uncommon here. Especially after winning a race. The prospects lowered my racing bike, Elektra, and placed her in the garage, where she'll get a thorough run down for next month's race. I run a hand over the gas tank and down to my seat before sliding my fingers along her perfect line all the way to her wasp-like tail end. "You did good, baby."

Next, is my daily bike, Philia. Pushing her to her spot, I back her in and toe the kickstand down, locking the handlebars. The sheepskin glove is hanging from a hook on the wall and once I start wiping her down, it almost feels like I'm cheating on her when thoughts of Cherry pop up in my head. Her sinewy body and tight little cunt take up permanent residence in my mind with every stroke across Philia's bodywork. I can still feel Cherry squeezing my cock like she wanted to strangle it, or maybe just suck up everything I had to give her. By the time I've wiped my bike down completely, I'm hard again.

This shit is going to get fucking old real quick.

"Prez! You should've seen this guy!" Sledge's voice roars out just as we walk into the common room where an entire wall is dedicated to a bar area. Across from that are pool tables, couches, and diner booths for grub time. "Smashed the shit outta that wanker from the Toxic Rebels. What a fuckin' stupid name for a biker gang." Every time he gets drunk, it's like his native country invades his tongue and his British accent just gets thicker and thicker.

"Proud of you, son! Keep that up and you'll be number one in no time." Prez slaps me on the shoulder and grins, his old lady—who's neither old nor a proper lady with the amounts of fucks she throws around this place—Vanessa, smiling wide, all her pretty white teeth showing.

Any other time, I'd be over the moon with this kind of praise. Racing is my happy place, the twenty seconds of freedom from all the chaos in my mind. But my Cherry Pie is holding my brain hostage and I'm too pissed off to enjoy this victory lap.

"Thanks, Prez. I'll make you proud, no doubt." We clasp hands and when I turn around to grab a beer, I run smack dab into a pair of tits, my eyes landing on the cleavage and taking a second to step away.

"Hey, Psycho, congrats on your win tonight." My only response to Rea is a grunt as I grab the offered beer from Violet, who's working the bar tonight. We've got a lot of women hanging out here at the clubhouse—in the heart of the Khaos Kompound—but there's a kind of hierarchy established between them. Vanessa is at the top of that pyramid and a few others hold jobs around this place that don't involve sucking our cocks. As a trained bartender, Vi is one of them.

"Thanks." You don't need to be a genius to know Rea is looking for dick. Whether it's in her mouth or pussy, she doesn't care and, any other night, I would have taken her up on her not-so-subtle offer but I can still smell my Cherry Pie's cunt on my fingers so, at this point, Rea is lacking.

"I can give your lap a winning blow, if you want."

My eyes narrow, making my brows scrunch up at her words. Why can't she just say a blowjob instead of using a ridiculous metaphor?

"Not tonight, get lost." Bringing my bottle to my lips, I take a long pull and turn my back to Rea, who's no doubt pouting. She'll get over it and find fresh meat elsewhere. I'm not worried about her. I am, however, worried that I just turned down pussy.

Frowning, I look around the room. The brothers of the Sons of Khaos are having a good time playing pool, throwing darts, recalling tonight's races, and some, of course, getting their dicks wet. Yet, here I am, with my beer in hand thinking about a girl who just...walked away.

Fucking hell.

After three beers and absolutely no hard-on for any of the girls here, I head upstairs to my suite and take a much needed shower. Our compound is an old psychiatric hospital that the founder of the Sons of Khaos bought with his best friend back in the seventies. Since then, it's been turned into a living and working space for the brothers, with personal suites where the patient rooms used to be and a big fucking kitchen to feed the sheer number of us.

Most of the guys have their own places in town or by the beach, but every single one of the patched-in brothers has a suite of their own here for when they want to crash without taking the risk of riding under the influence. The compound is divided into two main wings, the west is for brothers and eventually their old ladies while the east is for prospects and Khunts. Eventually, the prospects will move to our side but the Khunts stay in their shared rooms, unless they're fucking a brother then all bets are off.

When the charter was created, the idea of building solid bonds between brothers was at the center of all the rules, which means until they're patched-in, prospects have to live at the compound.

The hot water is like a blessing on my battered body. Racing always wreaks havoc on my muscles; the stress before the ride tenses up my shoulders and arms. Fucking usually relaxes me, especially if I grab a joint beforehand.

Tonight, though, my mind is stuck on two pigtails walking away from me after what sounded like a stellar orgasm.

Taking out my bong, I fill it with water and grab my stash of weed from the drawer of my bedside table before filling the bowl. The flames from my lighter lick at the bud and I inhale deeply as the sound of the bubbling water acts like a balm to my soul.

Ah, sweet silence. With my exhale, I expel all the white noise from my mind and finally, fucking finally, relax as I lay my head on my pillow and try to zone out. My hand traveling to my crotch, I picture three or four hotties all over my body, licking and sucking in all the right places. But it takes less than a second for those women to disappear like a puff of smoke and, in their places, the image of a perfectly round ass and two ponytails like handlebars appears. My sweet Cherry Pie.

Instantly, I'm raging hard again as my palm wraps around my dick and squeezes tight enough to make me grit my teeth. The mere thought of Cherry affects me more than any of the Khunts running around half-naked in the compound.

This is a problem for me. A huge fucking problem because I know myself. I know who I am. What I am.

And I know without a fucking doubt that once my focus is honed in on something—or some*one*—it becomes a bone, and I'm the dog that will stop at nothing to bite into it.

Watch out, little Cherry. You've just become my brand new, shiny obsession.

Chapter Two

Aleko

The gavel thuds against the solid oak table and, immediately, Prez has the attention of every brother in the room. Next to me, my best friend Bear sparks up the spliff he just rolled before passing me his gear to roll one for myself.

"Things have been running relatively smoothly," Prez begins, his deep voice commanding its usual respect.

"Famous last words, brother!" Shade chuckles, and as Prez's best friend from way back in high school and now the club's Sergeant at Arms, he's pretty much the only one in this room allowed to bust his balls and get away with it. They both have matching salt-and-pepper-speckled beards, but where Shade's dark hair falls to his shoulders in loose waves, Prez's is short, styled close to his scalp around the sides.

"Fuck off, Shade. If anyone's gonna jinx us, it'll be you, you crazy bastard." Crow—our Road Captain—pipes up, and as usual, his deep, booming laugh practically makes the table vibrate.

"Okay, brothers, time to shut the fuck up and listen so we can get the hell outta here. The girls are making breakfast and I'm fuckin' starved after last night. Speaking of..." He pauses and turns his attention to me. "Great race, you took the number two spot from Brick, which probably pissed the Rebels right off. Now we just need to call out their mystery racer for the number one." He grins, and I know he's genuinely happy for me to be so close to the top spot again.

If someone from our club wins, we get a large cash payout from the race chief—who holds the money from every rider who enters. There are side bets for all the individual races, too, and if someone wants a higher ranked position, they have to call out their opponent on race night with the chief as witness. Men and women who love to ride join us from all over North Carolina, some from other clubs, others just for the fun of it. It's not just about rank though. It'd be pretty shit for the ones who never make the top spots if we didn't have our side races and competitions. Pulling stunts down a straight track is one of my favorite things to do, my Elektra and I working as one to perform dangerous feats is a thrill like no other.

After joining the Sons of Khaos eight years ago, specifically with the intent to race with them, I found a brotherhood I never even knew existed. My actual blood brother was a fucking dick, the head of the Greek mafia in New York. He got too big for his boots and fucked with Marco Mancini of the Italian mafia, then I found out about his fucking trafficking side-quests—young girls, fucking children—and I shot him in front of the Italians and got the fuck out of Dodge.

I left everything behind to start a new life away from the shitty reputation brought on by the Kastellanos name. Away from the graves of my dead parents. And what I found is something pretty fucking special.

A year ago, I became the club's new Enforcer after we lost our brother on an illegal parts run that went wrong. Some fuckers got the jump on us on a highway just outside of town, and while we may have slaughtered every one of them, they got in a few hits of their own.

I've been taking my role seriously, so much so that I stepped away from the street racing circuit for about six months to concentrate on club business, therefore, losing the top position I'd held for so long. I had to start from scratch, but quickly clawed my way back into the higher ranks.

There is now only one rider ahead of me in the top ten rankings of the street racing circuit. One that belongs to our rival gang, the Toxic Rebels. He's never shown his face, not once in the nearly two years he's been racing. But this Cain, or whatever they call him, wears their cut. He was at the bottom of the ranks when I bowed out, and we began to take notice when he beat Sledge months ago.

We never see Cain anywhere other than at the races, not that we make it a point of hanging anywhere near the Rebels. They're in the next town over, in Stonebrook Falls, and we only tend to pay attention when they encroach on our turf. Which has been more often as of late. Their prez, Isaac Moore, recently tried to buy out the hardware store on the outskirts of Rockford Beach. We shut that shit down quickly when the owner, Ronald, came to us for help.

"First thing I wanna bring to the table is that the latest tire delivery from Cooper's was short. This isn't the first time, which means we need to pay them a visit." Prez brings my attention back to him as I lift and lick the glue of my rolling paper to seal it before bringing it to my lips and lighting it up.

"Fuckin' wankers," Sledge mumbles, shaking his head in disgust. He's pretty anal about making sure our suppliers are delivering, and I know for a fact that the Cooper's bullshit is messing with his head. No doubt Sledge is the one who broke the news to Prez after this morning's early inventory.

"Bear, Psycho, pick a Prospect, then take him and Grinder with you to Myrtle Beach this evening. Pay Cooper's a not-so-friendly visit and let 'em know we won't be disrespected like this."

"You got it, Prez." Bear speaks for us all with a strong nod of confirmation, and I can't help but smile. They may call me Psycho but guaranteed, Grinder is legit a psychopath and doling out punishment with him by my side is better than any amusement park in the nation.

I wouldn't say I crave violence, but...I crave violence.

It's been way too long since I last beat the shit out of someone. I've even been hanging around the club's strip joint—Rocks Off—more often recently, in hopes of one of the patrons stepping out of line.

"Next up customs. I know y'all have a couple of big jobs in at the moment, just let me know if you need any more help and we'll get some guys on it."

"We're good for now, Prez. Might ask one of the prospects to come in and be our bitch for the next few days though." Hoops, our Vice President, runs the legit garages we operate from the compound; Khaos Kustoms and Khaos Autos. He prefers to work in the customs side, says his days of repo-ing trucks and fiddling with shitty engines are behind him, but he still oversees the general operations.

We quickly run down the repo work on the schedule as Prez delegates the different jobs to our members.

"So, Bear, you had something you wanted to bring to the table about the strip club?"

With his black short-sleeve T-shirt showcasing the club logo tattooed on his inner forearm, Prez rests his elbows on the table—the same tattoo each patched-in member has somewhere, thanks to Shade.

We have all tried to encourage him to open up a shop, but he said he needs the right location for that kind of thing. Finding an empty building in Rockford Beach that he could use is like finding unicorn shit with sparkles, plus we all think he's got a thing for the tattooist in the next town over.

"Yeah, we've lost a couple of the girls over the last few weeks. One fell in love, and one decided she couldn't hack it anymore. I've asked Candie to set up some interviews next week and just wanted to approve new hires and make sure we were all aware when we see the new faces." Bear is our Treasurer, keeping track of the money coming in and out of the club from both our legal and illegal businesses. He continues explaining to the table who owes us money, meaning I'll be a busy boy over the next week.

Ninja, my pet rat who's more like my baby, jostles around in my hood, crawling up to sit on my shoulder and nuzzle into my neck. He's been asleep since I served him his favorite breakfast of cut up bananas mixed with grains and seeds all served in his orange ceramic bowl, not metal or else the ultrasound noises could hurt his ears.

I take a final drag of my smoke, passing it to Sledge to finish off because sharing's caring as I pick out a cherry-flavored lollipop from the pocket of my hoodie. I pull out an extra one for Ninja, opening it up and placing it on the table. Running down my arm, he gets comfortable and begins licking at his sweet treat. Seems like he has a taste for cherry now, too. It's been too long since I've tasted her scent and this is the only thing I can do to keep her close for now. Knowing I'm going to be busy chasing debts means less time searching for my Cherry Pie.

I'm hoping she turns up at the next street race night because, other than knocking on every door in town before expanding my search, I have no idea if she's even from Rockford Beach. Only problem is, that means I have to wait a whole fucking month and that's just not gonna work for me.

Prez calls an end to the meeting and we all stand, leaving the room that was once an actual chapel for the psych hospital. Smells of pancakes and bacon waft through from the large dining room beside the kitchen, and now I know why Bear is pushing through the brothers to get there. It's his favorite.

"Oh, yes! Come to Papa." Bear practically salivates over the food as he grabs a plate from the open-hatch counter leading to the kitchen, piling food onto it from the trays Sabrina and Vanessa have prepared.

"Save some for the others, Bear," Vanessa, the Prez's old lady, chastises with a small smirk playing at her lips. She exchanges a look with Sabrina and they both roll their eyes, communicating without words. Sabrina is mute and has been since forever. The club saved her from a shitty situation years before I arrived and she's taken on a kind of mother-hen role to the Khunts.

"My mama always said, 'You eat when there's food 'cause I don't cook for one.'" Sabrina cocks her head at Bear, then nods like his response should be our new motto.

For a silent woman in her fifties, she's a formidable force.

Bear doesn't bring up his mother very often and when he does, it's always obvious how much love he has for her.

"Hey, Psycho, want me to make you up a plate?" Rea, the red-headed Khaos Khunt sidles up to me, so close I can smell her overwhelming perfume. It's musky and spicy and everything my mystery Cherry isn't.

The distaste is difficult to hide as I just stare at Rea, a brow raised. I can't help but sigh, closing my eyes to hold back my crazy because she is disrespecting my woman, the only one who has a right to be this close to me. Okay, Rea doesn't know that yet, so technically, the disrespect isn't intentional, but I'm having trouble separating real life from my fantasies right about now.

"Is that a yes or a no, sexy?" If it was at all possible, Rea moves closer, her tits rubbing against my arm. Luckily, it's covered by the long sleeve of my lightweight zipped hoodie, but I'm going to need to wash this now so my mystery woman doesn't get jealous of another woman's scent on me.

"No, Rea. Get the fuck away from me." I move from my position against the wall beside the door, where I stopped to daydream about my girl.

The little huff Rea lets out isn't cute like she thinks it is, and I ignore her as I head over to Bear. He's ramming his face with syrup-covered bacon and pancakes, in fact, I'd go as far to say he's inhaling them.

"I'm going for a ride, I'll be back for the run to Myrtle Beach later." Patting the top of his back, I don't stop, heading toward the exit on the other side of the room.

"Later, Psycho." His words are muffled around the food and he raises a hand. He knows me well enough to understand that when I need a ride, I don't want human company. Just me, my sugary sweets, and my favorite long-tailed companion.

Being part of the brotherhood is amazing, one of the best things that ever happened to me, but sometimes I just need to be with my own thoughts. We all have those moments though. Not one of us is without his own traumas or fucked-up past. This is why we all have our own separate places in town, for down time.

It feels as though my skin is itching from the inside, eager for me to touch, taste, smell, hear, fucking *see* my Cherry in person again.

I need to ride. I need to hunt. I need to find her.

It takes me a few minutes to make sure Ninja is comfortable and secure in his travel pouch I had custom made to fit above my handlebars, because I don't plan on riding within the limits of the law today.

When I find a long stretch of relatively clear road, I twist the throttle and lift the front of Philia, pulling a wheelie and finger-waving at the kids in the back of a Ford Focus as I pass.

I wonder if Cherry wants kids. She'd look fucking amazing with my baby in her belly. It'd be a permanent connection between us that could never be broken. *Fuck.* I want to put a baby inside her. Kids aren't something I've ever really thought about, but I want to do everything with this woman.

Five fucking hours I've been riding and walking around town, checking shops, places of business; frightening the shit out of some people, and having a little catch up with others. Most of the people in this town know the Sons of Khaos aren't totally the evil bastards others may think we are. We keep the place clean of hard drugs and guns, and when the sheriff's department can't—or won't—handle a problem, the people come to us for help.

Except the ones who don't. The ones who would do anything to get us away from Rockford Beach, to get the hooligan motorcycle gang away from their expensive homes and precious children. Fucking pricks.

They're usually the ones who have begged to borrow money from us, only to not pay it back on time. So, of course, we've had to pay them a visit, remind them of the deal they made, and make sure they fucking remember who they owe.

It's almost time to head back to the compound to meet Bear, Grinder, and whichever prospect Bear has chosen to come with us, but I'm just gonna do one more lap of the business district again to see if she's one of the many leaving work around now.

The sound of sirens makes me growl under my breath, pulling over so the ambulance can pass; those few seconds of me not moving could mean all the difference between finding her and not. Ninja reminds me he's here as he pokes his nose out from his little riding pouch in between my windshield and handlebars, so I pet the underside of his chin. It calms me, somewhat. I may not be completely rational about what's annoying me right now, but the need to find her is almost eating me alive.

As this is only a ride around town, I'm wearing my half-face helmet, meaning my mouth is free and clear for my lollipops. I must've gone through at least twenty, but I stocked up on that shit at the supermarket about an hour into my search. It's the only way I can keep her cherry scent with me at all times.

With a sigh, and another unsuccessful search through the business district, I realize it's time to head back. Club business waits for no man, and as much as I need to bury my cock inside that crazy tight pussy again, I'll never let my club down.

I'll check Bar Alley when we get back. If she's not there, I'm knocking on doors tomorrow. I bet Sledge could draw me up one of those portraits based on a description like those cop artists can.

Yeah, that's what I'll get.

I'm not above making every one of these fuckers un-comfortable in order to find this woman.

There's no way I'll let her escape my reach.

CHAPTER THREE
ALEKO

By the time we hit the road, it's well past eight and even though mere mortals can expect the trip to take a little over an hour and half, we'll be shaving at least twenty minutes off that. And no, it's not all about the speeding, although there is that, but on bikes we can avoid all the summertime traffic that plagues Myrtle Beach. Hell, it's no better here in Rockford Beach.

Without Prez leading the pack, Bear and I take the lead, Grinder right behind me, and Bash, our wide-eyed prospect, bringing up the rear with the bike he built from parts when he first joined the ranks. It's a great machine, too bad it still looks like a piece of shit since he hasn't had time to pretty up the body work.

Outside of the street races, we tend to stay under the radar, but it's impossible to resist weaving and speeding down a two-lane highway with little to no traffic for most of the ride. Not to mention the high from taking the bike to dangerous speeds and feeling our bodies become the machine. The adrenaline is like nothing else in the world, at least for me.

It's total and complete freedom in every sense of the word. Freedom to place your life in the hands of your riding skills, freedom to feel the muggy air turn cool as it finds ways to touch your skin.

Now, I may be a crazy motherfucker but I'm not a stupid motherfucker. We all wear helmets on our bikes. We also wear leather gloves and jackets and a good pair of jeans and steel enforced shoes. Not a single one of us escaped the inevitable fall in the early days. Hell, the first time I hopped on, close to ten years ago, I almost fell on the spot. The weight surprised me but mostly the road was uneven and my right foot slipped. Those assholes I now call my brothers still rag on me about that shit.

The sun has set for at least twenty minutes by the time we slowly roll into the distribution center that looks like a legit business shipping out their goods. To be fair, it's exactly what these guys do, except there's nothing legit about this particular loading dock. In fact, we're supposed to be their only client, which begs the question...who the fuck is this asshole riding away as we all line up our bikes on the side of the building?

Trying to make eye contact with the guy is impossible since his visor is blacked out and he's dressed in all black leather, not an inch of skin to clue us in to who he could possibly be.

"That ain't ever a good sign, man." My only answer to Bear is a nod as my eyes follow the red flash of the rider's back brakes illuminating North Carolina plates before the booming sound of an open throttle through custom pipes triggers a nearby car alarm.

Pointing a gloved finger in the direction of the bike, I call out to Grinder. "Follow him, get his plates. I want information on this asshole." Grinder doesn't hesitate, speeding after the guy without giving me lip. Unlike Bash, who's just asking for a kick in the ass.

"Maybe he's just an employee going home for the night?" We all turn to the prospect, visors up and eyes shooting withering glares his way. "What? I mean, it doesn't have to be something bad, right?"

"Christ, this is why prospects are to be seen and not heard." Bear and I chuckle but it's half-hearted because while Bash is still living in a fairy tale where good things happen to good people, we know better.

If it smells toxic, then it probably *is* toxic.

"I'm just sayin'—"

"Well don't. Shut the fuck up, Prospect, and learn something." Bear's usually the happy-go-lucky one of us all, but that lone rider leaving our fucking supply hangar doesn't bode well for the club.

"Oh, so that's why we call you Bear? You look all cute and cuddly but then you show your teeth and bite a limb off."

Why is he still talking?

Stepping in front of Bash as Bear keeps walking toward the warehouse, I slam my helmet against his chest, making sure I have his full attention.

"Don't poke the fucking Bear, Prospect. If you do, we won't be able to bring your bike back to the compound. You get me?" Bash's Adam's apple bobs once, twice, before he nods with rising enthusiasm as his brain catches up to my threat. "Come on." I ruffle his mop of dirty blonde hair as I push him toward the building. It's time to get down to business.

We walk in as a unit. Three big guys with promises of death swimming in our eyes always get our work partners' attention, but before we dole out punishments, we want to make sure we're not wrong. It's the nice in us.

"What's shakin', Darryl?" Bear slaps on his million-dol-lar grin, the one that puts others at ease, while I take a little stroll around the too-empty warehouse. Bash follows me while Bear walks around Darryl and sniffs at him like a fucking dog.

Christ, he's creepy when he wants to be.

"Shouldn't this place be full of our shit?" Bash's words are barely loud enough for me to hear, just as the roar of Grinder's bike rumbles outside

"Yup." The merch is divided in two rows on either side of the building, mirrored in quantity. I mean, it could just be an organizational thing. I'm no expert in stocking and distributing but I can sniff out a con like a basset hound sniffs out blood.

In a matter of minutes, Grinder is at my side whispering. "Got the plates but I lost him in Myrtle Beach North." I nod, knowing Python will be able to find something on this guy soon enough.

"How're the kids, man? Taking a vacation this sum-mer?" Bear looks all relaxed and friendly but when he slides his hands into his pockets, I recognize his stance. The one that puts him up and above his enemies. The intimidator sizing up his prey.

"Good, good. You know, happy to be out of school." Darryl is pretending to be at ease but his eyes are following me and, even from here, I can smell the stench of fear seeping out of his pores. "We're looking at the Blue Ridge for a week or so. Gonna visit my sister-in-law around those parts so the boys can go camping and my wife can get out of the heat." Fuck, I hate having to kill fathers. I know what it's like to grow up without a father.

"Summers are brutal for sure, man. For fucking sure." Bear is toying with him like a cat messing with a petrified mouse.

"Yeah, and she's six months pregnant so it's even harder for her." Goddammit, expecting fathers shouldn't be this fucking stupid. Bear turns to look at me and without saying one damn word, we hold an entire conversation.

"Are we gonna spare him?" Bear starts.

"Because he's got kids?"

"And a wife preggers."

"Whose fucking fault is that?" I end our silent back and forth, feeling like I should feel some type of regret but not enough to disobey club law.

And that's the crux of the problem, isn't it? This douchebag made a conscious choice to betray us knowing damn well what the consequences of his actions would be.

This is not on us. Our laws are clear and they are explained before any deals are made.

"So, tell me something, Darryl." Bear takes a step closer to the guy and slaps him on the shoulder like they're about to have drinks and a smoke. "What's goin' on here?" One arm waves around the space like Vanna fucking White presenting the vowels on *The Wheel of Fortune.*

"Whattaya mean? I was just organizing, that's all." At this point, Bash and I are one hundred percent invested in this conversation. It's obvious he's going to lie but how far is he willing to go?

"Hmm, organizing. How old are your kids, Darryl?" From the corner of my eye, I see Bash turn to look at me and, sure as shit, his knitted brows scream confusion.

"Watch and learn, Prospect," is all I have to whisper as I mentally take out the popcorn and enjoy the Bear Show.

"Ah, eight, five, and three." Darryl speaks slowly and I can almost hear his mind whirring as he tries to figure out Bear's one-eighty in this conversation. Me? I just lean against the crates and grin.

"Damn, you've been a busy rabbit." We all chuckle but it takes Darryl a couple of confused seconds to chime in, looking like he'd rather give himself a poison ivy handjob than have this conversation with us.

I'm a little insulted, to be honest. We're trying to save his life and here he is, mentally insulting us.

"My Annabelle is beautiful so, ya know, it's hard to control myself. She only wanted two but ain't no way I'm using condoms."

Oh fuck. Shaking my head, as if I actually give a shit—I really fucking don't—I push myself off the crate and make my way over to Bear, who has now dropped all pretense of niceties. Knowing his past, this motherfucker right here just signed his death warrant. Any ounce of guilt Bear was having about leaving his kids orphans just poofed right into nothingness.

"Yeah, I gotcha. Showing her who's boss, huh? A man fucks his woman whenever he wants, however he wants, right?" Bear's laugh is nothing less than deadly but this asswipe thinks they're having a heart to heart.

"Damn straight! I tell her to shut up and take it." This time, I laugh outright, a roar that bounces off the steel walls and roof like a boomerang. Dude is dead-man-shaking in his steel-toed boots.

In a nanosecond, Bear has him pushed up against the crates on this side of the warehouse, his huge fucking hand wrapped around Darryl's throat, squeezing hard enough to get his full attention but not enough to kill him. Yet.

"You think because she signed a piece of paper that you can rape her whenever you want?" Bear's words are deadly but he takes control of his emotions and gets back on track as Darryl shakes his head vehemently. "Now, imagine I'm your five-year-old and explain what the fuck you're trying to do here, Darryl."

The subtle smell of ammonia makes me groan with frustration. Goddamit, dude's pissed himself. When I look down at his crotch, sure enough, the crotch of his jeans is a darker blue than the rest of the whitewashed denim. Fucking idiot.

"I-I-I was j-j-just trying to—" Bear slams the back of Darryl's head against the crate and grits out another warning. I swear, we're too nice for our own good.

"Lie again and I'll become your baby mama's new fuck buddy." That gets Darryl's attention but does he decide to give us the whole fucking story?

No. He fucking does not.

"The trucks left a little later than we anticipated. That's why the warehouse isn't full and that side—" Again, his head is slammed against the crate and this time, Bear's face is only an inch away from Darryl's trembling mouth. Is he about to cry? Jesus, Mary, and a fuckload of animals, he just might.

Taking a step forward, I decide it's time to be the good cop. Fucking laughable since you should always fear the quiet ones.

"Who was the guy leaving when we got here?" I swear to fuck, if he lies I'm going to put a bullet in the dead center of his forehead.

"Fuck." The single word escapes from between his lips like a silent fart in the middle of the night.

"Bear, I do believe he's catching on," I say, my eyes fixed on Darryl's face as fear replaces any trace of blood flow, turning his skin ashen.

"I didn't have a choice, I swear I didn't. He was gonna kill me—" Bear shuts him up with the roar of only one word.

"Who?"

"The Rebels. Toxic Rebels." Dude pisses himself again and for a second I wonder just how much coffee he's had today to make him piss like a fountain.

I look at Bear and shrug. The law is the law. Without a single word, I pull out my gun, silencer firmly in place, press it into Darryl's eye, and pull the trigger.

There's a reason we never take off our gloves...never know when business needs to get done.

Bear hands me his knife. His stone-cold grin reminds me of what exactly he's capable of doing.

"Thanks, brother." My tongue darts out to the side and my head cocks to the right as I apply myself, making sure my handwriting is legible.

The letter "T" is first, I capitalize it just like sweet Ms. Templeton taught me in first grade. To be fair, all four of the other letters follow suit since writing cursive with a knife on a dead man's forehead is way more work than I need.

THIEF

Perfect. At least the cops won't have to guess why he's dead. We're generous with taxpayers' money.

When Darryl's lifeless body falls to the floor, I hold out my hand to Bash and nod to the nearby table. "Hand me the pliers." Without a second thought, Bash hurries to the table, grabs the pliers, and slaps them into the palm of my hand. In this moment, I know he'll be a great addition to the club one day. This is his first kill, and contrary to other prospects before him, he doesn't even flinch at what's gone down tonight.

The bullet wound is a through and through, which was my intent. Using the pliers, I latch on to the bullet now encased into the container behind him and pull it out. It takes me a couple of tries, what with the blood and brain matter making it slick but it's all about patience and finesse. I've got that shit in spades.

A sudden image of my Cherry Pie flashes in my mind, making the pliers shake and the bullet fall to the floor, the metal against concrete sounding causing me to jump.

"What the fuck, Psycho?" I shrug at Bear's confusion. It happens.

"What about his wife?" Bash asks like he's wondering about what we're eating for dinner and not how an innocent is supposed to survive with three kids and one on the way without her husband's income.

"She'll be taken care of." Bear doesn't hesitate. He may be a ruthless motherfucker but when it comes to women and children, his softie teddy bear heart shines like a fucking beacon.

"Should I start calling you Step Daddy Bear?"

Asshole pushes me hard enough to make me lose my footing but not enough that I step into the rapidly growing pool of blood.

"Grab his keys." Calling back to Bash, I point to Darryl's jean pocket and hear the prospect groan. Another reason why gloves are great...nobody wants another man's piss on his hands. Well, unless you're into that shit, then it's just a matter of personal choices.

When Bash isn't immediately at my side, I stop and turn only to be greeted with an interesting scenario.

Grinder is giving Bash a tutorial on collecting trophies. With a quick glance around the outside property, I settle in and watch as Grinder takes the pliers and forces Darryl's mouth open.

"There are rules to this, Prospect," Grinder points the pliers to Bash as if what he's about to say is the subject of the essay Bash will have to write when we get home. "First, get to 'em quick before rigor mortis sets in. Anytime beyond four hours is just going to be a hassle and nobody's got time for breaking jaws. It's messy."

Bear brings his knuckles to his mouth, his wide grin pressed into his gloves as Grinder takes his hobby really fucking seriously. In fact, he's been looking for an heir to continue the tradition in case he's suddenly killed in action.

Dude's fucked up but we love that psycho.

"Rule number two, choose healthy teeth. They're prettier. Nobody wants rotting teeth in or out of the mouth." He's not wrong. "And last but definitely not least," Grinder pulls up his black nylon neck tube, covering up his mouth and nose making his next words muffled. "Dead man's breath ain't pretty."

Bash is too slow to act as Grinder pushes down on Darryl's jaw and inserts his pliers. One quick pull later, he's showing off his new prize like he's just won the lottery.

"Number sweet sixteen." Looking back down at Darryl, Grinder pats him on the cheek and coos, "You'll always be special."

Not sure what to expect with Bash, Bear and I are pleasantly surprised when his only reaction is curiosity.

"Holy shit, I didn't know you could take out the entire fucking roots, that's killer!"

Grinder looks over his shoulder at us as he exposes his face again, big grin and all teeth, "We've got ourselves a winner, boys."

That's our signal that Bash will one day soon become a full-fledged member. But nobody's telling him that, though. Not yet, not when there's still fun to be had.

After calling our crew to come pick up our merch—tires, muffler kits, small body parts—we close up and put the key in the mailbox that our brothers will have to rip open. It works out this way, keeps the cops guessing. Then we're off, riding like fucking kings on Highway 17, all the while keeping an eye out for any flashing red and blues.

We all have rooms at the compound but it's almost midnight and I'm still restless from the adrenaline rush. At least that's what I keep telling myself. What I really want is to find my girl and fuck her ten ways to Sunday with an extra five on Monday for good measure. I want to see how far I can take her, what her breaking point is so I can take her to the edge and drag her right back.

Once we've reached the city limits of Rockford Beach, we all go our separate ways as I turn toward Old Towne where my small one-bedroom two floors up from a popular bar on the strip awaits me.

Do I actually go home? Fuck no. Instead, I go straight to my garage where I leave my bike to rest while I go on the hunt.

I walk. Then walk some more. On a few occasions, I have to push a couple of college kids off me right before they puke their guts out. It may be summer vacation but this place has a healthy amount of summer classes happening and, some nights, it's worse than during the fall and spring semesters.

Grinning at the sound of an ambulance speeding by, I imagine some poor idiot drowning in his own vomit.

Lesson to learn, kids. Always know when to stop because getting slapped awake by paramedics ain't a good look.

Just as I reach the stopped ambulance, I see two paramedics heading for a guy slumped over someone's property, not seeming to move when they try to lay him down on the stretcher. Ah, the joys of living on Bar Alley.

The guy is taking vitals while the other one straps the kid in, her ponytail swishing from side to side as she checks out her handiwork. I grin, one eye on the kid, curious to know just how badly he's doing when it hits me.

Cherries.

It takes me two steps to register what I'm actually smelling before I react, turning to see the paramedics slam the back doors before speeding off toward the hospital, I'm guessing. The huge number one on the red and white ambulance tells me exactly where she'll be going next. So, like the patient man I pretend to be, I grin, turn due west, and think about all the different ways I'm going to make her pay for keeping me on edge all this time.

Chapter Four
Mackenzie

"When he woke up and caught me trying to change the bedding, I told him I'd just spilled my glass of water." Spence shakes his head, clearly mortified at himself for getting drunk enough to piss the bed last night—the first time his new boyfriend slept over.

"Did he believe you?" I faux-shudder, laughing at my best friend sitting across from me.

"Pretty sure he didn't because he was up and in the shower before I finished pulling the sheets off the bed. He did stay for breakfast though." Bright-blue eyes meet mine sheepishly and he shrugs with a grin etched across his face.

Last night was the first time I've shown him a little piece of my other world; the motorcycles, the racing, the thrill of it all. He had agreed to come with me for my birthday because, and I quote, "If you think I'm not getting legally fucked up with you for your twenty-first, bitch, please, do you even know me?" The new boyfriend coming along was just a bonus. Raheem is a fun addition to our little duo, though he's a little quiet so I'm not sure how long this one will last. That doesn't stop me from encouraging him.

"Oh, he's a keeper then, Spence. Especially if he's willing to stick around after waking up in your piss. Maybe he's into that?"

"He's not." We both laugh when the department alarm goes off, a voice coming through the speakers in every room letting us know we're up.

Someone has collapsed, unresponsive, requires paramedics. Spence and I gear up and head toward the garage, jumping into the ambulance before I turn on the engine and we're off, sirens blazing.

With it being after midnight, there is barely any traffic on the road, making it easier to maneuver the large vehicle around the cars that pull over to clear our path. Being the EMT in our duo, I tend to do most of the driving, which I'm happy with because Spence drives like an eighty-year-old man who forgot to wear his bifocals. He's a fully qualified paramedic, which is something I just don't have the extra time to study for right now. I'd love to, one day, but that's something that has to wait until I can free myself of my brother, Jake—which is coming around sooner than I thought it would.

After our dad died almost five years ago, Mom lost her shit and fell into a deep depression. She tried to commit suicide on more than one occasion and I did my best to look after her, but I was only sixteen and there was only so much I could do for her. Six months later, Jake took over all the finances when Mom had to be committed to the psych ward for her own safety. He also became my legal guardian because he was twenty-seven at the time.

The last five years have been a total shit show that I've had to grin and bear for the sake of my mom. My brother isn't a nice person, which is putting it lightly. If I'm honest, he's a giant fucking abusive dick—and not the good kind that bruises pelvic muscles. He's the Vice President of the Toxic Rebels motorcycle club in Stonebrooke Falls, and his position affords him a lot of privileges around town.

When the time came that I was old enough to look after myself, he began using his position as the conservator of Mom's finances and health to keep me under his thumb.

He holds too much fucking power and I hate it, but I can't do a fucking thing to stop him...yet. The money I earn as an EMT goes to him and the club as my payment for the trailer I live in, food to eat, and the motorcycle they allow me to ride. Anything I've earned in bonuses has gone into a secure box in the storage unit I've been able to keep hidden from my brother. It's about an hour out of town, heading inland, and holds some of my dearest possessions. If things go well over the next year, I'll be able to afford to pay for Mom's care myself and my own apartment.

It'll all be a giant fuck you to my brother dangling Mom's life over my head.

The same way he dangles Dad's death.

He blames me.

I blame me.

Dad was the whole reason Jake and I fell in love with motorcycle racing. He was a professional back in the day, winning around all the famous circuits, several trophies in his cabinet—which my brother has long since sold off, along with our family home, all to aid the funding of his motorcycle club. My dad was my literal hero, as cliché as that is. He taught me everything he could about racing before his accident, and I've done what I can to learn more since then.

Working outside of the club gives me a little more free-dom than Jake wants me to have, but he's not complaining because of the extra money I'm bringing in. It means that every three days, I'm unavailable for twenty-four hours and he fucking hates having to work around my schedule. As long as I answer to his every whim when I'm off, I can avoid a beating and my concealer stash doesn't get used.

His—or the club's—whims usually consist of me drug running, race night responsibilities, and working the homemade bar in the trailer park I call home—as do the club sluts for the Toxic Rebels. I detest every second, but a girl's gotta do what a girl's gotta do to keep her mom and herself alive. Not that the drugs I'm responsible for moving ever reach their destination. They're also stashed in my storage unit, along with the fake placebo replacements that actually do get delivered. Although, it's been about two weeks since I last did this, and it's usually a weekly thing. Either someone's been complaining about the quality of the goods, or someone knows what I've been doing. They've had me behind the bar more often lately, I suspect so my brother can keep an eye on me.

The hours he's been making me work means I've had less time to visit Mom lately, although she doesn't react to me being there half the time. On last week's visit, just before my birthday, she barely opened her eyes. That didn't stop me from telling her how excited I was to be celebrating my twenty-first birthday and what my plans were. She even knows what I'm plotting for Jake and the Rebels.

It's not like she's going to tell anyone.

"What's the ETA, Mac?" Spencer is on the radio to dispatch, informing them we're on the way.

"Ten minutes." I know these streets like the back of my hand. Only five minutes from the location we're headed is where Thursday night's street race was held—where riders from several clubs around North Carolina come together to determine who the best racer is. Occasionally, there's a solo racer trying their hand for the top spot because there's a huge payout at the end of the season in November.

The Rebels held the first two spots in the leaderboard up until Thursday, when a rider from the Rebels' rival club, Sons of Khaos, took the number two from Brick. It was some dude they call Psycho who's been off the racing circuit for a while so I haven't seen his face yet since I've only been allowed to go for the last year.

I tend to avoid the SOK guys like the plague, but this Psycho guy that beat out Brick was a fucking beast on the track. His helmet was full coverage, but I'd recognize it again in a heartbeat. The demonic design on his lid made him look like a badass. He didn't take it off to reveal his face before I moved away from the finish line, though. If any of the Rebels had caught me anywhere near their rivals of my own free will, my brother would issue another of his punishments.

That's about all I remember from Thursday night, considering I was almost as piss-the-bed drunk as Spence by the time I got home. Well, I also remember the hottie that made me come harder than I ever thought possible in the back of a pickup truck. Best twenty-first birthday gift ever. Jake allowed me the night to myself, being my birthday and all, so I took Spence with me to the street race. Obviously, we spent it as far away from The Rebels as possible or there's no way I would've celebrated the way I did. I could've spent the night in a bar or club, but there's just something about the smell of high octane and burnt rubber that makes me happy.

"On scene." Spencer's voice informing dispatch that we've arrived cuts through my thoughts.

I pull up the ambulance beside the nightclub, seeing straight away where the person we need to help is lying—if the crowd of bystanders is anything to go by. Rubberneckers with their phones out recording all the drama to post on their social media accounts for views. Fucking vultures.

"Let's see what we're dealing with." Spence is first out of the door, grabbing a med bag for any immediate assessments we need to make.

I quickly follow, making sure my work-issued cap is in place because I've had vomit in my hair on more than one occasion after attending a call in this area.

There's a man around my age lying on the sidewalk just outside the door of the club, thumping music blaring louder through the doors every time they open to let someone in or out. The bouncers are doing their best to back up the bystanders, and a woman who appears to be in her thirties is kneeling beside the concussed man, tears streaming down her face.

"Oh, thank God. He just fell, I don't know what happened. Please, save him!" She looks up, eyes widening when she sees Spence and me heading toward them.

"Okay, Ma'am, try and breathe. How old is he?" Spence takes control as I kneel beside them, quickly getting to work on checking the man's airways and pulse.

"Twenty-two. He's my boyfriend. We've been drinking since this afternoon and I thought he was okay, just a little drunk. He said he needed some air, and as soon as we came outside he was sick, he banged his head on the wall then fell. Please tell me he's going to be okay?" Her ramblings are surprisingly useful, and I know I need to get the stretcher so we can take him to the hospital for observation. Also, way to go, Miss Cougar. Internally,

I'm high-fiving her for her ability to give zero shits about conformity.

"I promise we'll do everything we can."

"Pulse is steady, but we'll give him some oxygen. His breaths are a little short." I relay the information to Spence after checking the guy's vitals.

"We'll take him in." Spence is all business while we're on the job, which is just one reason I love him. No bullshit.

I nod, standing and heading toward the van for the stretcher. Wheeling it out, I begin to help Spencer get the man in position so we can load him on and into our ambulance. After explaining to the woman what we're doing, she declines the invitation to ride to the hospital with us, letting us know she'll meet him there later. Fucking suspicious, if you ask me. But it's not my job to judge.

Just as Spence and I are finishing up and I'm about to close the back doors, a face in the crowd makes me pause.

A fucking beautiful face, with a tattoo just below his eye that I remember licking on my birthday, a tattoo above his eyebrow that I memorized, a black hoodie hiding a chiseled and tattooed chest, and shit...he's wearing a Sons Of Khaos cut. His blue eyes cut into my soul so deeply I have to force myself to look away, to do my job, and to forget all about him because it can never work.

I'm with the Toxic Rebels—well, if being their pawn is being with them—and he's with the Sons Of Khaos.

My brother would fucking kill him, making me watch before killing me too, all while knowing he would let Mom rot as my extra punishment.

I hate being that person, *oh it can never work* while secretly obsessing over them—not that I've obsessed over him at all—and if I'd known this guy was a SOK guy, I would've steered clear away. But fuck, why does life consistently fuck me up the ass with sharp and rusty implements?

Quickly pulling myself out of my stupor, I close the doors and climb into the driver's seat, leaving Spencer to stabilize our patient and prepare him for when we arrive at the hospital. Just as I pull up, the back doors open and our patient begins to convulse.

"Shit!" Spence curses, and I check my watch to time how long it lasts before helping to make sure the patient is safe.

Thirty seconds later, the convulsing has stopped and we pass over the patient to the ER doctor as we rattle off his vitals and information. From here, my job with this patient is over, and I'm thankful for that. I don't have the capacity to form long-term relationships with anyone other than Spence.

The drive back to the firehouse is quiet. A patient can do that. If it's a lively person, we'll be buzzing the whole way back, but with incidents like the one we just experienced, we tend to be reflective. Don't get me wrong, someone convulsing isn't exactly the worst patient we've ever dealt with, but it's certainly not a pleasant one.

"I hope someone's made breakfast or, at least, has the coffee pot on." Spence rubs his palms together. The thought of food or coffee always excites him. If he hadn't become a paramedic, his next choice was to be a chef, and I kinda feel like he missed a calling with that one. The sweet potato pie he made for the station on the last shift we worked was divine, and he taught me how to make some really tasty baked treats, too.

"It's like four in the morning, Spence. Coffee will be on, but nobody's making breakfast for another couple of hours. Unless you wanna do it. I could eat."

Spencer grins as I pull into the station and I mentally face-palm because now that he knows I could eat, I've inadvertently put myself on breakfast duty. He won't wait for the firefighters in the station to get on the task.

I turn off the engine and we carry out our vehicle and supply checks before heading inside. As suspected, the coffee pot is half full already and I can't help my groan at the beautiful sight of the black liquid. Spence grabs the mugs while I pick up the pot, ready to pour, and we work like the team we've been for the last year. Easily moving around each other, I take the eggs from the refrigerator and he begins toasting some bread.

"Smells like breakfast." Ryan, one of the firefighters on the Squad Company based here in this station, comes into the kitchen area and pours himself a fresh coffee.

"I take it you want in on this, even though it's ridiculous o'clock?" I smirk in Ryan's direction, because of course he wants to eat. He's a six-foot-six giant of a man with muscles on his muscles. He *always* wants to eat.

He helps by getting some plates from one of the cupboards just in time for me to serve the first now-cooked omelet.

"Dibs!" Spence shouts out as he's buttering some toast, letting the knife drop to the counter and picking up the plate. He sits at the table and scarfs his food like he's never eaten before, much like most of the guys in my brother's club.

"Would you like some help, Beautiful?" Ryan moves to stand behind me, his breath tickling the back of my neck as he presses a palm against my waist.

Ugh, I hate it when Ryan does this. He's handsome, yes, buff, yes, tall and sexy...yeah. Okay, I'm woman enough to admit he's a great catch, being some sexy-as-fuck firefighter. The thing is, I can't get involved with anyone for more than a fumble or quick fuck to try and replace the shit going on in my home life, because my brother just wouldn't allow it and it doesn't fit with my plans.

Ryan has been nothing but a gentleman, giving me space, time, being helpful and kind, even calling me sweet nicknames like Beautiful, but it gives me the ick and I don't know what to do with myself. I feel like there are only so many ways to turn a guy down.

"I'm good, Ry. Call the others through, see if anyone else is hungry."

He sighs and steps away.

The rest of my shift is relatively quiet, Spence and I only get called out once more before we head to our lockers at 2000. I shower and change out of my uniform into my light-gray sweats, hugging Spence when he leaves before me.

Rushing to get home is not something I will ever see myself doing, so I take my time brushing through my damp blonde hair before twisting it into a bun on top of my head. With nothing left to do, I sigh, pick up my bag and place it over my head so it hangs by my waist, and slip out of the building. Ryan and his team already swapped shifts at 08:00, they're on a different schedule to the paramedic crews, only occasionally leaving at the same time as us, and I'm actually thankful for that. The nights they're on a similar shift have been awkward with Ryan insisting he walk me to my shit heap of a car.

My car is parked five minutes away from the station because it gives me that extra few minutes to myself—most of the time. An extra few minutes away from the home I despise and can't wait to escape.

It's still relatively light out, but the setting sun has cast a pretty glow over the town. This time of day is one of my favorites, almost like an inbetweeny moment as the sun sets, the moon rises, and the sound of the sea crashes in the distance. There's something a little off about tonight though...and I've learned to trust my senses to some extent.

I'm being followed.

I may be a punching bag for my brother's crew, but that doesn't mean I'll allow that kind of shit when I'm out in the real world.

Leading whoever this is to my car would be a mistake. They're close enough that I won't have time to climb in, turn on the engine—if it even starts the first time—and speed off into the distance. There's a small alley just ahead, beside the coffee shop and drug store where I usually stock up on my milk duds.

I make a sharp turn into the alley and pull out my knuckle stun gun. It's illegal to conceal a stun gun in this state without the correct permit, but mine could easily pass for a cock ring if I'm ever actually caught with it. I mean, not if they inspect it closely of course, but at a glance...yeah. Cock ring.

The ring easily slides over my middle finger, and all I need to do is squeeze my fist and basically punch whoever this is to have them fucked up for a few minutes.

I've barely prepared myself when he walks around the corner, his eyes immediately finding mine as he stalks toward me like a man on a mission.

"Are you running from me, Cherry?" He pins me against the brick wall, caging me in with his arms on either side of my head. His eyes search mine eagerly. For what? I have no idea. Then he brings his palm to the side of my face and strokes my cheek with the pad of his thumb.

"Think you've gotten me confused with someone else. My name isn't Cherry." I try to insert as much sass as possible into my words.

"Sexy *and* an attitude." He wags his brows with a small grin tipping the corners of his lips. "You wanna come back to my place or fuck right here?"

"Oh my God! How could I ever refuse such a romantic gesture?" I deadpan, ignoring his amused expression before I continue. "Does that shit usually work for you?" I'm all bravado right now because, if I'm being honest with myself, then yes, that shit works for me. Especially coming from this tattooed beast in front of me.

I should be scared. The Sons of Khaos have a reputation for being ruthless, they've killed several of the Rebels over the years, stolen my brother's merch, fucked up his suppliers, and generally make life difficult for everyone. But instead of scared, I'm turned the fuck on. Which is fucking stupid considering what I put up with from the Rebels.

It seems this particular one has a superpower against me. And it can go fuck itself because I can't get into what I'm feeling around this man. Not now. Not ever.

"To be honest, I've never asked for a second round before, so you tell me." He shrugs, and I swear it looks like he wants to eat my face. Even that doesn't scare me.

"Okay, I'll help you out." I bring my empty hand up to his chest, sliding it between us and resting my palm against the leather of his cut. The patch there tells me he's the SOK

Enforcer, so I'm going to need to do this quickly—well, quickish. "It doesn't work. I bet I can change your mind though. Do you know who I am?" Here goes...I'm preparing myself for the hate to fill his beautiful blue eyes, to mar his incredibly tattooed face.

"I know you're mine. We'll figure everything else out along the way." That smile never leaves his lips, and the way he raises his brow accentuates the tattoo there. Images of our bodies working together...no...fuck! How is he doing this to me?

"I'm Mackenzie Wilson. Jake's sister. You know, the Vice Prez for the Toxic Rebels." My voice is firm as I explain, waiting for the inevitable moment that he swings for me.

His brows scrunch together in confusion at the same time his eyes widen, and before the hate for me can truly fill him, I squeeze my fist and press my knuckle against his upper thigh.

"Ah fuck!" is all I hear as he falls to the ground and I run like the wind toward my car, my heart racing in my chest.

Hopefully, the SOK Enforcer has gotten the hint and will leave me alone. Now that he knows who I am, I'll need to watch my back because I have a feeling that him leaving me alone is a wasted wish.

Chapter Five

Aleko

"Hand me that empty container, will you?" Bash follows my finger as I point to the pile of plastic five-quart oil and antifreeze jugs that we tell the prospects to cut out as receptacles for our oil changes. Recycling and reusing, we're all about the environment. Okay, fine, that's a stretch but shy of quitting our racing addiction, we do our part.

The garages at the front of the compound are where we have our legit businesses, the repair shops and body shops and paint shops. For a medium-sized town like Rockford Beach, it's insane the amount of business we get. Not to mention our unofficial and definitely illegal garage hidden way down in the back of the old—like nineteen-fifties old—psych hospital we've made into our cozy little home away from home. That's where we collect, sell, and delve into the black market for whatever our special clients need or fits our fancy.

Even though it's summer and hot as fuck, I'm wearing my sleeveless hoodie so my best friend can hang out with me, mainly by sleeping in it or hanging out on my shoulder. I've had Ninja his entire life, which is all of six months, but we bonded immediately. A client fucked up when he put two pet rats in the same cage without checking their sexes. Boom, it didn't take long to have a mischief of little baby rats—they're called kittens but that's just fucking lazy vocabulary skills—so I took this one. He's so fucking cool it amazes me that more people don't adopt them. He even purrs. It's fucking adorable. And today is beach day and Ninja loves hanging out with the brothers, but mainly he loves all the Khunts because they let him sleep in their cleavage.

After popping off the fairing on my Hayabusa, I unscrew the used oil filter, then wipe off the excess oil drops before lubricating the seal of the new filter.

"You missed a good party last night."

Glancing at Grinder, I smirk. I know what that means.

"Threesome? Coke? Fucking doing the helicopter with your dick?" Any of those things are possible with Grinder. As he begins telling me about some chick and her boyfriend that he brought back to the small house he rents out with Boner, I half tune out, concentrating instead on loosening the drain plug and making sure it doesn't slip from between my slick fingers.

"Because let me tell you, on their worst days, men suck cock better than women. Hands down."

Here we go. I'm about to get a lesson on the pros and cons of getting a blowjob from a dude. Spoiler alert: there are no cons according to Grinder.

"You know we've had this conversation about a dozen times, right?" And by conversation, I mean he talks and we laugh our asses off at the crazy anecdotes he always seems to have. At least he's taking my mind off the shit show that is my Cherry Pie—Mackenzie Wilson. Fuck me. And just like every other time the subject hijacks my brain power, I get more and more pissed off at how profoundly the universe has decided to fuck me up the ass.

"And yet you've never tried it, which means I haven't convinced you of the positive effects yet."

I sigh but tell him the same damn thing I always say.

"Dicks don't do it for me, Grinder. I'm all about the pussy." Getting up, I pull the ring seal off the bolt and replace it with a new one, all the while Grinder is giving me a play by play of how he got rimmed and sucked at the same time.

"Tag teams are the best, man." His sigh makes me chuckle. He's an equal opportunity manwhore and wears the badge proudly.

By the time the bike is ready and the fairing is popped back in, I double check that the holds are nice and snug. It would be a bitch if part of my bike ended up flying off on the highway. Then I bolt it all back into place and give it a little shine, ready to ride my baby once more.

"Speaking of pussy." Fuck my life, Bear is chiming in on this conversation and it feels like I'm about to be the center of attention. "Did you ever find the girl you banged on that guy's truck?"

The memory invades my entire body, making me hard in an instant. Grinder, who never misses a fucking beat, looks down at my crotch and grins. "Damn, looks like it was magical pussy, too."

I growl, full on possessed motherfucker with a pinch of murderous, before adjusting myself and checking on the oil. Fucker is against me too, dripping one lonely drop at a time as if I have all fucking day for this.

"Hey, Prospect!" My voice booms out around the garage until Bash pops up beside me like a good little free laborer. Ninja stirs in my hood, probably unhappy that I've woken him up.

"Yeah, Psycho?" He's looking around the garage, probably wondering what the fuck I'm going to make him do.

"Go help Vanessa and the Khunts with the shit for the beach." As if understanding the word "beach", Ninja hurries up to my shoulder and nudges my neck then my cheek before sitting up on his haunches and staring at Bash.

"He creeps me out."

I like fucking with Bash since he's afraid of rats, almost to the point of phobia. Every time Ninja stares him down, it's as if my little buddy knows exactly what he's doing.

"Keep talking like that and he might chew your nose off while you sleep." Ninja turns to look at me then stares at Bash again. It's like he understands me, even though that would be creepy, wouldn't it?

"Oh, shit, I need to run up to my suite and grab my Speedo." As if we're in a sitcom, we all turn slowly when Grinder runs out of the garage and toward the entrance of the main building.

"That dude is weird as fuck but, man, I can't wait to bust his balls." Bear laughs.

Ninja, just now noticing his favorite playtoy is here, reaches out with his little pink paws until Bear leans in, allowing him to jump on his chest and run up to his shoulder.

"With a Speedo on, he'll probably bust his own balls on the waves." We all chuckle at Bash's comment before we realize that he's a prospect and doesn't yet have the privilege of fucking with a member.

"Didn't I give you an order?" I swear to fuck, Ninja cackles as Bash runs out to help the ladies load up their cars.

"Come on, you grumpy fuck, sex on the beach sounds pretty fucking fantastic, right now."

I grunt, not wanting to give Bear any more ammo than he already has when it comes to my girl.

Yeah, *my* fucking girl. I've been thinking about this since she decided to give me a lesson on boundaries last night. Thirty thousand plus volts of pure electric shock running up my thigh wasn't even the worst part. That was when she bolted, disappearing down the street while I tried to regain control of my trapped muscles. You'd think that would be a cold shower for me but my brain or sex drive doesn't work that way.

Mackenzie Wilson is on my radar, and short of moving to another planet, I don't plan on letting her go anytime soon. Yeah, yeah, her brother being a selfish piece of shit who regularly tries to fuck with our business and sell his product on our streets *may* be a speed bump on my road to making her mine, but there's no obstacle I can't overcome.

My true problem will be Prez when he cuts off my balls for fucking the enemy's sister. No, not just fucking, obsessing over. Do I feel shame for being completely consumed by her? Fuck no. I don't do shit half-assed and I won't be satisfied until I get my fill of her.

"Last one to the beach has to clean up Grinder's used condoms." Fucking Bear. We take our dares seriously around here.

With my equipment on in a flash, I'm the first one out, waving my middle finger with pride knowing my ass won't be touching stale rubbers anytime soon.

Bear is quickly on my heels. The glossy midnight blue of his bike always shines bright in the North Carolina sun. When he tries to pass me, my left foot drops to third gear and my right wrist pulls back until all I'm showing him is my license plate and my fine ass. In my rearview, I see him swerving left and right, in and out of traffic, just like me, and pretty soon we've got three other bikes joining us. Grinder being one of them.

That's when I decide to put on a show. With Ninja secured in his pouch, I lift the front of the bike and lead the way down College Avenue riding on my back wheel.

Not to be outdone, I see in my left mirror that Bear has lifted his bike as well, followed by Crow to my right. Some of the drivers honk their horns, enjoying the show, while others, who can't help but be complete assholes, scream obscenities at us. Usually, we ignore them or else we'd be breaking noses every other weekday.

By the time we reach the beach, I've got about a dozen plans swimming in my head on how I can convince the brothers that this thing with Mackenzie is a great fucking idea.

Although, to be fair, none of those reasons take what's really important into account...the club.

"Come on, buddy, let's see if I can forget about Cherry pussy by diving into a willing Khunt."

Untying the velvet travel pouch where Ninja hitches a ride everywhere with me, I let him jump out and crawl up my arm so he can rest on my shoulder. He won't stay there long, though. He loves the beach because we're all there giving him attention and the sand is a great way for him to clean himself up. The best part is watching him swim and float in the ocean. Dude is a great wingman too.

"There he is!" Bear's already in his board shorts with a surfboard tucked under his arm as he holds out his hand for Ninja. Clearly, he doesn't give two shits about me.

My best friend grew up on the beach, and unlike me, he protects his body from the sun by wearing a rashguard and sun protection on his shaved head. I don't think I've ever seen it anything but perfectly bald and I know for a fact he's at the downtown barber shop every week catching up with his cousins and friends from his old neighborhood.

I've got everything I need underneath my jeans, sleeveless hoodie, and cut. Everyone in Rockford Beach knows who we are, the snake slinking in and out of the eye socket of a skull stitched onto our leathers with the club name, a clear indicator. Not to mention the identical tattoos if ever we're not wearing our cuts.

Star Point is the extreme end of the popular barrier island where Rockford inhabitants like to hang out on days like these. As soon as we get there, said residents make sure to leave us a wide berth as we settle in for the next few hours. Vanessa, Prez's own ride or die, made sure we had enough food and drinks—little alcohol so we don't end up killing ourselves—for the duration of our get together.

"Thanks, V, this looks fucking delicious," Hoops, our vice-prez calls out in her direction. We all hum our agreement as I take a mini pizza square for myself and one for Ninja.

"Hey, V, did you bring any sunscreen? I don't want my ink to fade." About ten pairs of eyes swing over to Grinder—in all his bright aqua-colored Speedo glory—and I can guarantee we're all thinking the same thing but only Bear actually speaks up.

"Brother, I don't know what's blinding me more, your pasty white ass or your neon bright ball clutcher." Obviously, we all crack up like a bunch of preteens but Grinder doesn't even flinch. Ribbing is the last thing that can possibly get his panties in a wad. Too much shit happened to him back in his teen years, this here is love for him.

"Yeah, yeah. One..." He pops out his index finger, staring straight at Bear. "We'll revisit this conversation when y'all are bitching about your skin cancer and I'm living my healthy life like a boss."

"I'm guessing you don't want to know about the dangerous chemicals in your sunscreen then?" Vanessa pipes up, and I swear to fuck that woman has comedic timing down to an art.

"What?" Grinder's confidence deflates right before our eyes.

"Hey now! Don't leave us hanging on your one, tell us more." Bear can barely speak through his laughter, straight white teeth gleaming in the sun's rays.

Grinder blinks a couple of times before shaking it off and popping up his middle finger to join the first.

"Two, this pasty white ass is going to get a butt-load—emphasis on the butt—of willing bodies back to my casa before y'all have time to say...sunburn."

We have no doubt. The guy must have a honey-coated dick that makes people's mouths water. I get a lot of pussy, but Grinder? Fucking hell, I'm not sure where he finds the time to fuck so much.

We all laugh until Grinder struts—fucking *struts*—down the beach once his entire body is covered in one hundred SPF.

"So, on a serious note, what's been going on with you?"

Aw fuck.

I glance over at Bear, sarcasm pouring out of every one of my words. "Is Dr. Phil in, now?"

Ninja jumps from Bear's shoulder to mine, nuzzles my neck, then runs down my arm and into my hoodie on the towel, where he settles in for a little nap. With a belly full of pizza, he's about to go into a food coma.

"You've never reacted like that"—he thumbs behind us like the compound is right there—"for pussy before, so spill."

"I told you, she tastes and smells like cherries." It's all I say and it's enough.

"Nice. You gonna make lollipops with her cum, now?" He says this like it's a joke, not knowing that, yeah, that's exactly what I did and will do again as soon as I fucking find her.

"Dude, I'm fucking kidding. What's the matter with you?" Bear's half laughing, half staring at me like I've lost my damn mind.

Wouldn't be the first time, to be honest. My lollipop addiction is real but at least I keep the candy store in business. In fact, I've got one in my pocket for my after-dinner sweetness. My brother once told me it had something to do with Freud's concept of oral fixation. Our mother died when I was just a baby so apparently my needs were unmet in early childhood. Maybe I'll quit the lollipops once I have Mackenzie's pussy at my beck and call, meeting all of my oral needs.

"It doesn't matter because I can't go back for seconds." I'm not sure who I'm trying to convince of this because I know myself well enough…there isn't much on this Earth that will come between me and my obsessions.

"So, what, you're going to stay a grumpy fucker for the rest of time?" He takes a can of soda, drinks a healthy dose, then belches loud and proud.

"Maybe." Honestly, I didn't mean to say that, it opens up too many questions and Bear jumps on that shit like a starving fly.

"Well that's gonna fucking suck. What's so special about this one that's making you more of an asshole than you already are?" The brief glance he throws my way says more about his worry than his tone ever will.

"It's complicated and, to be honest, it's not good for the club." That gets his attention, the handful of sour cream and onion chips freezing midway to his mouth.

"Why is it bad for the club, Psycho?" As with anything related to the wellbeing of our found family, Bear's tone turns deadly, his muscles contracting, ready to fight for us all.

It takes me a second to confess, knowing that not only will voicing the situation make it all too fucking real but it also means that she's no longer just mine. Saying her name, telling him she's that fucker's sister, will instantly make her club business. For some inexplicable reason, I don't like it.

But also, I won't keep secrets from my brothers. I fucking hate secrets.

"Her name is Mackenzie Wilson."

"Yeah, so?"

"As in Jake Wilson's little sister." I don't need to elaborate, everyone knows our enemy's name.

The silence that follows my words is deafening.

"Fuuuuuck."

"Yeah, exactly that." We look at each other, our silent conversation louder than when we were actually speaking.

"You have to tell Prez." He whispers those five little words, they sound innocent enough but I know that making this public will be the definite end of whatever this is with her. Not that her tasing my ass in the middle of an alley wasn't clue enough.

"I know. I'm going for a swim. You surfin'?" I look out to the waves and see they're regular but nothing mind blowing. Hurricane season has barely started, he won't see good waves for another month or so when the swells from hurricanes down in Florida start popping up here.

"Nah, think I'm gonna chill out under the umbrella Vanessa brought for us. I mean, the beach is cool and shit." He speaks loud enough for everyone in our group to hear him.

"Remember that when I ask you to help out at the compound!" V volleys right back without missing a beat.

"I'll be back in a bit, make sure Ninja doesn't run away." Taking my T-shirt off, I drop it next to my towel and jog out to the shore and run straight into the crashing waves.

Swimming is a great way to keep in shape, the movement making every one of your muscles work without pushing your body too far. Thirty minutes of laps just behind the crest of the waves and my muscles begin that delicious burn. Problem is, I'm hungry now and my stomach always wins against anything else.

Walking back up the beach to pile on a plate of food, I pick up the T-shirt I threw off before jumping in the water and slide it over my head. When I turn to head back to the party, I stop dead in my tracks, my eyes narrowing and my heart rate going double that of when I was actually exerting myself.

What the actual fuck?

Not fifty feet in front of me, I see her. Long waves of gold with just a hint of pink and blue whipping around her face, her lithe, muscular body on display for all to appreciate with only a few strings and triangles of cloth hiding her most intimate parts. The white of her bikini contrasting perfectly with her smooth tan skin may as well be a red flag to my interior bull.

My logic disappears.

My loyalty to the club gets swallowed up by my obsessive need to own her.

Above all of that is my self-control drowning under the sudden rage that consumes my every cell.

My little Cherry Pie isn't alone. No, that would be too easy. She's walking with two assholes on either side, one who dares put his arm around her shoulders before pulling her in and kissing her temple, making her giggle like a fucking school girl.

I don't think. I don't weigh the pros and cons. I don't even try to calm myself down.

Before I even know what the fuck is happening, my fist is connecting with a jaw and my arm is popped back ready to pummel this asshole who thought it was a good idea to touch my woman.

Guess I have my answer...I'm not done with Mackenzie fucking Wilson.

Consequences be damned.

Chapter Six

Mackenzie

"What the actual fucking fuck?!" Thankfully, we're far enough down the beach from the SOK members I hadn't noticed until now—that'll teach me to pay attention to my surroundings when having fun—and my yell doesn't draw any additional attention, but fuck.

Turning away from the devil in front of me, I fall to my knees beside Spencer, who's crouched down and holding his nose.

"Let me take a look." I encourage him to uncurl and gently move his palms away from his face. Fuck. "It's a mess but I don't think it's broken." He covers his nose again, glaring daggers up at the crazy fuck who just punched him.

"Ready to come home with me yet, Cherry?"

How is this man able to remain so smug right now?

"That would still be a no. Pretty sure punching the fuck out of a girl's best friend in front of his new boyfriend isn't going to win you any prizes with anyone. I have no idea what possessed me to even lay my eyes on you the other night." I shake my head, curling my lip in disgust at him as Raheem and I help Spencer stand.

"That would be my charming wit and winning smile." He raises just the one eyebrow several times, grinning sadistically. It shouldn't turn me on, but my panties would disagree and that makes me mad as hell.

"You're about as charming and witty as genital herpes, and the only thing you're winning tonight is your dick in your own hand." Stupidly, I turn my back on the devil to check on Spence again. "We can get this fixed up with a med kit."

"You're a crazy bastard," Raheem mumbles as he takes his T-shirt off and hands it to Spence.

"What the fuck did you just call me?" The SOK Enforcer grabs Raheem's beard and pulls him so they're nose-to-nose, and I swear Raheem just pissed himself.

Not that I blame him.

This devil man is pretty fucking scary, but he seems to like me, so I do the thing my brain is telling me isn't sensible and insert myself between them. I push him back and away from Raheem.

"Stop being a bully." I poke at his rock-hard chest and stare him down for a few seconds before turning back to Spence. "Keep pressure on it. Hang on." I sigh, digging into my bag for my pen-knife so I can slice some material small enough to pack his nose.

Once again, I face the devil. And I'm either really fucking brave, or really fucking stupid, but I'm doing it...

I grab the hem of his T-shirt and use my knife to cut the material I need to roll up for Spencer. It's a little damp, but it'll work. The Enforcer keeps his eyes on me the whole time, I can feel them burning into every inch of my soul even though I completely avoid his gaze. Amusement at the situation is evident in the way he's standing, and when I do glance up, that smirk is firmly in place. Brushing my knuckles—completely by accident—against his hard stomach absolutely does not make me wish I was wearing something other than white panties and a bikini top right now. Okay, it totally does. My nipples are like twin peaks and I'm pretty sure it won't be long until my panties are see-through.

I fucking hate what he's doing to my body.

Still ignoring him, I slowly move away Raheem's scrunched up T-shirt from Spencer's face, I use the non-bloody parts to clean his nose a little before pushing the first of the scrap of material up his nostril.

"I thought you were cheating o—"

"Shh. I'm very busy and you are annoying me." I interrupt the Enforcer trying to gain my attention behind me and continue to pack Spencer's nose. "You might wanna go home and get an ice pack on that and pack it properly if you need to. It doesn't look out of shape at all, so you know the do's and don'ts. It'll heal right up in about three weeks."

"Thanks, honey." Spence's voice is pained, but he's a tough nut. The clearing of a throat behind me gains my attention again and I close my eyes, taking a deep, calming breath before I turn my attention to the devil.

"*You!* If he has to go to the hospital or receive any kind of medical attention, you'll be receiving the bill. Understand?"

He's so close to me, if I breathe in my nipples will inevitably brush against his chest. My eyes are forward, focused on his tattooed neck instead of his swirling blue irises.

The sound of a deep inhale makes me think I may have just pushed my luck a little too far. This is a dangerous man who knows I'm the sister of his rival. I'm in fucking stupid territory right now.

"Is this the part where we pinky swear, my little Cherry Pie?" I can't decide if I want to throat punch him or deep throat him. Since my gag reflex can't be trusted, throat punch, it is.

Except he brings a hand up, cupping my chin between his thumb and forefinger to lift my face, and every violent bone in my body pauses to *awww* at the gesture. Fucking traitorous body. I keep my gaze focused downward, my teeth clenched as I prepare for a beating. At this point, I'm used to men and how they get their own way.

"Look at me."

It's not a demand, as such, but I want to defy him anyway.

"I am." He didn't specify where to look at him.

"Eyes, Cherry, look into my eyes." His voice is so soft, calm, yet it's also full of need and want and all the things it shouldn't be.

"Why? You gonna try and hypnotize me or some shit?" The way the greens and blacks and blues of his neck tattoo swirl together remind me of the light crashing waves beside us.

"Why not? You scared or some shit?" He crouches down slightly, crooking his neck so his face is level with mine, his grip still firm on my chin.

It's impossible to not look in his eyes. So I do. And I fill my gaze with such hatred and stubbornness, my breaths become heavy and my chest literally heaves like a fucking damsel. With a deep sigh, I begin to step away, but his hand is on my waist and his lips are on mine so quickly I almost think I'm imagining it.

There's no way my imagination is this good though. His tongue demands immediate attention, the piercing I had forgotten about adding an extra thing to play with inside my mouth. His grip on my waist tightens, likely leaving bruises that will be a reminder of this forbidden moment between us. He moans into my mouth and I'm pretty sure I whimper, feeling just as needy for him as he seems to be for me. He tilts my head to the side, giving him easier access to nip and suck and bite into my neck, my collarbone, all while continuing to knead into my waist with his bruising grip.

"Want a hand with that one, Psycho?" A tall man wearing an aqua-colored Speedo calls over from behind...Psycho?

Immediately, I step away, embarrassed that I allowed myself to be caught up like that. Heat creeps across my chest and face as Psycho growls in the man's direction, and I swear he's about to kill someone.

"Fuck off, Grinder. She's mine." Without taking his eyes away from mine, he lifts a hand and flips off Speedo Guy. "Wanna come for a swim?" There goes that one eyebrow again and he's suddenly calmer than a lake in summer.

His switch from kill-a-bitch to chilled-the-fuck-out is impressive.

"No, I don't want to swim." I raise both of my eyebrows in challenge, mainly because I can't do just the one. That's not a skill I possess.

This is the moment I walk away, when I forget everything about this man and focus on what's important: my mom and my plan to get away from my brother.

Spence clears his throat behind me, reminding me that he and Raheem are still here watching our little show, and fuck my actual life. What am I doing? This isn't me.

"Thanks for that, but it can't, and won't, be happening again." While he's distracted, I make for a quick getaway, dragging Spence and Raheem with me to our pile of clothes.

"Come back to my place. Stay with me." Psycho grips my wrist, making me pause and look over my shoulder at his pleading eyes, almost the same color as the ocean surrounding us.

"Desperate much, Psycho? Even if I wanted to, which let's be clear, I don't, I have to work."

"I'll pay you whatever you'll earn at work if you don't go." He doesn't loosen his grip and I glare at him.

"Don't mistake me for one of your club whores." I am not, and will never be, that girl.

"What happened to the pink and blue pigtails?"

Is this guy even listening to me?

"Not that it's any of your business, you fucking psycho, but it was just hair chalk." I run my fingers through the strands making sure to get some of the pink on my finger before I shove it in his face. "Happy?"

"Hmm. Where are your clothes?"

This has got to be a fucking joke, where's the camera?

Glancing to my left, where Spence and Raheem are picking up our things, I raise my brows as if to say, "duh, use your eyes."

"Let me dress you."

"Fuck no." I pull my arm away from his hold and storm over to the guys, who are patiently waiting for me with scowls on their faces.

Grabbing my clothes, I unfold my pink summer dress to slide over my head when it's snatched away from me.

"What the fuck do you think you're doing?" Spence, bless his heart, tries standing up to the devil in disguise, who practically snarls at him in response.

"Dressing my fucking girl is what I'm doing."

"Pretty sure she told you no." Stepping forward, Spence places a hand on his hip, while still holding Raheem's T-shirt up to his face, muffling his words a little.

The fact I'm standing so close to the psycho biker is the only reason I even hear the menacing growl that sneaks out from between his lips like a dangerous animal ready to pounce. I have no choice but to intervene.

"Maybe *Psycho,* here, got too much sea salt in his ears." I say his name like an insult, as though venom is dripping from my tongue.

Narrowing his eyes, he gives me a half-smile as he tries to figure out which way my dress goes on before stepping into me. "Arms up."

"She sai—"

"It's okay, Spence. Let him get it out of his system." If this is what it takes so we can walk away without dying today, then this is what happens.

I want to defy him, but I also need to get away from him. He's the most confusing creature I've ever encountered and that is not in my plans.

Raising my arms, I glare at him, allowing him to pull the dress over my head. It's a simple design, pink and white tie-dye with thin spaghetti straps on my shoulders and the full skirt falling just beneath my ass cheeks.

"Thanks."

"Take your panties off."

It's so out of the blue, I almost think I heard him wrong.

"What the actual fuck?"

"I've had my cock inside your beautiful pussy, Cherry, don't tell me you're too shy to give me your panties?" He pulls a lollipop from the back pocket of his damp shorts, unwraps it, and pops it into his mouth.

Memories of what he did with one of those heat my cheeks, and I recall sucking on said candy as I walked away from him the first time.

There's a challenge in his intense gaze and I fucking hate it. It's almost like he knows this is my kryptonite because backing away from a challenge is not in my nature.

"I'm not about to hand my panties over to some creeper who just punched my best friend."

"Please?" He raises a single brow and grins, just one side of his mouth curving upward.

"Oh, so you do have some manners?" I don't know why I'm still standing here.

"You're mine, Cherry, I'll always treat you with respect, even when I'm spitting on your beautiful pussy and decorating your chest with my cum." He grins again as though what he's saying isn't all kinds of fucked up.

"I'm not yours." For a start, it's not safe for me to be this close to the enemy.

"You are."

I sigh, steeling my spine and forcing all my bravado into my face as an idea hits me. "It's been fun." Then I bend down and lift the hem of my dress as though I'm about to do as he asked, right before I grab a fistful of sand and throw it at his face. "Run!" I whisper-yell to Spence and Raheem before we all run as fast as we can across the sand toward my car. My flip-flops are in my hands because there's no way I could run while wearing them.

There is cursing behind me, fading a little as I unlock my shit heap and we all jump in.

I don't even look back.

I can't.

It's been a long fucking night serving the Rebels drinks with Mona. Thankfully, with it being almost three in the morning, most of the guys have gone home or are shacking up in one of the "fuck trailers" here on site. Of which I have the pleasure of cleaning, along with the other club sluts.

I hate calling them that, but they own that shit so I'm happy to go with it. I'm not exactly a club slut, being the VP's sister, and I'm not expected to put out like the rest of them do, but that doesn't excuse me from other duties.

If I want to stay alive, I do what they say. If I want a roof over my head, my mom to be safe, food to eat, and a non-beaten body...I do what they say.

That doesn't mean I don't find ways to bite back. I've been playing the long game because I needed time to find people who could help me without putting Mom in danger. And I'm so fucking close I can almost taste it.

Earlier tonight, I handed out some of my homemade cookies to a few select members with their drinks, making sure Mona didn't try to swipe any for herself because they were special. Just for Jake's two besties. The thought of them makes me shudder in disgust.

Cam, the Toxic Rebels' Sergeant at Arms, pouted when I told him I'd run out of cookies, but I promised to make him his own batch later in the week. They'll be normal cookies, of course, not the kind baked with special ingredients from my garden.

"Do you have nothing better to do than stand there and be useless, Kenz?" My brother bangs his empty glass against the bar top—which is basically a hole cut out of a trailer and a slab of wood to make a counter.

The vitriol coming from his tone makes me grind my teeth before turning to face him while I continue to dry off the glasses I'm pulling out of the small washer.

"Bourbon?" I pick up the bottle and begin filling his glass without waiting for a response, not using the usual measurements because I've been slapped for that on more than one occasion.

He doesn't say thank you. Instead, he picks it up and takes a large gulp, resting it back down again, palm still against the glass. "Just heard about the next race night, it's on the fifth of July. Make sure you're ready. You're not missing two in a row."

"I'm working until eight that night, so if I don't get stuck out on a call, I'll be there." Because I have to be. I'm useful. For now.

"You insolent and ungrateful little brat." He smashes the glass against the bar, sending liquid and broken shards everywhere.

Great. More for me to clean up before I can go to bed.

"You will fucking be there. Do you understand me, girl? Or do I have to remind you what happens when you let the club down?" His lips are curled up in a snarl, his eyes full of hatred and anger. Still, to this day, I don't know why he detests me so much.

I get that he blames me for Dad dying; I was on the back of his bike when we crashed. The road was slippery, black ice, and it was a complete accident. But maybe I could've been a better passenger, or leaned a different way and everything would be okay.

I broke my leg and had a small concussion, while Dad lost his life from internal bleeding.

"I understand, Jake. I'll be there." I nod, agreeing with him because it's the easiest thing to do. The quickest way to appease him so he fucks all the way off.

"Too fucking right, you will be."

I flinch back when he slams his fists onto the bar—hopefully cutting himself on the broken shards of glass—and stands, snatching the bottle of bourbon I'm still holding before storming off to his motorcycle. He's way over the limit, but I'm not going to be the one to remind him how dangerous it is to ride while that fucked up.

After five minutes of standing here, wondering where Mona is before remembering she went into one of the trailers with Brick, I realize I'm still trembling and give myself an all over shimmy. It doesn't get rid of it completely, but I'm calm enough to clean the bar up and head over to my own trailer in the far corner of the property.

The only luxury I have.

I turn off all the floodlights and walk toward my trailer, pausing near my little secret garden patch when I spot a new weed growing that shouldn't be there. After pulling it out, I nod contentedly, my hand on my hip as I admire my tiny patch of evil hiding in plain sight.

Panic shoots up my spine when a large palm covers my mouth, preventing me from screaming as an arm snakes around my waist. I kick and try to reach into the bag at my side for my taser ring, but I'm restricted.

"Shh. I'm here now."

CHAPTER SEVEN
ALEKO

I have done some stupid shit in my life but this? This right here takes the fucking grand prize, the number one slot. I am standing on Toxic Rebel territory, my palm pressed against the VP's sister's mouth—and what a fucking mouth it is—and I'm here alone.

Well, I have Ninja with me in Vanessa's truck outside but I'm not sure he could have my back the way I'd need him to.

Without even waiting for the sand to stop attacking my retina, I flew to our side of the beach, scooped up my jeans and hoodie—careful not to jostle Ninja too much—and grabbed my boots and cut before yelling out for the nearest truck. Just as I got my eyesight back to normal, I saw my Cherry Pie squealing out of the parking lot in a dingy, beat-up sedan that looked like it was built before the Berlin Wall came crashing down.

Of course I fucking followed her. Ninja settled up on my shoulder watching the road the same way he watches our video games when Bear, Grinder, and I are in my suite at the compound.

Pulling up alongside the wooded area a couple of hundred feet behind, I walk down the road as though I belong there, searching out where Mackenzie parked her car.

Barely in her trailer for five minutes, she flew back out like a fire had been lit under her ass and ran into another trailer in the middle of the half-moon shaped property. From the boisterous cries and laughter coming from the place, it wasn't a stretch to guess she'd gone to the club hangout.

Is that where she works? Fuck, if I had a sister I wouldn't expose her to that kind of shit. Then again, I'm the guy who shot his own brother in the head because I didn't like his business choices.

"You're a fucking psycho, you know that?" Mackenzie whisper-yells now that we're inside her trailer, fear and confusion fighting for dominance with every expression on her face.

I shrug. "I've been called worse."

"You need to leave. Jesus! Did you, for one second, consider what would happen to me if any of those assholes found you here?" She's frantic, running to every one of her windows, quickly pulling the strings to the blinds to give us privacy.

The panic written all over her face has a fiery hatred unraveling in my stomach, but I push it down. I don't want to be responsible for adding more fear in her beautiful big blue eyes.

"I want you to meet someone."

"Oh my fucking God. No. I can't—"

I cut off her protests with my mouth slamming against hers. There's no resisting, no pushing me back, no slapping me away. That's how I know this thing between us isn't just me, she feels it too and the relief that flows through me is palpable.

"'No' and 'can't' aren't words I respond to very well." Winking first to keep it real, I slap my palm back over her mouth and grin at her wide eyes. Staying here is too dangerous, too many variables, but with her so adamant about not leaving, well, it doesn't leave me much of a choice, now does it?

Turning her around, I wrap my forearm around her neck and apply pressure on her carotid artery, all the while keeping her airway clear so she can keep breathing. I want her pliable, not dead. Obviously.

Right before her knees give out, I hear her mumble something that sounds closer to a death threat than a declaration of love.

Next time, she'll be more pliant and leave with me.

Maybe. Unless she kills me when she wakes up.

I'll step over that little speed bump just as soon as I reach it.

In mere seconds, I have her over one of my shoulders, head down toward my ass while I keep a strong hold of her thighs. I don't waste time getting the fuck out of there, leaving through a hole in the fence that I cut earlier when I realized this was her trailer.

Running to the truck, her body bouncing with every one of my steps, I open the passenger door just before placing her with gentle hands into the truck's cabin. Thankfully, the truck is too old to have a fob that beeps every time you unlock the doors, it's all old school where I have to put the key in the hole and turn to open.

It isn't long until she stirs, her nearly limp hand rising to her face and pushing her hair away.

When she opens her eyes, her entire body freezes and I can't help but grin. She's so fucking cute with her nose scrunched up and her brows slanted in confusion. No doubt, she's probably wondering what the fuck just happened so, being the gentleman that I am, I explain.

"It wasn't safe in your trailer so I brought you here." My smile doesn't falter, this is what she does to me.

"You mean...you kidnapped me." Speaking through clenched teeth, I see the moment she tries to sit up and push me away so she can bolt.

Yeah, that's not happening. These little disappearing acts are getting old and we need to have a serious conversation.

"You say this like it's a bad thing. Weren't you the one who said getting caught over there was dangerous?" Raising one brow in challenge, I sink my top teeth into my bottom lip and fight with every ounce of control that I have to not bring her back into my arms and fuck the confusion right off her face.

With a growl that says she's pissed but backing down, I watch her as she takes in the interior of Vanessa's truck. It's nothing new. In fact, I'm pretty sure this is the same vehicle Vanessa had when she met Prez and refused to give it up no matter how many times he protested.

"This is yours?"

It's cute how Mackenzie scrunches up her nose like me being on anything but a bike seems too strange for her. Hell, it's weird as fuck for me, too.

"Nah, it belongs to the Prez's old lady. I...borrowed it." Her scoff at my words has me shrugging.

"Yeah, like you borrowed me." This time she looks at me, hooking her fingers with air quotes.

"Touché." I don't let her continue as I close the passenger side door and run to my side of the truck.

"Where are we going? I can't leave with you, he'll fucking kill me." She's still whisper-yelling, even though we're safe and closed off inside the truck cabin.

"Nowhere, I just wanted to talk." She raises her brows at me—both, not just one, which is confusing because I can't tell if she's surprised or being sarcastic.

"By 'talking' do you mean your cock spilling its guts inside my pussy?" If she's trying to gross me out with her description, she's gonna have to up her game.

"No, smart ass, I mean talk. Like a regular couple." Just as I finish my sentence, she screams then jumps high enough to hit her head on the roof of the truck. Fucking Christ, I can't be that disgusting.

Then I get it.

Ninja runs up my arm to my shoulder and burrows inside my hoodie, scared shitless.

"Hey, buddy, it's okay. She won't hurt you."

"*She*? There's a rat in the truck and it's afraid of *me*?" With her feet up on the seat, her knees pressed against her chest and her arms wrapped around her shins, she looks so young that I'm suddenly worried she could be a minor. No, I've seen her drink, right?

"Now, now. No need to insult him. He's terrified of you, Cherry." Ninja peeks his head out and slowly crawls up to my shoulder, his tiny black marble eyes watching her every move.

"Well, I'm terrified of it, too."

"Mackenzie, I'm gonna have to put my foot down and make something clear or else this thing?" I motion my index finger between her and me in quick succession. "Won't work."

"That's what I've been trying—" I cut her off because fuck that, this thing *will* work, she just can't go around hurting Ninja's feelings.

"Not an 'it', baby, a 'he'. His name is Ninja and he's about six months old. Smartest pet I've ever had." Okay, also the only pet I've ever had but that's beside the point.

Ninja wraps his pink tail around my neck and backs into me, his nose going a million miles a minute as if he, too, can smell the cherries on her. It's his favorite fruit.

"I mean, he's cute now that I'm actually looking at him." Her body relaxes a little, her feet going back to the floorboard and her body leaning slightly in our direction. With her eyes darting all over Ninja's form, I can practically hear the cogs in her brain assessing just how dangerous my pet rat might be.

He's harmless.

"Do you want to hold him?" Holding my hand out, Ninja jumps on and curls his tail around my wrist for balance as he sits upright on his haunches. Meanwhile, I try to keep him relaxed by running a finger down his back and lightly scratching behind his ears.

They both lean in, sizing each other up. This feels like a monumental moment for me. My club is my family and, no doubt, I'm going to need to make adjustments for Mackenzie, especially knowing who her brother is, but this is something that feels more intimate somehow.

She's meeting my baby boy and if they don't get along it'll make life difficult for me, not to mention for her since Ninja has never had to share a space with anyone but me.

Sex in my bed might be an adjustment. I've never brought a woman to my place, always fucked them at the compound, so Ninja is pretty much the only constant in my everyday life.

"Hey, buddy, this is Mackenzie. She won't hurt you." Mackenzie reaches out a tentative finger and waits for Ninja to sniff it, his teeth taking her by surprise as he nibbles the extremity with affection. Rats have an excellent sense of smell so that cherry scent she's got going on is definitely playing in her favor. "See? He's grooming you. That means he likes you."

When Mackenzie's face lifts up to me, I'm taken aback by her sheer beauty. Yeah, her face is gorgeous with her big blue eyes, regal nose, and high cheekbones, not to mention those pouty pink lips that could bring any man to his knees, but that's not what gets to me. It's the genuine smile that she beams at me as though me telling her that Ninja likes her is akin to me telling her...fuck. I have no idea what would make her happy.

"I like him, too. You, however, I still hate." There's barely any venom in her words, unlike at the beach, but I guess punching her best friend in the face didn't earn me any points.

"That line between love and hate is mighty thin, baby-doll, and I wouldn't be opposed to you straddling it for me. If you could have anything in the world, what would you want?"

That beautiful smile vanishes immediately, a frown marrying her flawless features. I don't like it. I don't fucking like it one bit and I want to kick my own ass for causing it.

"Freedom." The silence in the cabin of the truck is stifling until Ninja saves us from the dreary mood by running down the side of my body and making his way up to her shoulder, where he nuzzles into her neck.

Mackenzie only squirms for a second before she's giving me that beautiful smile and, in an instant, the world is right again. Then her one word answer comes back to me and I have to ask.

"Freedom? What does that mean?" If someone is causing her to feel trapped, I'll cut their fucking arms off.

Wait, hopefully she's not talking about me.

Ninja is making her giggle, running up and down her arms and squeaking away like he's at Disney. Finally, he settles in her cleavage and I can't help the burst of laughter at the shocked look on her face.

"Is Ninja a..." She lowers her voice and tries to shield his ears. "Pervert?"

Oh fuck, she's so fucking cute.

"No, he likes warm and comfortable places to sleep." And sure enough, just as I say this, he curls up and starts to purr.

"I think I'm in love." Her words come out nonchalant and I swear to fuck, I make it my life goal to hear those words aimed at me.

"Mackenzie." My voice is rough, almost like I'm jealous of Ninja's privileged position, but I can't get distracted. "Freedom from what?"

With a sigh, she speaks, all the while staring at Ninja, as though not looking at me makes it easier for her to answer.

"Let's just say my brother hates me and I think he hates our mother even more but I'm not really sure why." She shrugs and the movement makes Ninja stir but doesn't wake him. "The only thing I can think about is that I was with our dad when he died so maybe he thinks I caused it somehow?" I frown at her admission. That's a bold accusation on his part.

"Did he tell you this?" Hate isn't a word I'd use when thinking of Jake, more of an animosity and general disdain for the way he chooses to interact with others. Now, though? The fact he's causing Mackenzie grief makes every one of my molecules boil with uncapped rage.

"No." Crossing her legs onto the seat, she leans her head back then rolls it to the side so she can look at me. "I'm like some weird version of Cinderella, except I don't live in a castle and there's no magical fairy godmother to save the day. And just like Cinderella, I have no idea what I did that was so wrong." Her smile can barely be called that, it's a fraction of what it was earlier when she and Ninja became besties.

"Well, I don't have the skills to be a fairy godmother and, to be clear, I'm far from being a prince, but I can kill him if you want."

Her chuckle tells me she thinks I'm kidding. I'm really not but I pretend like I am because losing her now isn't on my agenda.

"Look, you're..."—she waves her fingers around in my direction, pausing like she's choosing her next words wisely— "all that, but I don't need or even want a prince. I've got a plan in place, I'm getting myself out of this mess even though I didn't create it."

Leaning in, I'm about to tell her that she doesn't have to do a damn thing, I'll do it for her, keep her hands clean...when her palm rests softly on my cheek. She's taking this whole kidnapping thing quite well, to be honest. If her gesture says anything at all, it's that being with me isn't a hardship. I can work with that.

The warmth and tenderness of her touch is like nothing I've ever felt. There's no bolt of electricity or zing of fate. It's like the heat from her touch is spreading on all sides, down my neck and over my chest to where my cold heart beats only for survival's sake. But this touch? Her tenderness in this steel bubble where only the two of us exist? It melts away a chunk of that ice and gives my heart a new reason for beating.

"As much as you being here is a welcome distraction, it's also going to get me hurt. So, please, Psycho. Please, just let this go."

"Aleko."

"What?" She turns in my direction, confusion swimming in her beautiful blues.

"That's my name. Aleko. Aleko Kastellanos."

"Aleko. It suits you."

Our whispers keep this moment almost sacred, like we don't want it to be ruined by reality.

"Look at me, Mackenzie. I'm not letting you go. I can't do that. But here's what I am willing to do. Give me your boundaries and I'll..." Fucking hell, I haven't negotiated shit in years, I'm not even sure I know how. "I'll *try* to respect them." It's the best I can give her right now.

As she starts shaking her head from side to side, I take her hand and place it back where it was a second ago, basking in that heat again. "I'm not a good man, Cherry, but I'm an honest man. I've never had a need to lie, mainly because I don't give a fuck what people think of me and, in general, I don't give a fuck about anyone except my brothers." The way her attention is solely on me is giving me some strange version of stage fright but I ignore it. "Then, one night, you show up and all of a sudden...I give a shit."

I'm trying to be profound but all I do is make her chuckle.

"That's the most romantic thing anyone's ever said to me."

I smile, pressing her palm harder against my cheek.

"I give a shit, Mackenzie."

It's barely there but I'm staring so hard at her that it's impossible to miss her tiny nod. She gets it. She fucking gets it.

When she pulls her hand from my cheek it feels like the sun has died and my soul has fallen into the ice age. Picking up Ninja, she nuzzles his cute little nose as he makes squeaking sounds like she's the best thing since pizza and warm cleavage.

"He's really adorable." She's speaking to me but only looking at Ninja, like she doesn't have the courage to say her next words to my face.

This can't be good but if she thinks I'll let her go, she clearly hasn't been reading the room very well.

"Look." Her spine straightens by a fraction but I notice. In fact, I notice every fucking thing she does. "I'm not interested in whatever you think this is. I've got too much shit going on in my life to have to worry about one more thing."

"Trust me, babydoll, you won't need—" When she cuts me off, I legit growl. This woman is going to drive me insane, but at least I have her full attention now as her eyes hit me like twin missiles ready to annihilate me.

"Are you fucking kidding me? You show up at my work." I'm going to bite that index finger right off if she doesn't stop enumerating. "You punch my best friend." Her middle finger joins the first. "You follow me back to my home." When she raises her ring finger, I realize a diamond would look fucking amazing right there. Then her pinky finger pops up. "You. Kidnapped. Me." Ah, so she *is* holding that against me. "You are the fucking definition of a problem."

I'm so busy wondering where I could find a ring that is unique and exceptional, just like her, that it takes me a second to realize she's stopped talking and is now placing Ninja on my lap. Next thing I know, she's out of the fucking truck. That definitely gets my attention as I practically fly out of the driver's side, careful to put Ninja back on the passenger seat.

"Mackenzie." She stops, whipping around with her finger at her lips silently telling me to shut the fuck up. "Do not fucking walk away from me."

With her shoulders rising and falling like a frustrated kindergarten teacher trying to keep her patience at an acceptable level, she walks over to me and pats me on the chest. Fucking hell, is she placating me? Does she think I'm going to fall apart?

"Look." Nothing good ever starts with that word. "This isn't happening. My brother is dangerous and his moral compass is so far south that even the devil has to look down at him. Maybe one day, when I've left this place, I'll give you a call."

Motherfucker. I mean, if I kill him with one bullet to the brain, all of these fucking problems would be moot.

I'm about to tell her just that when she shushes me. Fucking shushes me like I'm fucking five. "You can't kill him, Aleko. He's my responsibility."

Two things happen in that moment.

Hearing my given name breathed out from between her lips does something to me. There's some kind of inexplicable shift somewhere in my chest and a drop in my stomach so close to a rollercoaster ride that I have to brace myself against the hood of the truck to keep myself grounded.

Then, her last two words act like a magnet to her strength. She's not afraid of me killing her brother, no. She's keeping it as her duty. Her job. Her kill.

Fuck. I think I'm in love.

"I have to go. Please stop following me or showing up at my place or whatever it is that stalkers tend to do these days. When I'm ready, I'll get in touch." At the finality of her words, I stand to my full height and cross my arms over my chest to trap them so I don't reach out and fucking kidnap her—again. Taking a step back, she nods like this conversation is over and she got what she wanted.

Yeah, not even close, babydoll.

I watch her walk away until her silhouette disappears, all the while planning my next move.

As soon as I get back into the truck, Ninja jumps on my shoulder and nuzzles my neck like he too is bummed that Mackenzie is making this harder than it needs to be.

"Yeah, buddy, I know. Next time, you need to amp up your charms. I can't be doing all the work here."

"Church, five minutes," Shade calls out just as I sink the eight ball right where I wanted it and hold out my hand for Bear to pay up. Thankfully for him, we never bet much or else he'd be pushing his bike instead of riding.

"Fucker."

I barely hear Bear's insult as he slaps a Hamilton into my awaiting palm, making a beeline for the chapel at the back of the compound.

"Come on, Bear, don't be a sore loser." My booming laughter echoes in the halls making Bear, Grinder, and Shade all stop and turn. "What?" Looking down at my clothes, I don't see anything wrong so I bring my hand to my mouth, but there aren't any crumbs stuck to my face either.

"Why are you so giddy?" My snarl is instant and it's aimed at Grinder, whose attention is back on his phone. "Hold please." His thumbs are flying a million miles a second but it's his slow rising smile that promises holes will be filled and soon that takes all the attention off of me and right onto him.

"Who you textin'?" Shade rolls his eyes and doesn't wait around to find out Grinder's answer to Bear's question, instead he continues down the hall toward the chapel.

"Nunya," is Grinder's one word reply.

"What are we, five?" I clip Grinder in the back of the head as Bear and I leave him behind, still texting, still smiling.

"You didn't answer the question, don't think I didn't notice."

I shrug at Bear's words and pop a cherry sucker in my mouth like the cocky asshole I am.

Only once everyone is sitting at the large oak table built with love and tenderness by our founders' hands does the gavel silence the laughter and chatter.

"Shut the fuck up! We've got business and I don't have time for all y'all's bullshit." All eyes are to the head of the table as we go through our different tasks from the week.

"Python, where we at with the security system?" My sucker still in my mouth, I turn to the prospect who wouldn't normally be here, but his techy brain is the only one capable of getting our cameras and surveillance shit set up. He'll be gone for the rest of our club business.

"Yeah, so, I made a spreadsheet for our risk management process with overall IT security strategies in one tab, goals in a second and, of course, our control obje–" Python is interrupted by Prez who, like the rest of us, has had enough of the kid's geekfest monologue.

"I don't give a fuck about spreadsheets and risk management. That's your fucking job. Is. It. Done?"

"Yes."

"Good, now get the fuck out."

I try not to chuckle as Prez shows his rank. He's a big believer in tough love and being too easy on Py won't help him beat his addiction...keeping him busy will.

"And, Py." We all wait as the prospect looks over his shoulder, one hand on the door knob. "Good job."

Well, fuck. I take it all back.

"Going soft in your old age, Prez." Shade is the only brother ballsy enough to mention Prez's age.

"The only thing going soft is your dick." Prez's attention is back on Python's retreating back, waiting for the heavy double doors to close again before he continues the meeting. "All right, what's going on with the distributor?"

"Well, Darryl couldn't keep his mouth shut and his pockets empty so he's no longer of this world." Grinder shoots his one sentence explanation with exactly zero regret.

"Bear, I get it, man, but fuck. Did you really need to go the whole nine yards on him?"

Bear shrugs.

"Don't look at me. This psycho killed him and Neon Ass Flosser over there thought it was a great teaching moment for the prospect. All I did was hand the knife over to him." Bear's thumb is pointing at me, accusation loud and clear.

"Look, I just told it like it is. Guy's a thief, thought it'd be good for the dudes in the afterlife to know it." One fist bump later, Prez gives up, sitting back in his chair on a heavy exhale.

"Well, we've got the shipment but that ain't gonna last long. What's our back-up plan?" The answer to Prez's question comes from the back of the table.

"Remember my cousin, Jed?" Boner pipes up, his right hand up like he's in fucking middle school.

"Yeah, up in New Bern?" We all nod at Prez's words.

I remember this. Boner came to us a couple of years ago, saying his cousin had opened up a distribution center for automotive and motorcycle parts but since Darryl's shit was working well for us, we put the idea on the back burner.

Guess it's time to heat up the sauce, so to speak.

"Yeah, Prez. It's doing good up there. He's hired a few new employees this year and even bought the store next door so he could expand."

Taking the candy out of my mouth, I tap it to my lip and hum loudly enough for all to hear.

"What's on your mind, Psycho?"

"I mean, it all depends on where he's located. New Bern is growing, got a lot of old folks retiring on the waterfront since it's cheaper than this place." I voice my concerns and watch as Prez takes it all in. It's what makes him ideal for this role. He's not a loose cannon like Grinder or blood-thirsty like Shade. Definitely not walking the line of morality like Bear and me.

"Yeah, old folks have lots of time on their hands and notice every fucking thing." Pointing to me, Bear, and Boner, he makes his decision. "You three go up to New Bern and check out the location, get a read on..." Prez looks to Boner.

"Jed."

"Right, get a read on Jed, see if his balls have dropped and make sure he knows that anything goes wrong, Boner pays the price." We all nod then continue on with the next order of business.

Twenty minutes later, we're walking out the door when Prez calls out.

"Psycho."

I turn. "Yeah, Prez."

"Take Python with you. I don't want him getting bored."

"Sure thing, Prez."

By the time we're on the road, I've convinced Python to set us up with cameras so we can feed his favorite social media platform, LibPost, where it's easy to hide IP addresses and most content disappears after twenty-hours. It's where a lot of us do our crazy shit on bikes, post it, and laugh at other people's reactions.

That's what I'm doing right now, on Highway 17, heading due north. Cars are in both lanes and tourists are taking their time visiting the great state of First Flight. You can't live, or even just be, in this state and not know the Wright Brothers had their first powered plane in the air for twelve seconds in Kitty Hawk, North Carolina.

In our own way, we're doing the same thing with our speed and our death wishes on wheels. Going almost a hundred miles an hour, I lower my head into the small bubble windshield, hop one knee on the seat and extend my other leg like a fucking ballerina. Python is filming me as I pass him and just before I return to a normal position, I flip off the camera and everyone watching.

No doubt, Py will add some catchy tunes to the video and the shit will go viral again.

It's my winning personality and my great body.

It should have taken us less than an hour and a half to get here but Bear was picky with his stunts and Python had to stop a couple of times to adjust something or other, who the fuck knows?

Needless to say, our late arrival in New Bern was noticed since my phone lit up with fifteen calls from Prez.

"Fuck. Daddy's mad." Everyone cackles, but once I have him on the phone, I just put all the blame on Py since he's the least likely to get the shit beat out of him.

Shade wasn't wrong, Prez has a soft side for him, although none of us know why. It's adorable, in a papa-bear-ready-to-shoot-someone's-face-off-for-disre-specting-his-old-lady kind of way.

Immediately, my mind turns to my Cherry Pie and my smile is automatic.

"Brother, you are no longer pussy whipped. You're fucking tied to her bed like a goddamn starfish." Bear's laughing, thinking he's funny as fuck, but I'm wondering if she'd be into that shit. I mean, I would definitely tie her up to my bed and eat her pussy until she's crying and begging and screaming for me to stop. And even then, I don't think I could ever get enough of eating her raw.

Then my smile disappears when I remember her words, *"I'm not interested in whatever you think this is."* I don't know if she's lying to me or to herself. One thing is for sure, though, she's fucking lying to someone because the way her body reacts to my touch is the only truth I trust.

"All right, assholes," I call out, "Let's get this shit done." Our bikes are all aligned at perfect intervals from each other, as if they're watching us walk away but eager for us to return.

"Yeah, Psycho's frothin' at the mouth for some puss-ay!" I love Bear, he's my brother in every way that counts, but if he continues to talk about Mackenzie like she's some cheap Khaos Khunt, I'm going to throw down and hurt the motherfucker.

"Keep talking, Bear, and you'll be eating through a straw." They all *ooooh* and *ahhhh* at my reaction but they have no idea just how close I am to acting on it.

"All right, all right. I gotcha, Brother. I gotcha." And he does because he lets it go. He gets me, and thank fuck for that because I don't want to have to kill him for disrespecting my woman.

"Felix!" We all turn to the booming voice and it takes me a second to remember Boner's real name. "Glad you're here, man. Was happy to get your call." Jed is nothing like Boner. In fact, they're polar opposites. Where Boner is basically skin on bones—which is where his club name comes from—with hair well past his shoulders, Jed looks like he's enjoying all the barbecues and Sunday dinners life has to offer. His cropped hair reminds me that he served. The high and tight must be hard to abandon.

"'Sup, Jed? Been a while, man." They hug, slapping each other on the back and shooting the shit for almost five minutes, making me impatient. I'm all for family re-unions but this is business. Boner can catch up with the three-point-five kids and new boob job for the wife at a later date.

"Is there a place we can talk in private?" I hate to cut short the lovefest happening but...yeah, no. I don't actually hate it. I'm eager to get back home and surprise my Cherry Pie by showing up at her place and burying my cock so deep inside her delicious cunt that she'll forget all about her lies.

"Oh, yeah, yeah. Of course. Come on, I've got the conference all set up. You boys need some coffee?" Bear and I look at each other with matching "What the fuck?" expressions. This guy is like a Beaver Cleaver dad. Does he even know what we do?

I hang back a few steps, my hand on Boner's shoulder pulling him toward me.

"Ex-military, good guy with a legit business? I'm thinking this is a bad idea, Boner." His only response to my worries is a wink. If this shit goes south, I'll kill him myself.

As soon as we walk into the conference, Jed's entire demeanor changes. Gone is the happy-go-lucky automotive shop owner, in his place is down-for-business Jed who wants to double his income without paying taxes.

Hmmm, I don't trust greedy people so I do what I do best. I watch and assess.

Unwrapping a sucker with slow, measured movements, I listen while Bear introduces us and Python, not so discreetly, checks out the security system. There are two cameras in opposite corners of the room, the shades are pulled halfway down, and the air in the room has shifted to something less cozy and more gritty.

We all decline alcohol. We're driving back on sports bikes, we're not that fucking stupid.

Meanwhile, Jed serves Bear and Boner each a cup of coffee from what looks like a complicated machine from Italy. The thought has Marco Mancini's shocked face flashing in my mind from the day I pulled out my gun and shot my older brother right between the eyes.

The day I tasted freedom for the first time.

As the don of the New York City mafia, at the time, Marco was trying to figure out where my family stood on the war that was about to break out in the Big Apple. That's when I learned that my brother, Yiannis, was trafficking young women, having them abducted from fuck knows where to sell them to the highest bidders.

I didn't hesitate. I didn't negotiate.

There are few moral high-grounds I pretend to stand on, but that? No. Innocent people aren't our pawns and they aren't our currency. Everyone at the table joins willingly, their fate is their own.

My brother chose to break our pact so I ended him. Plain and simple.

"When Felix called and said y'all had an opening for distribution, I was all in. Our business is thriving all on its own so me doing some side jobs won't be suspicious." From across the table, Bear eyes me with legitimate questions in his eyes.

The one thing that keeps bouncing around my mind is that old adage: "If it's too good to be true..."

Instead of pushing my chair back and walking away from this potentially fucked up situation, I let my curiosity get its fill.

"Ain't nothin' suspicious about buying in bulk." Bear is throwing a line out to see if Jed bites. On this, we're on the same page. Those cameras are either for legit business reasons or we're being set-up.

"Right, right. Just tryin' to stay afloat on taxes and such." I breathe a little easier on my end when Jed doesn't try to push us to admit to something that could potentially land us in jail faster than you can say *bend over*.

"Mind if we take a look around the premises? I'm a sucker for businesses that are...what did you say? Thriving?" Boner rolls his eyes, knowing exactly what my deal is and Bear nods, completely on board.

"Oh yeah, of course. Be my pleasure." Everyone stands, Jed taking the lead to walk out of the conference room while Bear waits long enough to be out of earshot.

"Thoughts?"

I shrug, not wanting to say anything with cameras trained on us.

"We'll see what he's got to offer."

"I'm gonna go take a piss." Python doesn't wait for us to answer, he's already running for the bathroom. My eyes narrow as I watch him. His gate is quick, his hands raking through his hair, scratching at his scalp making my lip rise in a snarl. That's a brotherly beat down waiting to happen, right there, if he's doing what I think he's doing.

"Come on, let's go." Bear clips me at the back of my head and I punch him in the side laughing when he coughs, effectively distracting me from that time bomb.

Boner's walking with his cousin as they cross the building. One side is like a huge automotive shop with products lining the walls, neat little price tags aligned on the tops and bottoms of the rows.

Once we're out of the conference room, I speak but keep my voice low so that only Bear can hear me.

"The meeting in a closed off space with cameras? Not a good start, Brother."

"Yeah, and I ain't likin' the whole Dr. Jekyll and Mr. Hyde thing he's got goin' on." I stop walking, taking my sucker out of my mouth and waiting for him to realize I'm not at his side anymore. When he finally does, he turns and frowns. "What?"

"Have you been reading behind my back?" It's a running joke. Bear talks like he's crawled his way out of the boondocks but the man's culture is impressive. I bust his balls all the time since before he joined, I was the only one not playing video games and passing my quiet time with a book or ten.

"Not hard to do these days, Psycho. You've been distracted." And that's all he says about that.

Also, he's not wrong.

When Python catches up to us, he looks calmer, which makes my hands twitchy with the need to smack some sense into him.

"You." I point to the prospect and just as I expected, his eyes go wide and his body language tells a whole story about his addiction. "Get over here."

As if he's got springs on his boots, he runs over to me, one hand scratching at his scalp, the other in his pocket. "Whassup?"

"What were you doin' in the bathroom, Py?" My eyes don't leave him for a second, trying to read every twitch and every move he makes.

"Uh, taking a piss. Why?" He's staring straight at me and all of a sudden I question myself. Did I read too much into this? His eyes aren't dilated or glassy, and it's not like it took him long to answer, like he was looking for excuses.

"I'm gonna ask you once, and only once. Are you using again?" At my words, Python jumps back like I've just shocked him with a defibrillator.

"No, man. Of course not. I promised Prez I wouldn't. You know he'll kick me out if I do. I ain't takin' that risk." Fuck, maybe I'm just being paranoid. His speech is coherent, his gaze steady without glassy or bloodshot eyes. I mean, the kid's not even in his twenties yet, so being cagey could just be the norm at nineteen.

"All right." I ruffle his hair and chuckle when he bends at the waist to get away from my hand. Python's a pretty boy, he doesn't like it when we mess up his pretty locks.

For the next hour, we get the grand tour. From the warehouse where he keeps his stock to the small garage where he's got a couple of mechanics doing diagnostics and adjustments with minimal repairs. Any considerable jobs are sent to a partner across town, which seems ridiculous. They should expand that here, hire more mechanics that can do the hardcore repairs and keep the clients for themselves. But fuck, ain't my circus.

"So, there you have it. We have the space and I have three men I trust to my core." Jed slides his hands in his pockets and nods to a few men chatting right outside the garage. They look at us then at our bikes and the appreciation in their eyes is evident. They're fans of sports bikes and we get it. Speed makes me hard, too.

"Well, any business needs to be put up to a vote so Boner will let you know the deal." Bear shakes Jed's hand and we all follow suit, not giving him anything one way or another.

"Of course. Y'all be safe ridin' back." We all nod, knowing damn well we'll probably do some stupid shit. Par for the course.

Python's the first on his bike, blowing his nose like he's suddenly caught a virus while Boner is giving his cousin a bro hug with lots of back slapping and shoulder punching.

On the ride back, my brain alternates between analyzing every detail of this meeting and wondering just how I'm going to fuck Mackenzie into submission.

By the time we make it back to Rockford Beach, I'm ready to seek out my girl and show her that it's going to take a fuck load more than late night speeches and lies to make me back down. I don't give a shit what her brother wants, I will bury that motherfucker then apologize to her for taking away her kill, but one way or another, her wish will come true.

Well, kind of.

She'll be free. Free from her brother's hold but not free from me.

Never that.

I'm about to tell the brothers to have drinks without me when Python gets off his bike, stumbles two or three steps, then falls flat on his face.

CHAPTER EIGHT
MACKENZIE

Deaths occurring while I'm working my EMT job aren't unheard of, but they're usually few and far between. It hits me hard when we have to escort a lifeless body to the ER. When I got home from yesterday's shift, I dove into my stash of Milk Duds from the drawer beneath my bed and still haven't moved. And now the sun is shining through my flimsy curtains, the dawn of a new day and all that shit.

I shouldn't allow myself to get so affected by death, it happens every day. I'm aware my brother and his club aren't exactly angels, but last night...it was just a kid. He was barely seventeen and the seizure seemed to come out of nowhere.

Banging on my trailer door makes me jump, spilling Milk Duds all over my bed sheets as I quickly stand. Still wearing the sweats I left work in last night, I step out of my tiny room that barely fits my queen-size bed and move to open the front door. The handle is halfway down when my brother barges inside, pushing me out of the way and heading straight to my fridge. He grabs a beer—of which I make sure to have plenty for occasions such as this—and he gulps down over half the purple can before sitting on my old navy-blue couch.

"Got a job for ya, Kenz." Leaning back, he lifts his feet and rests them on my dark wooden coffee table.

I don't speak, gently clicking the door closed behind me because the other club members can be nosy fucks if they happen to be walking by.

"You're twenty-one now, yeah?" He's my brother, this is information he should know, and a passerby would assume he's being hypothetical. He's not.

"Yes. I turned twenty-one a week ago." My voice is monotone, emotions are wasted on Jake.

"Good. I need you to do some undercover shit for me. The grapevine says Rocks Off over in Rockford beach are looking for some new girls, so go get a job. Bring me information on the Sons of Khaos." He's speaking as though it's the simplest task in the world. Like he's asking me to grab him some sugar from the supermarket on my next trip.

"You told me to stay away from them because they're dangerous. Now you want me to work for them?" It's difficult to keep the bite from my tone, his hard stare telling me not to argue with him on this.

"I do. Get close to them, find out how they run their businesses, and relay everything back to me for the club. Simple." He shrugs, still not grasping the enormity of what he's asking me to do.

"What about here? You know the other girls are too slow behind the bar when it gets busy. They spend most of their time flirting to get out of work." I'm grasping at straws because it's clear by the set of his jaw that there's no getting out of this.

"Are you questioning me, Kenz?" He cracks his knuckles and I prepare myself for some kind of impact. "You know, it's been a while since I've visited Mom." The way he says *Mom* makes the hairs on the back of my neck stand and a rock forms in my stomach. "Brick loves older ladies. Especially practically comat—"

"Okay, I'll do it. Just stop. Please." I hate begging him, and when it comes to myself I can take it. But when he brings Mom into it...no.

Her heart is broken enough, I won't allow him to break her body and mind any more than she's done herself.

Jake chuckles, a sadistic sneer curving his thin lips, the darkness of his lashes and hair highlighting his bright blue eyes. If it wasn't for the shadow of hate that surrounds my brother, he'd be the spitting image of Dad, whereas I'm a mixture of both our parents. I have Dad's blue eyes and Mom's thick blonde hair.

"Yes. You will. You can go in as soon as they open at three for the afternoon crowd. Get an application and do everything you can to make them hire you." Crushing the can of beer in his fist, he stands, throwing it into my sink before pushing me against the wall and pressing his forehead into mine so hard it hurts. "And if you think this means more freedom for you, little sister, you are very fucking wrong. You know what happens when you disappoint me." His malice-filled words are spoken through gritted teeth, his eyes pools of pure darkness and hatred before he steps back and slaps my cheek. It stings, but I don't flinch away from him, instead staring directly at him before he turns and walks out the door. He doesn't close it behind him because he's a giant anus.

Interactions like this with my brother are just reminders of why I need to get out of this hellhole. Adrenaline courses through my veins and I'm more determined than ever to follow through with my plan. But I'll do what he asks, for now. I was originally on Rebels dinner duty this afternoon before tidying up the property and working the bar, so I guess I could drag this out and pretend there are reasons I'm not back in time to work tonight. Silver linings...

Although, it does mean the Prez, Isaac, and Brick, the Rebels' Enforcer, won't be getting this week's round of the shits or vomiting from my latest special recipe. Lucky for me, they put it down to the amount of general shit they ingest into their bodies willingly. Drugs, alcohol, way too much food, it's surprising they can still ride their motorcycles at all.

Brick's one of our top riders in the street races because he has no respect for his motorcycle, it's always in the garage being fixed up for stupid things, and holy shit!

The connection to last week's new number two spot has just caught up in my brain. Psycho! Aleko. Damn, he just became one of those memes, *he's a ten, but he's a badass on the track, so he's a twenty.*

The warm water cascading down my body in my tiny shower relaxes me after my encounter with Jake, and I notice the marks Aleko left on my shoulders and neck last weekend are fading into nothingness. Honestly, I'm a little sad about it. My last reminder of my own personal *Romeo and Juliet* moment of a forbidden encounter.

It's a good thing I have a large stash of different colored concealers for marks on my body—it's a whole color wheel theory thing; greens cancel out redness, purples cancel out yellows. But every time I've covered these particular marks, the memory from that night makes my nipples peak. Then I remember the other crazy shit that possessive man has done since and I find myself smiling—right before telling myself off for such thoughts. Putting my foot down the other night and telling Aleko there is no hope for us was absolutely the right move.

Hair washed, dried, and now with loose bouncing curls, I finish applying just the right amount of makeup. What I'm really hoping for with this whole thing is that the people at Rocks Off will turn me away from the strip club, tell me I'm not what they're looking for, but my brother will no doubt want to check me over before I leave. To make sure I've made adequate effort to do what he has asked, so I have to make an effort with the way I look. To be honest, I've always loved an excuse to get dressed up. It's like an opportunity to be an elevated version of myself that isn't practically rolling in crap every day.

The half-length mirror in my bedroom is all I have in this shitty little trailer with more leaks than Niagara Falls, and I spend a minute analyzing myself. Tight black booty shorts, fuck-me heels in my hand because driving in them would be a death sentence, black thigh-high socks with three pink stripes around the top, and a matching pink and diamanté bra-style top that makes my ample cleavage look amazing. Yeah, this will do. Paired with my smokey eyes, glossy lips, and gold hoops in all five of each of my ear piercings, I look pretty fucking hot.

I wish I wasn't driving tonight because I wouldn't say no to a joint to calm my nerves. With a deep breath, I pick up my small bag with all my essentials and leave my poor excuse for a home in search of Jake.

Who I see first, is not Jake.

It's almost two thirty in the afternoon now and a lot of the Rebel members are finishing up their construction jobs or are just done for the day. They're beginning to congregate around the bar area, with Brick and Booker pulling donuts on their motorcycles around the large empty space in the center of the yard.

Isaac is the one who makes eye contact with me first, wolf-whistling in a way that makes me want to vomit in my mouth.

"Looking sexy as hell, Kenz. Come and sit on Daddy's lap like a good girl." He pats his thigh where he's sitting half-on his motorcycle on the outskirts of the larger area.

Trying really hard not to roll my eyes and visibly cringe, I move toward him, bracing myself for whatever's about to happen. He may be the President of this club, but he is not a good man. In fact, I'd say he's worse than my brother.

Most of the other members don't know the extent of my beatings from my brother and his merry band of dickheads. They may see me get reprimanded from time to time, but most of my punishments are dealt out in private. They like to build up the suspense before they take turns slapping me around for shits and giggles. But the joke's on them. My punishment for them will be a lot more permanent.

"I need to go, Isaac. Jake has me on a club task and I can't be late." I keep a smile on my face, my tone sweet, so as not to rile him up or anger him in any way.

As I get closer, he reaches out and grabs my wrist, tight enough to bruise, pushing the silver bracelet I'm wearing into my flesh.

"You can give your Prez a little something before you go though, right?" Pulling me into him, he wraps an arm around my waist, letting go of my wrist to paw up my thigh.

"I really don't have time. Jake said it was importa—"

His fingers dig so deeply into the flesh of my thigh just beneath my pussy that I almost cry out with pain, but I clench my teeth and remain deadly still. They don't cross that line with me, though they may get close, and I don't want to do anything that would push him right now.

"Fine. But you owe me. Ungrateful little slut."

I almost fall over as he shoves me away from him, forgetting all about me as Mona sidles up to him with a purple can in her hand for him.

Jake is nowhere to be seen, so I'm guessing he's either gone home or is out somewhere. Meaning I can leave without the ridiculous inspection of my outfit choice.

The wreck I call a car starts up after only two tries, and as I drive away, I think about how it's going to feel when I can finally do this for real. Like, never come back. Gone. Poof. Leaving my brother and his club up shit's creek without a paddle because I also plan on exposing every illegal thing they do to the cops—I just need to keep trying to find actual evidence of this.

It's a twenty-minute drive to Rocks Off, the strip club owned by the Sons Of Khaos, and there's a small parking lot to the left with plenty of spaces available at this time in the afternoon. I arrive at the double doors with impeccable timing because I watched them being unlocked as I approached.

A beautiful, tall woman with a lavender afro greets me when I walk in, and I lift my hand in an awkward wave.

"Hey. I'm Candie. I didn't realize they'd hired someone new already. I haven't even interviewed anyone yet, but I'll show you around." Her smile is genuine as she looks me up and down, no hint of malice etched within her features at all. It's refreshing.

The sluts at the Rebels' compound may tolerate me, and I may respect them, but let's just say that I'm never going to be invited to girls' night out with them.

"Sorry, no. I'm not new. Not yet anyway. I was hoping to fill out an application?"

Stepping further inside, I allow the doors to close behind me, taking in the grandeur that is the blacks and glittering silvers of the club. The entrance is surrounded with sparkling black curtains on the walls, a large shining black desk and coat check-in area. From my position, I can see through to the main strip club area, with several mini stages surrounded by booths and a larger stage in the center, a walkway leading toward it from a wall with yet more curtains. Though, I'm guessing there are actual changing rooms or something behind those.

"Ah, okay. Sorry about that. If it was up to me, I'd give you a job on the spot, but you might be a serial killer or some shit, so yeah, I'll grab you a form." Candie faux-grimaces when she says I might be a serial killer, quickly replacing it with a wide smile I can't help but like.

Walking behind the desk, she shuffles through some drawers before pulling out what she's looking for, passing me what I'm guessing is the application form.

"Thank you. Can I fill it out now?" Once I'm done here, I've already scoped out a great-looking coffee shop about five minutes away where I plan on sitting for as long as possible to avoid going home. I'll make up some bullshit excuse about needing to do a trial run or something because I know Jake won't send anyone here to check on me tonight. That'll come later, if I get the job. "Absolutely. Do you have a pen?" Without waiting for me to answer, she holds up a black ballpoint, waving it around enthusiastically.

"I don't. Thank you for this." I take the pen and place the form on the waist-high desk space. There's no sitting here, it seems.

"I'll leave you to it, have to finish setting up the bar and make sure the girls are ready before too many people start coming in." Candie waves way more elegantly than I did earlier before practically skipping off into the main room, her skin-tight red sequin pants reflecting the lights as she goes.

I bring my attention back to the form, and the surname part almost makes me falter because it won't take long to put two and two together if I use my real last name, the one I share with my brother. Instead, I use my mom's maiden name, Monroe. There's no way the Sons of Khaos would give a job to the sister of their rivals.

"I'd recognize that ass anywhere."

And I'd recognize that voice in a heartbeat.

Aleko.

Slowly, I stand straight and turn to face him, almost jumping backward when I realize how close he already is.

Leaning into me, he inhales deeply, pressing me against the tall desk so I have nowhere to go.

"Mmm. Cherries."

If I'm honest with myself, a part of me wanted to see him, but I also hoped he'd do what we discussed and stay away from me. Boundaries and all that.

I'm in his territory now though, it's a whole new ball game over here.

Instead of worrying about my brother and his friends trying to fuck me over, I have the notorious Sons of Khaos to worry about. Aleko is obsessed with me for reasons I can't comprehend, and I wish I was madder about it. I guess I'm attracted to chaos. Ha. Ironic but true.

"Why do you keep smelling me?"

His lips are hovering over mine as he continues to cage me in, and I want to trace the tattoos on his face with my fingers...which is exactly why this job is a bad idea. Not only are the Sons dangerous in general, but this one in particular is deadly for so many more reasons.

"Because you smell fucking delicious. Good enough to eat." As if proving his point, he thrusts his hips a little while biting down super close to the tip of my nose. "Did you come to kidnap *me* this time, Cherry?" There goes that damn single eyebrow again. It's an art form, I swear.

"Ha, no. I'm not a psycho like you. I came to fill out an application."

He backs off slightly, glancing behind me to the paperwork I've been completing.

"You don't need to finish that." He turns his head toward the entrance of the main area. "Candie, ready to do an interview now?" His voice is a little raised, but still raspy and sends chills through my bones.

"No. I'm waiting for Bruno to arrive so he can work the bar. I'm holding interviews on Sunday afternoon." She appears in the entryway to speak before disappearing again, then music starts up and another beautiful girl dressed in a sparkling black tux comes from a door I hadn't noticed before. She stands behind the tall desk and clears her throat.

"Are you done here, Miss? I have guests to check in. Hi, Psycho." The way she says hi is filled with a lot more lust than I find necessary.

"Come on, Cherry. I'll interview you." Completely ignoring the red-head, he shoves a lollipop into his mouth from fuck knows where then gently grips my hand as though it's made from porcelain, grabs my form, and leads me through the new-to-me door.

"If by interview, you mean a fuck in the office, then no. Not today, Satan."

He chuckles as we step into a large space that looks a little like a lounge/refreshment room with a fridge, coffee machines, and several places to sit and eat I suppose.

"I'm not Satan, sweetheart. I'm far more dangerous. Just call me Aleko." He pulls me onto his lap as he takes a seat on one of the two-seater couches.

"Get off me, Psycho." I struggle to free myself of his hold and stand again, resting a hand on my hip as I turn to stare down at him. "I thought I already explained that this can't happen."

"Aleko." There's nothing but a victory smirk on his stupidly handsome face. The upside down cross beneath his eye twitches as his cheek moves and the stick in his mouth tilts upward as he sucks.

"What does your name have to do with anything?"

"No one calls me Aleko anymore, it's special. Just for you."

"I don't need a special name for you because I don't want to be around you." I'm lying, I know it, and he knows it too if his fucking raised brow is anything to go by.

"Okay, Cherry." He leans forward, resting his elbows on his knees, and gestures to the office chair in front of the desk. "Now, about this interview. Why do you wanna work here? I thought you had a job or two already."

Huffing, I resist rolling my eyes and sit down, feeling like I should be interviewing him rather than the other way around.

In one quick move, Aleko stands, grips the arms of the rolling chair and drags it over to the couch, sitting back down so our knees are touching.

"I don't think we need to be this close for an interview, do you?" I narrow my eyes and tilt my head, enjoying the challenge this man brings.

"Yes, I do." He smirks again, his hand coming to my jaw and squeezing hard enough to make my lips part wide. Expecting some caveman kissing from him, I blink in surprise when he slides his ever-present candy on a stick out, sucking once for good measure, before placing it on my tongue. When he releases my jaw, my lips automatically close around the sugary ball and, on instinct, it's my turn to suck on it. Just as quickly, it's gone and back in his own mouth. I'm pretty sure he's an actual psychopath.

"Whatever." I sigh and actually do roll my eyes this time. I'll do the interview, but as much as Jake wants it, I can't work here. It's already causing more problems than I want to juggle.

"So you have experience behind the bar?"

I didn't expect him to actually interview me...

"Yeah. Three years."

"But you've just turned twenty-one? What kind of bar allows an under-age girl to work there?" He furrows his brow.

"The kind that is a private one. C'mon. You know I'm with the Rebels, I work for them. Why are you even entertaining me for this?" Using my feet, I roll my chair backward until it bangs against the desk behind me.

"Figured you were leaving your brother's club and coming to join the darker side." He wags his single brow, that smirk fully in place.

This is fucking torturous insanity.

Why didn't I think this through at all? Not that I had much choice.

There's only one way out of this, and that's to get him to say no to employing me. Then I'll never have to come back and see him again. Jake may be initially angry about it, but when he has his other spies checking up on me to see if I'm telling the truth, he'll know I wasn't lying.

What I'm about to say could likely earn me a beating from the Sons, but I can take it. I may despise them because of who they are, hate the way this man in front of me makes me feel, but I can't see him this often and do what needs to be done. I can't be the spy Jake wants me to be.

"You don't want to hire me, okay? Can we leave it at that?" As soon as the words leave my mouth, I know they are wasted, because of course this obsessive man can't leave well enough alone. I quickly stand, ready to head out the door, but Aleko stands too, moving just as quickly and caging me in against the wall. He's not touching me, his palms to either side of my head, his breath tickling my cheek, the heat from his body causing a reaction inside mine that I'm trying so hard to deny.

"There's no way in Hell you're working on the stages. I'm okay with anyone admiring what's mine, but trying to touch it, sully it with their misguided thoughts...I'll cut every one of their dicks off." The possessive vibrations of his chest roll right through me as he crunches down on the rest of his sucker.

"It's settled then. I'm not hired. Thanks. You can let me go now." I try to move, to turn and walk away, but he doesn't let up. Shoving his nose into my neck, he sniffs and growls, holding me hostage.

"No, no, no. Now you need to tell me why we don't want to hire you. I just gave you a truth, now it's your turn." Fuck my life, Aleko is a persistent man who knows exactly what he wants.

I'll bet the truth would put him off though. Who wants to date someone sent to spy on their precious club?

"Okay, Aleko. Here it is. Jake heard there were vacancies, sent me to apply for a job so I could bring him personal and financial information about the Sons Of Khaos. So I'm basically a spy." I sigh, actually feeling a little lighter having gotten that off my chest.

"Don't give me that shit. If you were one of them, you wouldn't be telling me all this. But you are because, guess what? You belong to me, whether or not you get that yet. There's nothing Toxic about you, baby, you're a Khaos Old Lady, nothing less." He begins placing soft, gentle kisses across my throat, then my jaw, before he bites my bottom lip hard enough to draw blood. I know because there's a metallic taste in my mouth that immediately follows.

"Ow!" I pull back, shaking myself free of the lust this man seems to evoke by simply existing, and respond to his fucked-up words. "Hold your horses there a minute, Aleko. I'm not anyone's old lady, and did you forget what I told you a few nights ago? I have to go home."

"But you don't want to do that." It's not a question, but I answer anyway.

"It's not often that I get to do what I want to do, Aleko."

Gripping my chin between his thumb and forefinger, he forces me to look at him instead of trying to find a way out of here.

"You look at me now, Cherry. I will do whatever it takes to give you the fucking world and everything you never thought possible, but you need to let me, because if you do, you'll realize how high you can soar." He kisses me then, slamming his lips against mine with a hungry passion I can't help but match before quickly pulling away.

"Aleko, this can—"

He shushes me by placing a finger against my lips, a finger I casually suck into my mouth and bite down on. Aleko doesn't flinch or try to remove it, watching with rapt fascination as I twirl my tongue around the tip clenched between my teeth. I don't know what's come over me, but my inhibitions seem to fly away when I'm around this man.

"Baby, you're mine. I'm yours. There's no denying what we have. I'll find some bullshit information for you to tell your brother in a few weeks. In the meantime, you're hired."

CHAPTER NINE

ALEKO

Two hours into Mackenzie's "trial" shift and I'm regretting my decision to hire her. What a stupid fucking move on my part thinking I could handle all these horny, drunk motherfuckers looking at my girl and trying to touch her ass every time she passes their tables.

Not gonna lie, I've already slammed one guy's head into the wooden table and let him know his night was over, time to go back to his wife sitting at home waiting on his worthless self.

With Ninja sitting on my shoulder, I stand at the bar, my gaze fixed solely on Mackenzie and my stash of sweets dwindling down to almost nothing. I think Ninja wants one, too, but if I can't have another, neither can he.

"What happened?" Candie leans against the bar to my side, nodding to the empty space where the douchebag used to sit. No doubt she knows exactly what's going on. The girl is too smart for her own good.

Ninja reaches out to her, begging for an ear scratch or a back massage. This little guy is like a rockstar here.

"We have rules in place for a reason. No touching the staff." I'm trying to go for nonchalant, the manager looking out for his employees. When I glance her way, it's clear she's not buying it.

"Right, that is definitely the rule." She nods then confirms my suspicions. "That no one enforces unless it causes some kind of commotion."

I scoff but there's no escaping her truth. My fingers are running up and down Ninja's soft fur as I watch my girl.

"She's pretty." Her words are simple, but the meaning behind them is as complex as quantum physics.

"No, she's not," I start, surprising Candie who's now giving me her full attention. "She's fucking stunning."

"Ah, yes. She is that." We stand there watching Mackenzie working the floor like she's been doing this her whole life. For all I know, she could've been working for him for years and years. Like she reminded me, her brother's bar is private so no one is going to bat an eye at her working there.

My thoughts are interrupted by Bash asking me if I want something to drink.

I do but I'll get something later. Right now, the only thing I want is Mackenzie.

"Take Ninja, I've got something to do." Kissing Ninja on the top of his head, I hand him off to Bash who promptly gives him a raw carrot stick to distract him, as I make a beeline for Mackenzie, ignoring Candie's quip.

"Or some*one*."

We meet halfway on the floor, her tray is empty and her smile is plastered on her face.

She's perfect.

"Come with me." My fingers at her elbow, I guide her to the bar where I take her empty tray, place it on the wooden top, then lead her to the back of the club until we reach the office.

"What are you doing?" Squirming, Makenzie tries frantically to get away from me, but I'm not letting her go. I'm never letting her go and she needs to understand this. "Aleko, stop being a fucking crazy person."

"It's the law that employees have a twenty-minute break during an eight-hour shift." I have no fucking clue what I'm talking about but it sounds better than, "I'm about to fuck you until your knees are too weak to finish the night." I lock the office door and give my girl one hundred percent of my attention.

"No it's not. North Carolina law doesn't require em-ployees to take breaks."

I stop, looking at Mackenzie and wondering how the fuck she knows this.

She shrugs like she can read my mind. "I read the entire work manual when I got my first job."

This girl. Fuck my life.

My mouth is on her in seconds, my need to have her all consuming.

Fighting me, she tries to push me away.

With her wrists trapped in my closed fists, I pull her impossibly closer.

"Aleko." Her one word sounds like a mixture between begging and ordering.

"Tell me you don't feel this pull." My eyes are daring her to lie.

"I can't do this with you." She's shaking her head like her body is in complete disagreement with her own words.

My lips are so close to her mouth, I can taste her without even touching her.

"Your lies are delicious, Cherry, but your truths..." I pop off the button to her ridiculously short shorts, pulling everything down in one smooth move. "Well, I think your truths are going to be the best fucking thing in the world."

With those words, I let the few things on the desk fly off with one sweep of my forearm before I've got Mackenzie's ass on the faux-wood—legs spread and pussy open for my taste-testing.

If I needed proof that this thing between us isn't only one sided, her wet cunt would be the first piece of evidence I would present to the court.

The first swipe of my tongue along her slit has the same effect on me as a line of coke to an addict. The rush is immediate, the calm after hours of raging storms inside my chest is everything I needed and more.

When her hand lands on the top of my head, nails indenting my scalp with the force of them, I fucking know she feels it. "Your honor, I present my second piece of evidence."

"What?" She croaks out one word and I realize I just said that out loud.

"Proof, baby. Proof that you're fucking mine whether you accept it or not." Time for talking is over, it's time to make her come.

Wrapping my arms around her open thighs, I pull her close enough to feel her heat on my lips and bury my face in her sweet-smelling pussy. I don't just lick and bite, I fucking consume her. I take everything she's giving me and I throw it back tenfold.

Every time Mackenzie squirms, I squeeze my hold on her and dig my tongue just a little deeper inside her. There's no inch of her cunt I won't explore. No drop of her cum I won't pillage and take as mine. Before I'm ready for it, her back arches toward the ceiling, her hips thrusting against my frantic mouth when the cry that falls from her lips almost makes me come in my fucking jeans.

"Oh God, oh God, oh God." Fuck that. I'll be her god, her devil, and her savior all at once.

"Say my fucking name, Mackenzie."

"What?" Her breaths are heavy, her cum spilling like a tiny river from her open pussy lips.

"My name. You say *my* fucking name when I make you come." Licking up the trail of what I just did for her, I hum in pleasure.

"Aleko." My eyes land on Mackenzie's and the way she whispers my name is my new favorite thing in the world.

"Fucking right."

It takes me two seconds flat to unbutton my jeans and take out my cock—hard and throbbing— before I waste no time slamming it inside her pussy. Bending closer to her, I wrap my hand around her throat and dig my fingers where her thigh meets her hip as I thrust in and out, in and out of her throbbing, pulsing cunt.

It's only when my lips slam against hers that I feel complete. Fucking her mouth with my tongue, allowing her to taste the sweetness of her, is next level for me.

I never kissed the Khunts, never gave that part of me to any of them. But Mackenzie? Fuck, she can have every inch of me. Every fucking molecule I have to give.

We fuck like time is nothing and we're in our own little part of the world where no one and nothing can get to us. Right here, right now, we only exist for us. For this. For the pleasure we give to each other.

The next time I make Mackenzie come, I fall down the rabbit hole right along side her and it's fucking epic. It's wet and frantic, but it's perfect. My entire body stills as she wraps her legs around my waist and pumps her hips up and down, begging with her pussy to get closer, for me to get deeper. But I can't. I'm as deep as humanly possible and still, it's not enough. Still, I want more, she wants more.

"Fuck!" I roar out my orgasm, pushing away from Mackenzie and pressing one hand to the base of her stomach while I pump every fucking drop of my cum inside her pussy.

And goddamn, if she doesn't squeeze my cock like she never wants to let it go.

On that, we can agree.

The only reason I allow Mackenzie to go back onto the floor is because it's impossible to win an argument with that woman. Shy of throwing her over my shoulder and hauling her off into a private dungeon where no one but me can touch, look at, feed, or fuck her, it was clear early on that she was going to do what she damn well pleased.

I don't like it. Not one fucking bit. But I'm the asshole who hired her, as she so eloquently reminded me.

"You look like you want to murder someone."

With a new sucker puffing out my cheek, the corner of my lip lifts in a mock smile at the Deputy Sheriff's comment, because the dude at the corner table is dangerously close to being my first victim. Mackenzie does some kind of swirl-and-avoid move that helps me to relax. When she looks over her shoulder at me, like she knows exactly what's going on inside my mind, the smile she offers instantly appeases the monster inside.

"Well, that would be bad for business." This time, my grin is genuine when I give Celia Shipman my undivided attention. "Plus, I'd hate for you to have to work on your time off." I give my cherry-flavored sugar ball a lingering lick and suck, feeling appeased by the taste of my girl on my tongue.

Celia's grin is tired but no less sincere. We may be on opposite sides of the law but respect is something that is earned, no matter our circumstances, and this woman has mine.

"Time off," she scoffs, taking a large gulp of what I'm guessing is ginger ale. "What the fuck is that?"

"Fuck if I know, but you should. Aren't there rules and regulations?" I take a sip of my whisky, the same one I've been nursing for the last hour.

"Right, well, we've got a situation on our hands but we don't have the manpower to deal with it. It's actually why I'm here." Her relaxed demeanor from earlier vanishes like cheesecake at the compound.

"What's the situation?" I'm weary asking this question because nothing good ever comes from the law coming to criminals seeking advice. Just as I ask, Ninja jumps from Bash's shoulder and runs straight into my hoodie, where he curls up and, no doubt, quickly falls asleep.

"Jesus, Psycho. That thing violates half a dozen hygiene regulations."

I raise a brow at Celia, my teeth gritted.

"Are you calling my rat dirty? I bet he's cleaner than all of us put together."

"Christ, not my circus." Taking another drink from her glass, she adds, "There are suspicious deaths happening right now. Drug related, of course. Someone's distributing free pills to college kids: at bars, night clubs, hell, one of them got a baggie at the coffee shop on Sterling Drive just past the White Flag grocery store. The common denominator is a purple smiley face sticker with crosses for eyes."

I'm racking my brain but we don't deal in pills, at least not in this area. It was part of the deal. Keep our city clean and the Sheriff's Office turns a blind eye on our side business as long as we don't put a neon sign over it.

"And you think we have something to do with this?" My spine stiffens at the idea that Celia would look in our direction for putting dangerous shit on the streets. We sell weed, good fucking shit that's home grown most times, but that's it. And it's not a huge revenue for the club since the sales go back to the grower with a small percentage for us.

"No, of course not. You may not be innocent of a lot of shit but killing innocents isn't on your to-do list." Arching a brow at me in confirmation, she gives up when I give her nothing.

"It's not our kind of business, you know this. What happens to these kids?" I'm curious, an image of a college kid passed out in Old Town when I found Mackenzie that night flashes in my brain.

"Well, some of them pass out, have a small reaction to the mix in the pills with puking and head spinning, others fall into a coma or have seizures. A couple died on the spot. The pills have different effects on different people but we don't have the data to understand it, yet."

Bash, who's been listening to the deputy, straightens, face ashen, but I'm not about to ask him anything in front of the deputy. Club business stays club business, and I have a sinking feeling this has to do with Python and why he passed out at the beginning of the week.

"There's something else." This time, Celia leans in and speaks so that only I can hear her. "You wouldn't know anything about a dead body in Myrtle Beach, would you? We got a phone call from local police there saying they have eyewitnesses placing a few sport bikes with North Carolina plates."

I shrug.

"We certainly aren't the only bikes in this state." Meaning, I'm not answering any questions at this time. But we do need to have a club meeting, and very fucking soon.

Our deputy reads the room like a fucking champ, turning her attention away from me and on my girl as I crunch down on the tiny ball remaining on the white stick.

"She's too pretty for the likes of you." This time, I laugh out loud, surprising even myself.

"What, you think she's just right for you? I'm sorry to say, Deputy Shipman, that woman over there is a big fan of cocks." I frown. "Let me amend that. She's a big fan of *my* cock." Much fucking better.

"Hmmm, too bad." She barely gets her last word in when all Hell breaks loose. Bash jumps over the bar like a fucking Hollywood stunt man, passing me the baseball bat while our dear deputy follows us, one hand on her gun. Ninja jumps from my hoodie to the bar, the sudden noise not to his liking.

My control is barely restrained when I see Mackenzie in the eye of the storm and some piece of shit holding her by the front of her shirt that's currently fisted in his hand.

I don't hesitate. My bat flies over my head and right down onto his arm, just where his elbow used to be. I say used to, because it's now just crushed bones.

"Deputy Shipman here, requesting back up and an ambulance at Rocks Off, immediately." Celia's call into the station is barely audible before she's trying to yell over this motherfucker's screams. The only reason I'm not killing him for touching my woman is because said woman is using her entire weight to pull me away from him.

"I swear to fuck, Mackenzie, if you don't let me go, I will fuck shit up." My words aren't spoken, they're roared like a maniac off his meds. Next thing I know, Celia is slapping handcuffs—fucking handcuffs—on my wrists and pushing my torso against the nearest table. I fight her hold and am almost free when the distinct *thud* of a baton hits the backs of my knees just hard enough to get me under her control.

"Motherfucker!" I scream out in pain and unbridled rage as I watch Mackenzie giving that fucking douchebag of a Toxic Rebel first aid. My entire body feels like I've been standing too close to the sun, heat invading my chest and neck while my jaw is locked hard enough to lose a tooth.

"I'll take him to the hospital." If I thought I was losing my shit before, Mackenzie's words as she rushes the

Rebel out of our club without a single look back at me has every one of my muscles pumping adrenaline like a lion on crack.

Someone's gonna die.

I'm just not sure who at this point because the list is fucking growing by the second.

Chapter Ten

Mackenzie

"You're gonna need surgery, you need to go to the hospital, Goblin." It's three in the morning and I need a fucking sandwich. I'm trying desperately to not think about the anger on Aleko's face, the promise of death in his eyes, the way his cock filled me so completely...

"What's the point in you being a fucking doctor if you can't fix me up yourself?" Each of his words are spoken through clenched teeth as he tries to breathe through the pain of his shattered elbow. Goblin occasionally joins in with a few swift kicks to my ribs when I'm taking a beating from my brother and Isaac, and I won't say I'm not happy that he's in so much pain right now.

"Sur-ge-ry." If I spoke any slower I'd fall asleep behind the wheel of my car, and I have told him I'm not a doctor on more than one occasion. "We're here." I pull up outside the local hospital in Stonebridge, keeping my eyes forward and waiting for Goblin to get out. I don't dare turn the engine off to help him inside in case it doesn't start again. The last place I want to be right now is stuck here, with him.

"Your brother's gonna find out about your shit attitude, Kenz." His lips are curled up into a snarl as he opens the passenger door and climbs out of the car. I have to hold back a laugh when he nearly falls over because his balance is off.

The threat of my brother doesn't scare me per se, but it does worry me a little. Depending on Jake's mood, I may be able to talk my way out of a harsh punishment. Especially considering I was technically working "undercover" to benefit the Rebels. If anyone is getting punished, it should be Goblin for fucking it up the way he did.

I had assumed Jake wouldn't send anyone to check on me tonight, but we all know what it is to assume. Fucking stupid.

Luckily, Goblin didn't see me anywhere near Aleko because explaining that to my brother would be difficult. I can't even explain it to myself.

I don't wait to watch Goblin go inside, but I do have to unbuckle my seatbelt to lean over and shut the passenger door that he rudely left open. It doesn't take long to drive back home, with the streets being basically empty of vehicles at this time of the morning, and if I was riding I'd have made it last a lot longer.

Dad and I used to go riding for hours at a time, taking random routes and having no idea of our destination, knowing only that we'd have to be home for dinner or Mom would be mad.

I park my car outside of the trailer park, in my usual space by the side of the road, before grabbing my over-the-shoulder bag and quickly walking toward home. I say home, but it doesn't really feel like that. It's more of a prison that allows me day releases for work purposes or good behavior.

Between my trailer in the corner and the metal fencing surrounding the property is my small garden. I check on it regularly, making sure nobody has messed with my special plants. They're easily undetectable, passing as regular plants, and they each give me the means to kill every member of this club if I wanted to.

I wouldn't, of course, because club members like Booker and Cameron don't deserve that, they're nice enough people who just choose to hang around with sadists.

Without my gardening gloves, I'm careful not to touch the plants. The horse nettle in particular could cause an allergic reaction from the sharp spines it's covered in. It's one of my favorites. The fact it's a member of the night-shade family makes it sound cool as fuck, and is the only reason it's part of my little growing collection.

Satisfied that all is well, I turn and walk toward my trailer. I need a shower and my bed because I have to work the only job I actually enjoy tonight at eight. I have a twenty-four-hour shift every three days, and it's my respite from the Rebels and my brother. It's also the only reason Jake and his asshole club brothers try to avoid marking my face when I'm being smacked around for whatever reason they find.

The best part about my job as an EMT is Spencer, he's six years older than me but he really is the best friend I've ever had.

I unlock and open my trailer, using the small step to get inside before closing the door behind me. The sun will be rising within the next couple of hours so I need to pull down my blackout blinds or I won't be sleeping.

A knock coming from my bedroom has me on alert. It sounded like a drawer closing, making my heart race at a million miles a minute...

Slowly and quietly, I open the utensil drawer, and with my eye on my bedroom door, I grab for one of the big knives and take a deep breath. Being such a small space, it only takes me a few gentle steps to get to my room. Won't lie, I'm a little scared. With the exception of my brother, the Rebels don't usually come into my trailer, especially not my bedroom. It's the one place I am allowed solitude and peace from my life here. With a deep inhale, I grip the small handle and throw open the door, holding the weapon from the drawer high above my head.

"Get the fuck out of m..." I pause, furrowing my brow in confusion.

"Come here." The man is wearing a neck tube decorated with a colorful half skull over the bottom of his face and the black hood of his sweater pulled over his head, leaving those bright blue eyes boring holes into my soul.

A pair of my red panties are in his left hand and my underwear drawer is open. Psycho fucker has been snooping.

"You know you can't be here. Didn't you get arrested? You're gonna get us both killed if someone finds you on this property."

The way he's glaring at me says he's not listening, and when he pushes my panties up to his face and inhales, using his right hand to rub his growing cock over his jeans, I'm not quite sure where to look.

"What are you doing?" I finally lower my weapon-wielding arm, unable to do anything other than watch as he grips the back of his hoodie and pulls it over his head, revealing my new Achilles heel. His beautiful tattooed chest, the light happy trail from his belly button that disappears beneath his jeans...which he is now unzipping, pushing down, stepping out of...I may need to fan myself but I refuse to be the girl that swoons.

"Come here, Cherry. Don't make me chase you."

Something about the way he says that sends a thrill through me that, normally, only the open road can give me, making me shiver in anticipation of what he could do to me. He's still wearing the neck tube, and I kinda don't want him to remove it. Instead, I'm imagining what him wearing a full face mask would do to my rising libido.

No. No I'm not.

"You shouldn't be here. Go home." I speak firmly, but there's a wavering uncertainty that even I can sense.

Aleko growls under his breath, the sound coming from his chest as his eyes narrow on me. Two quick strides later, he's in front of me, we're toe-to-toe and I have to tilt my head back to see his half-covered face. Lifting a hand, he strokes his fingertips from my cheek to my chin before pushing the pad of his thumb against my lips, encouraging me to open up for him.

This is seriously all kinds of dangerous, but for some reason, I find myself not caring as much as I know I should. Aleko has a way of making me feel safe in situations that should scare me.

"You gonna put that wooden spoon down or spank me with it?"

He pulls down his neck tube, revealing his half-smile that almost renders me speechless—or it would if I were that girl—before blowing me a kiss and pulling it back over his nose. Instead, I'm more confused. Wooden spoon?

"What the—?" Looking down to my hand, I deflate a little when I realize the "knife" I grabbed is actually not a knife at all. "Fuck sake."

"Hey, if you wanna do knife play, baby, I've got a switchblade you can use." He lifts my chin for me to look at him again, and I just know I'm going to regret what I'm about to let happen—again. But I can't find it in myself to care. He makes me feel good, alive, wanted, needed, and not at all like the burden I know I am to my brother.

I drop the wooden spoon and the thud on the floor seems to ignite him as he roughly lifts my arms above my head. Then he spins me to face the wall, unzipping my little pink top before pulling it off me.

His warm breath hits the back of my neck, moving lower with his fingertips until he reaches my ass and begins to pull down my booty shorts.

"You can keep the socks on, they're fucking sexy." He lightly spanks my ass with his palm, shocking me and making me jump.

"You can keep the mask on so I can pretend you're someone else." The next spank is more of a sharp slap, quickly followed by the gentle rubbing over the newly sensitive area. A mixture of pain and relaxing pleasure makes me needy for more of him. Why isn't he touching me where I want him yet?

"No, you won't." He chuckles as I step out of my shorts, and his hands slide up my legs from my ankles to my ass to my waist and up to my breasts, where he squeezes them and pinches my nipples. He's so sure of himself, and honestly, he's probably right.

Because, here I am, with absolutely zero will-power against this man's advances. I hate him, I hate how he makes me feel, I hate that he makes me feel at all. This prison of a life I'm in is designed by my brother to break me, to make me pliable to his every whim, and I just need to put up with it for a few more weeks before I'm out of everyone's life for good.

Then Aleko came along and he refuses to leave. Telling me I'm his and he's mine. It's all bullshit, but for this moment, right here, right now, I can allow myself a small reprieve from my life, a little happiness before everything is gone. The kind of reprieve I've only ever felt with Aleko. Damn him.

"Hey, where'd you go, Cherry?" Spinning me to face him, Aleko pins me with his haunting blue eyes, raising that brow that makes my knees weak. But it's not the seductive move it usually is, it's more curious, concerned, questioning. "You spaced out for a second, baby. What's wrong?"

Ugh, he's ruining it. Why can't he just fuck me and fuck off?

"I'm fine. You should go." Suddenly feeling self conscious, I fold my arms over my chest and sit on the edge of my bed, crossing one leg over the other.

His eyes lock with mine, and they're so expressive, as though he's having a whole conversation inside his mind before he decides what to do.

"I should go. But I won't. And don't lie to me. We don't do that, you and I. No secrets, no lies. Understand?"

He moves to kneel in front of me, completely at ease with his own nakedness, his cock still rock hard and standing to attention.

"Hey, eyes up here." He grips my chin and lifts my head, making my gaze move from his impressive dick to his amused eyes. The crinkle in the corners gives him away. "No secrets, no lies. Do you understand?"

Slowly, I nod.

"Words." With his other hand, he begins to trail his fingers from my neck to my hip, where he squeezes so hard I know he's adding more bruises. More of his mark on me.

"I understand. But I sh—" His finger is over my lips before I continue, pushing between them, and I narrow my eyes. Smirking at him, I bite down on the tip of his finger, flicking the part inside my mouth with my tongue.

His next move is so quick I barely register what's happening as he pulls down his mask, revealing his soft pink lips, which are pressed against mine with a hunger I return. Lips, tongues, teeth, the way he owns my mouth has me opening my legs, digging my nails into his shoulders to bring him closer. I'm also leaving my own marks on him. Two can play the marking game.

My pussy practically weeps for joy when I feel him circling my clit with his thumb as he pushes two fingers inside me. Fast and hard. He pumps them in and out, in and out, then my pussy weeps for a whole other reason when he pulls them away, removing them completely.

All contact stops and he moves to stand, lifting the mask back over his face. This feels a little like role play, though I know it's really not, but my past experience is a little lackluster and what we're doing now is thrilling in a way I never knew existed.

"Move up the bed, head on the pillow, and raise your arms."

I do as he says, lifting my knees so my feet are flat on the bed, but I must not open my legs wide enough because he sighs, shaking his head like a disappointed father. Maybe I do have daddy issues because that singular move has way too much effect on me.

"How am I supposed to fuck you into a coma with your legs so close together?" He bends to pick something up from the floor and crawls across the bed toward me. Gripping my thighs, he squeezes and strokes, his fingers so close to my pussy it's basically purring for him. Then he moves them apart, putting me on display for him to feast his eyes on. And fuck...does he feast.

The lust in his beautiful blues seeps from every pore of his deliciously naked body, and he's turning me on with barely a touch. I lift my hips a little, letting him know with just my body what I want. He doesn't take it. Instead, he crawls farther up the bed, wagging his brows when he shows me my red panties dangling from his finger.

Gripping my wrists, he begins wrapping my underwear around my forearms, securing them together.

"What the ac—"

"Shhh. Your beautiful pussy is dripping for me, your body is calling out for me, but you lied to me. Don't tell me you're fine when you're not." He gently lowers my arms and rolls me onto my side as confusion swirls around my head.

I thought we were about to have sex, but now he's...what? Punishing me?

Why do I like that?

"Aleko, either you're going to fuck me or you're not, but you need to do it quickly because you ca—"

"I said, shhh. We'll talk more tomorrow. But for tonight, I'm going to play with your pussy over and over until you pass out."

The fact that I can only see his eyes makes this whole moment that much more intense. Every emotion and every expression translates through his glare. There's no denying he's pissed, but contrary to any other man in my life, this anger doesn't scare me the way it should.

"You need to shut the fuck up, Mackenzie. The time for talking and telling truths is gone. There's a fuckload of issues we need to address, like the fact you fucking walked away from me with. Another. Man." He punctuates his last words with the tightening of my underwear around my wrists, to the point of delicious pain. "Then, you fucking lied to me."

I squeal as his fingers push inside me again, his huge cock rests against my bare ass cheeks and his arm is across my body, playing me like his favorite toy.

"So, now you get to shut your pretty little mouth and take what I give you."

He slides his other arm beneath me, cocooning me in all that is him, using that hand to reach and grab for one of my hardened nipples.

An orgasm quickly builds, my hips moving to the rhythm until he stops, pulls his fingers out, and spanks my ass.

Then he starts again, and I'm trying desperately to be quiet, because these trailers have thin walls.

Except the fucker stops...

His fingers find my clit this time, circling gently, spreading my arousal around my pussy as he parts my lips and pushes inside me again. Then he stops and I want to scream.

"Stop fucking around and make me come." My tone is harsher than I intend, but all he does is chuckle behind me and I want to look at him. To see him.

"I'll stop when you learn not to lie again," he whispers seductively into my ear, his voice the deepest grumble of pure sex.

Pushing two fingers back inside me, he groans lowly behind me, rotating his hips against my back, his dick pressing against my asshole. The sensation is strangely nice, effective, even, as he begins moving his fingers in and out of me again.

This time, the orgasm takes mere seconds to creep up on me and my whole body feels like it's spasming as electricity rolls through me. Just as my orgasm hits, he pulls his fingers out and they're quickly replaced with the head of his cock. He lifts one of my thighs to give him better access as he begins to fuck me from behind.

His movements are lazy and slow, like he's taking his time to learn every sound I make, every move, inspecting every inch of my body with his roaming hands. When he reaches around to tweak my nipples and rub my clit, I come again. I didn't think this many orgasms in one session were possible. My body is tingling, twitching as he continues to pump into me, his thrusts getting deeper, harder, faster. His hand comes up to my mouth and I take the opportunity to bite down on his fingers, struggling not to scream out loud.

With a low grunt, he comes just as he pinches my clit, forcing yet another orgasm out of me, causing my world to spin and leaving me barely able to catch my breath.

"Sleep, my Cherry Pie. I've got you."

I must have blacked out because there's a warmth between my legs and I think he's cleaning me up before climbing back behind me and wrapping me in his arms. It's so warm and cozy...

My eyes fly open as a thud against my trailer wakes me and I struggle to sit up, still being held close to Aleko's chest as he grips me to him. There's a gun in his hand and it's pointing toward my bedroom door as noises come from my kitchen.

Fuck. Someone's here.

I may be relatively safe in my trailer, but there are two people on this compound that would still come in uninvited. And they are for very different reasons. One worse than the other.

One is my brother when he needs me for a job.

The other...

Means I need to get out of here. Fast.

CHAPTER ELEVEN
ALEKO

"Jesus Christ, Mac." Some skinny dude with jeans barely hanging on to his hips and a Duke cap on backwards is staring at me like he wants to skin me alive. *Same, dude. Fucking same.* "You're fucking a SOK?"

As soon as she woke up, Mackenzie threw my clothes at my chest, whisper-yelling that I needed to get dressed and get the fuck out, all while she put her own clothes on at record speed. My gun never lowered as I stepped back into the living area and came face to face with this kid. I say kid because he looks fucking twelve.

"Cam, please. This is not a good time." Mackenzie is frantic, trying to push my gun down and get me out of her hair. It's not happening.

"It's never a good time to get in bed with the enemy, Mac. Seriously, what the fuck were you thinking?"

If this kid doesn't shut his mouth, he's going to be fucking this gun I've got pointed straight between his incredulous eyes. When Celia put me in cuffs, it was mainly for show. As the deputy, she couldn't just let me get away with assault but she never patted me down or took away my weapons. I'm still pissed off she let Mackenzie leave with that piece of Rebel shit, though.

"I was thinking that orgasms save lives, ergo…"

"Yeah, keep joking, little girl, and you'll get the shit beat out of you again. Do you remember the last time Jake fucked you up? And for less than…" His arms are swinging all around like he's painting the picture he's seeing in front of him. "All this shit."

Now, I'm a reasonable man—okay, not even close, but for argument's sake, let's say I am—however, there are triggers that send me into a blind rage of nuclear proportions. Hearing that my girl gets regular beatings—fucking *beatings*…in the plural, no less—from the one person on this planet who should be protecting her, has me rushing for him in a fraction of a second.

Before he has time to react, Skinny's neck is imprisoned by my fingers, my face so close to his that he can probably count every single one of my lashes.

"What did you just say, motherfucker?" I don't yell, there's no need. Sometimes, the lower you speak the quicker they piss themselves.

"Which part, asshole?" The much needed oxygen is barely getting through with my fingers cutting off his supply, making his voice breathy and barely audible. Despite his predicament, he chooses to back talk.

Brave kid. Also, stupid.

Without thinking, my fist recoils like a spring as I back up just enough to punch him in the jaw. Behind me, Mackenzie whisper-screams at me to stop, which only pisses me off more.

"Dammit, Aleko, he's been helping me!" Wiggling herself between us, she stands with her back to the kid and her baby blues staring straight at me. Expecting fear or maybe a few tears tracking down her cheeks, I blink back my shock at the venom swimming in her irises. If it weren't for the fact that it's impossible, I'd believe she's actively trying to murder me with her glare. Fuck, she's hot.

My rage takes a back seat while I get my control back. Less than two weeks ago, I wouldn't have given two shits about my rage and going over the top. Not even a little bit. Before I met Mackenzie I would have killed this punk just for being in the same space as me. Guilty by association. If you're a Rebel, you're fucking scum. End of. Mackenzie doesn't count, she was Khaos before we even met. She was never a Rebel because she's always been mine.

Yet, here I am, maturing and shit. So, I take a deep breath but I'm sure as fuck not letting him go. I ain't that mature and definitely not that trusting.

"All right, Cherry. Quit tryin' to murder me with those sexy blues of yours." Still half-choking Skinny Dude, I bend down and trap her lips with mine, reminding her that she belongs to me. She doesn't fucking need her brother, I'll protect her. But first...

"Kid, I'm going to ask nicely." He scoffs and I just want to punch him all over again. "What the fuck did Jake do to her?" Saying his name gets my blood pressure rising all over again.

"Don't answer him, Cameron. Not a good idea." We both look down at Mackenzie, who's now standing with her fists on her hips. It's a good thing she's wearing shorts and a tank or this Cameron guy would be going blind from my fingers scooping out his eyeballs.

"He needs to know, Mac. Either way, he needs to know that him being here could get you killed. Or worse." My eyes narrow at his words.

"What the fuck could be worse than her being killed?" I do not like where this is going and before he even answers my question, I know. I fucking know.

"He's always threatening to have her gang raped." And there it is.

"Oh, please. Those threats have been going on for years, he's all tal—" I don't hear her next words because I'm flying out of that fucking trailer like a fire-breathing dragon ready to raze the Earth of all the scum. Starting with Jake fucking Wilson.

Maturing is a process. One step forward, two leaps back with a vengeance.

"Jake! Come at me, motherfucker!" It's late afternoon so there are people milling about this run-down trailer park and at the sound of my booming voice, every single one of them stops in their tracks. As they should. Our bodies are built to detect danger and run from it.

I am danger. And they *will* run.

The first shot fired comes from my left but whoever aimed at me needs fucking lessons.

"Where are you, you fucking coward?" If he's here, he can hear me. Every fucking body around can.

When shots start ringing from all around, I duck behind a car so I can assess the situation. One of them is shooting from a trailer across the courtyard. Another is behind a wall and a third one is straight ahead and coming for me.

Obviously, I did not think this through before I went *Die Hard* in an open space full of enemy fire.

The purring sound of a four-cylinder gets my attention and when I turn, ready to shoot whoever is trying to come up behind me, my mouth drops in an instant.

My girl rides.

My fucking girl rides and she looks like a damn warrior doing it. We'll talk about why she kept this from me later, if we get out of here alive.

"Get on!" The visor of her helmet is open a crack and the only reason she's not taking a bullet right now is because she's spinning the bike around so she can be ready to haul ass out of here. Goddammit, I hate riding bitch but I hate dying more. Just as she brakes, I jump on the back, one arm pressed against the tank and the other pulled back, shooting aimlessly behind us.

As we pass Mackenzie's trailer, I see Cameron hiding behind her door, one hand on his neck, but he makes no move to shoot us. He could, very easily, take us down and the fact he doesn't earns him another day alive.

In mere seconds, I'm dropped off at my bike as she hands me my keys before we're both speeding down the road heading back to Rockford on Highway 17. There's no mistaking the sound of multiple bikes not far behind but we've got enough of a head start that we'll be back to the compound before they reach us.

Leading the way, I constantly check my rear-views for my girl, smiling as I admire her line, the way she handles the bike. Fuck, it's a turn-on. Our only saving grace throughout this shit show is that on the way, we don't cross paths with the local police. Getting stopped for not wearing a helmet would only get us killed at this point.

At least one thing is clear. Mackenzie is no longer going back to that fucking dump. The only place she'll be living is with me and I'm not fucking sad about it.

"Christ, son, you got a death wish? 'Cause I can grant it without gettin' the whole damn club killed." Prez is fuming, but when I look him straight in the eyes, there's more concern than actual anger in them.

"I may have gone guns blazing without actually thinking it through."

At the compound, it doesn't take me long to get everyone up to speed on the situation. Mackenzie is standing beside me, taking it all in and probably scared out of her mind knowing she's been raised to see us as the enemy. Ninja chooses this moment to welcome me back home by jumping from Bear's shoulder and settling into my hood for his first nap of the day.

"Aren't you going to introduce us?" Vanessa smiles at Mackenzie, a warm and reassuring gesture she's mastered since I've known her. The introduction is on the tip of my tongue when my girl decides to steal the show.

"I'm Mackenzie Wilson, my friends call me Mac. Jake Wilson's sister. If you want me to leave, I will completely understand." With my brow raised at her little speech, I look down to see her chin raised high, her lips in a thin line, and her eyes clear and ready for the worst. I want to kill Jake just for making her feel like she's less than perfect.

"Don't be silly. The way I figure, you're Psycho's old lady, now. You're ours to keep." My eyes never leave her as Vanessa makes her point clear, so I don't miss the moment Mackenzie's jaw clenches and she blinks back what I'm guessing are unshed tears of relief.

Leaning down, I whisper in her ear just as Sledge hands me a beer, "You're mine now. There's no escaping that fact." Before she has a chance to answer, Vanessa takes her hand and brings her under her wing, introducing all the brothers around us.

"Let's start with Griffin, their Prez. He's my old man and I don't share." With a wink, Vanessa blows a kiss to Prez before she continues. "The big guy with the receding hairline is Bear."

"Prez, c'mon now. I thought we were a club of respect. Why's Vanessa dissin' me like that?" It's a running joke between those two. Bear once told her he liked her crow's feet, they made her look wise or some shit. Apparently, in no world is that a compliment. Yes, he was drunk. No, he did not enjoy the rest of the night. Or the rest of the month, for that matter. Since he'd disrespected a woman, he wasn't allowed to touch one for thirty days. Let's just say, I felt sorry for the first one he fucked after that. They didn't come out of his suite for three days straight—like me, he's never taken a woman back to his home away from here.

Ever since, Vanessa gets teasing rights even though finding a physical fault with that motherfucker is hard so she has to make shit up. Hence, the imaginary receding hairline. Unlike the rest of us, Bear keeps his head shaved clean to incite the fear of God in his enemies. Whatever the fuck that means.

"The quiet one, here, is Shade, our Sergeant at Arms. He's been Griffin's closest friend for over three decades. I count on him to always bring my man back to me in one piece." Shade inclines his head and smiles at Vanessa. We don't know much about him but we do know that he and Prez went through some shit together back in the day and this club saved their lives.

Saved us all, to be honest.

"My brother never speaks so highly of his crew. They don't call themselves brothers." Mackenzie looks around before she takes a step closer to me, allowing me to wrap my arms around her shoulders, her back to my front.

"That's because he's a cunt." The thick British accent cuts through the chatter like a knife through warm butter. "No offense, love." When Sledge gives my girl his famous, panty-dropping lopsided smile, I almost drop kick him on the spot.

"Keep that fucking smile to yourself, Brother, or I will come at you." Speaking through clenched teeth, I'm not even aware of the aura of danger I'm putting out there until all eyes are fixed solely on me. "What? Any of you fuckers would do the same thing." With one arm firmly wrapped around Mackenzie, I point the neck of my beer bottle at Sledge.

"Yeah, yeah, mate. I get it. She's yours." His chuckle, like he truly does get it, helps me to relax. Just a little.

"We've got church in an hour so make sure all you fuckers are sober enough to make good decisions." And just like that, Prez dismisses us while he and Vanessa leave for a while.

"So, Mac, what about your parents?" My head snaps up, the glare I'm throwing at Python should make him wither away into nothingness. Instead, he's happily sipping on his beer and shooting the shit with my girl, who has immediately stiffened in my arms.

"My dad died six years ago and my mom is...well, she's sick." I don't know the story about her mother and, to be honest, I hate that I'm learning about it at the compound, drinking a beer with the fucking prospect.

"Yeah, my grandma had cancer, she died three years ago. It's fucking Hell losing a parent. She was like a mom to me since my mother never gave a fuck about me."

I stare at Python, my eyes narrowed. How did I not know this shit?

"I'm sorry..." Mackenzie pauses, realizing she has no idea what to call him.

"I'm Flint but everyone calls me Python." Clueless when it comes to social cues, he leans and whispers. "It has nothing to do with the size of my dick."

Mackenzie spits her Coke out through her mouth and nose, coughing furiously as I pat her on the back and shoot fucking atomic bombs through my eyes.

"What?" Python shrugs then walks away. Fucking hell.

"Well, that was interesting." My girl is half laughing, half coughing as I scoop her up and take her to my suite so she can get ready for her long-ass fucking shift.

Twenty-four hours without her is going to suck. Speaking of…I'm about to grab a sucker when I decide that I'd rather go straight to the source. Burying my fingers in Mackenzie's long strands, I turn her gorgeous face to me, mirth and playfulness lighting up her features, and kiss her deeply, like she's the only thing in my world. To be fair, she *is* my favorite obsession.

As soon as we're in my room, I look at the place through her eyes. A large bed taking up most of the space, a closet that's mostly empty except for some workout clothes, a couple of overalls for when I'm working on bikes and a few pairs of shoes in case I need to change and don't have time to go back to my apartment. Ninja peeks out of my hood and, in seconds, he's running down the front of my body to attack his food bowl next to his tiny bed.

"It's so…impersonal." She turns to me, looking almost sad.

"It's functional. I'm not here all that often, you know?"
I stalk toward her, enjoying the way she takes a step back
like she knows she should be afraid when it comes to me.

"When are you here? What do you use this room for?"
Her eyes grow big and round, like the answer just came to
her and she doesn't like it. About to open her mouth, I cut
her off before she breathes out her first word.

"Don't ask questions knowing damn well you're going
to hate the answers." I keep moving but she's now frozen
in place

"Okay." That's all she says. Just that one word, telling
me everything I need to hear.

My entire palm rests against the side of her face, my
thumb just under her chin, lifting it so she can only see
me.

"You are mine, Mackenzie. There have been no women
before you, their existence holds no space in my head or
heart. It's all for you. You." My lips graze hers, just briefly
so she can hear and feel my next words. "You're staying
here, now. I'm your home."

"Oh, is that right?" Her words are just as softly spoken as
mine, as if saying anything loudly could break our bubble.

"Yes. This is happening."

"Don't I get a say in it?" The corners of her lips tick up and I know I've got her.

"No, Cherry. Not about this. Also, for my sanity, your trial period at Rocks Off is over and you are not hired." My teeth sink into her bottom lip as I pull it back enough to tease her. "Now, get ready for your real job so I can take you there. Tomorrow, you're getting fucked nine ways to Sunday in every available hole."

"Is this your way of saying you love me?" She's joking, maybe testing the waters. It doesn't matter.

"Yes." And that's the fucking truth, right there.

CHAPTER TWELVE
MACKENZIE

What a fucking whirlwind of a forty-eight hours. Well, if I'm being honest with myself, it's been more like a week and a half. Since the day I turned twenty-one and fucked the enemy in the bed of a pickup truck. I feel like one of those fucking women in stories or movies that lose their mind and cause their life to spiral all because of a man—which in itself is a giant red flag...for both of us at this point.

Yes, I had my ducks in a row. Kinda. I had a plan. Still do. I perform the tasks asked of me for now and nothing more, stay under the radar...

Well, after high-tailing it out of the Rebels' compound and straight into enemy territory, I've gone and put a massive target on my head.

The doctor I spoke to in New York a year ago—when I told Jake I had to attend a work thing for my EMT position—is under the same impression as me. My mom shouldn't still be as sick as she is if she's getting regular treatment for her mental state; I showed him videos I've secretly recorded on some of my visits with Mom. The doctors at the psych ward have said she'll never get better, that I should give up on her, but I know in my gut that Jake has his mouth to their money-grabbing ears. If I can get $75,000 together, I can get her out of there and to a real nice place in New York where the doctor thinks he can make drastic improvements within a year.

I may be reaching with my expectations and hopes, but I've got to do something. She's rotting away in there.

Now, though, fuck...the sun is rising as I drive Spence and I back to the station. The patient died on the way to the hospital after a really bad seizure. Fucking horrible to watch. But there was a moment watching him where I envisioned that being me. Dying in the back of an ambulance. Would anyone really care? It'd really fuck up Jake and the Rebels' plans for the racing season. And Mom...Jake wouldn't have a reason to treat her like shit anymore because it's always been my fault.

I know what I did yesterday is going to have consequences, repercussions, but the fallout could be huge, or it could be small. If I'm gone sooner than I planned, then there's nobody for Jake to punish. Although, Aleko shooting up the yard will probably level up their rivalry from intense foes to full-blown murderous enemies.

The ambulance radio beeps before Anthea's voice comes through, pulling me from the intrusive thoughts and back into the real world.

"Mac, there's a man here named Jake, says he's your brother, he said he needs to speak to you but he'd wait until you get back."

Never have I mixed the life I've built for myself with the one I was born into. Apart from Spencer and Human Resources, the details of my family life are unknown to everyone at the station. Jake turning up like this is going to have people asking questions. We're based in Rockford Beach, which means most of them are aware of the rivalries the Sons have with the out-of-towners, AKA the Toxic Rebels from Stonebridge.

"Thanks, Anthea. If there's an empty office we can use, can you ask him to wait in one of those for me, please?" I know the conversation isn't going to be one I want any of my colleagues to hear.

"Sure thing, Mac. Do you have an ETA?"

"Five minutes. Thank you."

I slide the radio back in its slot on the dash and sigh. Without taking my eyes off the road I silently flip Spence the bird because I can feel his judgey gaze on the side of my head.

"You've got five minutes to tell me what happened. I knew there was a reason you've been quiet all shift. Out with it." His tone is harsh although not unkind, and this is just one reason he's my best friend. No bullshit.

"It's a lot to tell in less than five minutes, Spence." I force a smile briefly in his direction as I pull up to a stop sign.

"Then tell it quickly." He's not messing around and I feel a real smile tugging at my lips.

"Okay, condensed version it is. Aleko found out where I live, kinda kidnapped me but took me home again. I told him we can never work because he's a SOK and I'm a Rebel. Jake made me get a job at Rocks Off to spy on the SOK guys, Aleko knows about it but gave me a job anyway. One of the guys came to the strip club while I was working, got his elbow smashed by Aleko about an hour after he fucked me senseless in a back office. He was arrested, then miraculously not arrested because I found him in my bedroom sniffing my panties. He fucked me again, made me pass out. Cameron walked in...you know, one of the nice ones in my brother's crew that I've told you about. He casually mentioned my brother has threatened some fucked-up stuff, Aleko went batshit and started shooting up the place. I grabbed one of the motorcycles the Rebels keep in the garage and rode Aleko out of there in a storm of dust. Went straight to the SOK compound where I spent a couple of hours making friends with the fucking enemy who should have wanted to kill me but didn't before coming to work at eight last night. So, Jake probably does want to kill me, which is why he's come to see me at work." I inhale and exhale deeply, shrugging as though everything I said is completely normal and not at all fucked up.

"Wow. I have so many questions. First...how can you only be kinda kidnapped? Second, passing out from orgasms, I approve. Third, girl, that man has it bad for you and again, I approve. Fourth, your brother is a *Jake*ass..." He chuckles at his own joke. "Get it? Seriously though, we can probably call in some favors and get someone to get your brother away from the station if you don't wanna see him. We can detour to avoid him."

I shake my head lightly. "I can't avoid him forever, Spence. He pretty much holds my world in his hands and he won't hesitate to crush it, but he needs me just as much as I need him right now. If the Rebels win the top spot in the current street race season, it'll get them out of a lot of money shit they've dug themselves into."

"Want me to get Ryan to stand outside the office door if the fire fighters aren't out on a call?" Even though I'm not looking at him, I know he's wagging his brows. He's just jealous because he thought Ryan batted for his team when he first joined the station crew, tried all his best moves on him, only to get shot down—politely—because Ryan had his eye on someone else...*me*.

It is a point of fun conversation though. We like to wind up and tease each other about it on the regular. It's just a small thing that helps our shifts go by more quickly.

"That'll probably make the situation ten times worse. Honestly, I'll be fine. He doesn't have the Rockford Sheriff's Department on his side. Technically he's on SOK turf right now." That, and he's not stupid enough to try anything in a fire station full of first responders who would absolutely press charges on him.

"Hmm. I'm not convinced. I feel better about letting you fuck the dude that punched me in the face than leaving you alone to deal with your brother." And I know that's only because Aleko's chest probably had Spencer as mesmerized by it as me.

"I love you, Spence, but I can handle my brother."

"Like the time you handled him when you came to work with a black eye because he was too angry to care about the

'No marks on her face' rule?" He folds his arms across his chest, taking a deep breath. I get it, he cares what happens to me, and if the same had happened to him I wouldn't be so calm.

I side-eye my best friend and blow him a kiss before concentrating on the road ahead. We're two minutes out from the station and my heart is thumping in my chest. I'm telling Spencer I can handle it, but I'm not positive. I really fucked up. Big time.

"Okay. I'll let you deal with it, but I'll be in the office next door with my ear against the wall. I won't hesitate to get someone in there if I need to."

We both chuckle, because he's a nosy ass motherfucker, but I won't deny him because it will actually be nice to know he's looking out for me in the room next door.

The station comes into view and I take a deep breath, preparing myself for what I know is going to be a verbal beating from my brother. We take our time checking the vehicle over once I'm parked, resupplying it with anything we used on our last job, then there's nothing left to do.

"Go on, girl, I'll be right behind you." Spence winks, a forced smile on his handsome face and worry clear in his eyes.

I nod, steeling my spine for the conversation ahead of me. Anthea texted me to let me know in which office Jake is waiting, so I head through the kitchen area and toward my doom...I mean, the room.

The door is ajar and I tenderly push it open, stepping inside and closing it behind me.

Jake is sitting behind the desk, a scowl etched into his features. It doesn't belong to anyone in particular, this is an office space any of us can use if we need to, so it's mostly empty. But it has the bare essentials, a dark wooden desk, a soft black chair, a computer, and some shelving. The walls are a light gray, and the outer wall has a small window overlooking the large lawn outside.

"Took your fucking time. That nasally bitch said you'd be back in five minutes. You whoring yourself out to the firefighters as well as the fucking enemy, Kenz?" He's practically snarling at me as he lounges back in the chair, his feet propped up onto the desk like the disrespectful bastard he is.

"We had to do our vehicle che—"

"I don't give a fuck what you had to do, Kenz. How are you going to explain what happened at the compound yesterday afternoon? Did you really think you could steal one of our motorcycles after fucking the enemy, letting him shoot our members, then helping him to escape?" Each of his words are spoken with such vitriol, even I'm a little shocked. Well...no, I'm not.

"I didn't fuck the enemy." Lie. "Or let him shoot anyone." Not a lie. "And I had to go with him, he's my boss at Rocks Off." Also not a total lie. "You wanted me to get close to them. It would've looked real bad if the one that came to see me died, wouldn't it? There would be no chance of finding out any information, and getting a job there would have been a waste of time." Inside, I'm fucking trembling, while also applauding myself for coming up with a relatively believable excuse for what happened. I rest my hand on my hip, as if to say he should have known why I helped Aleko escape.

"You think you're so fucking clever, Kenz. You'll work the bar at our compound tonight after your shift." He stands, walking around the desk and toward me, standing so close I have to look up into his face. Then he bends a little so we're nose to nose, his eyes narrowing, his mouth thinning. "I don't give a fuck if you're tired. You work for us." Spit lands on my cheek as he speaks and I'm trying really hard not to wipe it off or back away from him, showing zero weakness because this is how I play it with him.

If I show even a hint of being scared, it becomes fun for him. A game.

Straightening himself up, he curls his top lip at me in disgust before pushing me aside and reaching for the door. "You start at ten, I'll let you get a shower first. You fucking stink." Then he walks out of the room, taking all of the tension with him, and I deflate onto one of the chairs in front of the desk.

Okay. I can deal with this. I expected a harsher punishment than having to work the bar on my night off, even with my lame-ass excuse. Rubbing my eyes and cheeks, I attempt to pull myself back together. To stop trembling with adrenaline or fear or anger...I don't even know at this point.

I need to remind myself why staying under my brother's thumb is worth all this shit.

Mom.

Not having to look over my shoulder for fear of being killed by a Toxic Rebel member who I've been assured *will* find me if I run.

Somehow, they don't feel like good enough reasons anymore. I love my mom so, so much, but I know she wouldn't be okay with this. Hell, I'm not okay with the way *she's* being treated either, so up until this point, I've stayed because if they think I've run away, it'll be worse for her.

"Aargh!" I yell out loud, attempting to release some frustration, then Spence pops his head around the now-open door.

He doesn't speak at first, but he does sigh, a sad, sympathetic sigh, as he walks toward me and crouches in front of me so we're face to face.

"Why don't you get off early? We'll put it down as a family emergency. I'll tell them the ward called about your mom so you'll still get paid." Holding my hands inside his larger ones, he moves forward and kisses me on the cheek. "Love you."

My smile feels as sad as his sigh, but it's a great idea. It solves one of the problems I have today...that being Aleko will no doubt be waiting for me after work. He told me I would not be going back to the Rebels' compound ever again, but he doesn't seem to understand why I need to do exactly that.

His friends are great and not even a little scary, as I'd imagined. The way my brother and his club talk about the SOK guys, I thought they were worse than the Rebels. But they're actually a real brotherhood, not the whole my-dick-is-bigger-than-yours crap that goes on in Stonebridge. That doesn't change the fact that I have to stay with what are now seemingly the bad guys. The other shoe would eventually drop with the SOK guys anyway, someone would decide they hate the Rebels so much that killing me as revenge is their best option.

"Thanks, Spence. Love you too." I return his cheek kiss before wrapping my arms around his neck and squeezing tightly.

I know exactly what I'm going to do with my free time this afternoon.

My car is still parked where I left it, outside of the Rebels' compound, after Aleko insisted on driving me to work yesterday evening. It's like he doesn't trust me not to return to the Rebels or something...ha. Yeah, I wouldn't trust me either, seeing as that's exactly what I'm planning to do when I'm finished here.

Wearing my usual after-work sweats, I thank the Uber driver and get out of the car to look up at the looming building that is Mom's home right now. There are four floors of patients, gradually getting worse as the levels get higher. Mom is on the second floor. It's a very tra-ditional-looking building, lots of brickwork, large win-dows—barred off—and plenty of greenery in the sur-rounding gardens.

I'm pleased to see Maggie at the check-in and informa-tion desk when I get inside. She's usually on an afternoon shift, so I had hoped to see her. She's the only nurse in this place that I think I can rely on when it comes to keeping my visits on the downlow. Today is especially one I'd like to keep quiet because, technically, I should be at work.

"Hey, Mags. Here to see Mom. How is she?" I pick up the pen for the sign-in sheet, holding it poised over the paper.

"You're covered, Mac. Here's a pass." She smiles, taking the pen from between my fingers and handing me a visitor lanyard with a conspiratorial wink. "Well, your brother and his friends haven't been here for almost a month." She leans forward, beckoning for me to come closer. "Three days this week she was lucid for a couple of hours. That's almost more than the last year combined." She raises her brows and purses her lips, a knowing look in her eyes. And Maggie is just one more reason I sought out another opinion on Mom's situation.

"Thank you." Nodding knowingly, we share a look before I tip my head to her, salute her with the lanyard, and turn toward the stairs.

After letting myself into this section of the second floor with the pass Maggie gave me, I walk past several rooms, some with doors open, some closed. My focus is on finding Mom, who is usually in her room or looking out of the window in the common area.

She's in her room today, lying on her small double bed after their early dinner at six, half an hour ago. They have a strict routine and allocated wind-down time, as though the patients are children. Don't get me wrong, I'm sure it works for some of them, but for others, not so much.

The TV is on, commercials rolling so I have no idea what she's been watching.

"Hi, Mom."

Pushing all thoughts that scare me aside, I concentrate wholly on my mom, who turns her head to look at me when I say hi. She doesn't respond, not talking is one of her favorite things since Dad died, but her eyes seem to twinkle in acknowledgement, letting me know she's still with me.

"What are we watching?" I pull up the cream-colored armchair from the corner of the room to beside the bed, sitting down and reaching out my hand to hold hers.

The look she gives me this time is almost disapproving. Even in this state of mind, with pills rattling around her body, she knows me. She knows I have a lot to say since my last visit the day before my birthday.

"Okay, okay." I chuckle, squeezing her hand. She returns it ever so lightly before I continue. "I met someone." Why I start with that, I don't know, but it looks as though Mom's head slowly nods for me to continue. "I met him on my birthday, and he's kinda like gum in hair. Impossible to remove unless you cut it out. I don't think I want to cut him out though, Mom. He makes me feel..." I'm struggling to find the right words. I've used Mom as a dear diary of sorts since she's been here; her not replying nor having an opinion helps. "He makes me feel like I'm invincible." Case in point, riding through the middle of a fucking shootout to save him. "He makes me feel like I am capable of anything. Like Dad did." Oh, God. I think this confirms my daddy issues.

That is not something I want to delve into right now, or ever.

The small smile on Mom's face says a thousand things, but ultimately, she's happy for me. Let's see if she's still happy when she hears the real kicker to this story.

"Trouble is, he's the Enforcer for the Sons of Khaos. You know, Jake's rival club from Rockford Beach? Yeah, them. Which means I obviously can't see him again." And I don't know why that thought hurts so fucking much. "Jake would be angry an—" Mom's squeezing my hand, sadness and pain now in her eyes, and she lifts her arm, placing a palm gently against my cheek.

I lean forward into it, embracing the lucidity Mom's showing because it feels like so long since I've seen or felt any real emotion from her. She looks at me then, really looks at me, then slowly blinks.

"Don't...be..." She pauses, and I'm desperately trying to hold my tears at bay. This is the first time she's spoken in years and I'm not sure how to handle it. "Like..." Her words are spoken so slowly and are so soft I barely hear them, but each one is like a precious gift to my soul. Then she gestures to herself, seemingly worn out from the effort as she rests back into her pillows.

I don't call the doctors or nurses, because I'm unsure which ones are on the Rebels' payroll. Instead, I cherish the moment, despite her sad words, and stand a little to place a kiss on her forehead.

There's not a chance I'll be divulging any of the bad crap that's going on, definitely not now. This is a moment to remember and I won't tarnish it by continuing to talk about Jake.

Her smile is small, barely there, but I see it. I see every inflection her features make, and I understand every one of them.

"I love you too, Mom."

Chapter Thirteen

Aleko

It's half past eight, over twenty-four hours after I dropped Mackenzie off for her shift, specifically instructing her not to leave here without me. It doesn't take a fucking genius to put this text and her absence together.

I read the message again as if this time it'll say "On my way" instead of this bullshit.

Spoiler alert: It doesn't.

Ninja, who is sitting straight up in his open pouch, cocks his head at me like he fucking knows I'm pissed off.

"Yeah, dude, she's gonna get a spanking for this stunt."

If I thought spending an entire night and day away from her was leaning on this side of torture, waiting for her to answer is the seventh circle of Hell. I bet Dante wrote *The Divine Comedy* about having to wait months before some asshole could deliver him a letter from his beloved.

Me: I swear to fuck.

Me: You better fucking answer.

Maybe she's doing some last-minute shit inside. I can be patient. I'm not a fucking child, I can wait for two minutes. Plucking a lollipop from the inside of my leather jacket, I don't bother sucking, just go straight to angry crunching.

Me: I'm going inside.

Me: You better fucking be there.

Okay, so two minutes is asking for a lot.

Parking the bike out of the way, I hop off and head straight for the entrance, with Ninja now settled into my hood. My eyes scan the huge hangar for the trucks before I see my girl's ambulance parked on the end, to the right. Well, at least I know she's here. Maybe her message was about being late. Maybe she's sorry because she's making me wait.

I'd wait an eternity if it meant the other option wasn't on the table. Because the thought of Mackenzie going back to her brother's shithole makes me want to bleed that fucker out for days.

"Can I help you?" Slowly, I turn toward the voice to find a firefighter dressed casually in gray slacks and a light blue polo with the Rockford Beach insignia. Right above it, stitched in red, is his name. Ryan.

"Yeah, I'm looking for Mackenzie. Her shift ended a few minutes ago." The first sign that I am not going to like this prick is the immediate steeling of his spine like he needs added height to go into battle. The second is the tone he chooses to use on me. It's a classic move. Making himself taller is supposed to give me some kind of alpha vibe from him.

Except, *I'm* the fucking alpha and his savior complex needs to be aimed elsewhere.

"She's not here." Now, his hands are on his waist, one leg bent slightly as though he's all relaxed and shit. He's not.

Two other guys come out, eyeing me like I'm about to start throwing gasoline all over their station and lighting shit on fire. The third guy who walks out of the double doors I do recognize and fuck, it's the guy whose nose I broke at the beach. Well, fuck.

"Ryan, it's all good. I know him." My staring match with Superhero Ryan doesn't end. If anything, it intensifies.

"He's a biker."

Well, now I'm offended because that tone is nothing less than condescending.

"Let it go, man." Beach Dude...fuck, what is his name? Terence? Stan? He's walking toward me until he's standing right in front and blocking the view of Ryan. "He's her beau."

Ryan and I both look at...Lance? There's no hiding the pride in my grin. My girl has been talking about me. About us. And that warmth in my chest that only exists for her grows tenfold. Fire dude, though? He's sportin' a scowl that turns his friendly face into douchebag territory.

"She's with...him?"

"Don't sound so surprised." I cup my dick and grin. "She knows a good thing when she sees it." Then I add fuel to the fire by throwing a conspiratorial wink his way. I'm being an asshole to distract my growing desire to beat the shit out of this guy for even entertaining the idea that Mackenzie could be with anyone *but* me.

"Get this guy out of here, Spence. We don't need trouble." Lifting his chin, Ryan shakes his head and walks away. Then the bells ring in my brain.

Spence. That's it, Spencer.

"Sorry about that. He's a little...overprotective." Scoffing, I raise a brow at my girl's best friend as if to say, don't bullshit a bullshitter. "Okay, yeah, he has a thing for her. He's a good guy, though. It's just that he's had a crush on her for months and you just broke his little boy heart."

Fuck, now I feel like a dick for punching this guy the other day because I instantly like him.

"Hmmm, sucks to be him. How's the nose?" I nod to the bridge where he's got a bandage to support what I expect is a broken bone. Seems I did some damage, after all.

"It'll heal but this..." He points to said nose and gives me his best scowl. "Is very inconvenient for blowjobs."

I almost choke on air at his words, jostling Ninja as I cough, noticing his little head looking over my shoulder.

"Sorry about that, but I'm sure you'll be making dudes happy again in no time." I think back to Grinder and grin. "In fact, I bet I know someone who'd be down with helping you out with that."

"Thanks, I'll keep that in mind." His brows meet his hairline and I can practically hear the Spaghetti Western music as Ninja and him have a stare down. "You do know there's a rat on your shoulder, right?" I don't miss the way he leans away slightly, putting a little distance between himself and my pet.

"Ninja, Spencer, Spencer, Ninja." I introduce them quickly because we have more important shit to talk about.

"Don't you people tend to kill rats?" Spencer now leans in like he's observing a science project.

I scoop Ninja up and cover his little ears. "We're not the fucking mafia, dude. Ninja is the most loyal animal you'll ever meet."

"If you say so..."

We're both quiet for a while, Spencer's eyes darting from one side to the other, and the rage that had settled just enough to keep me calm and collected starts to rise yet again. That's the look of someone about to deliver news that will send me into a tailspin.

In three.

"About Mac..."

Two.

"She left early because..."

One.

"Her brother—"

Without listening to the rest of that fucking sentence, I turn and jog back to my bike, slapping on my helmet and squealing my back tire out of the space before speeding straight to the SOK compound. If I go to the Rebels now, I'll probably die there, which will do fuck all to help Mackenzie. No, I need to be smart about this. Wow, I really am maturing.

There's no *I* in Khaos. It takes all of the Sons for that shit.

The whole way back, my sole focus is on forcing myself to not detour to Stonebridge and slit Jake's throat open just to watch him bleed out. To be fair, the last time I went guns blazing, my Cherry Pie had to come save me. As hot as fuck as that was, I'd rather do this more efficiently.

Lining up my bike with the rest of the club, I tear off my helmet, grab Ninja, and stare into absolutely nothing in front of me. The compound is surrounded by trees on three sides with the only road leading to this place running in the front. There are only two more houses that use this road so when a car or bike comes up, it's noticed.

"What's up, Psycho?" Python is walking up from the front doors, his eyes on his phone before he starts scanning the area. We're watching him closely after the faceplant during our last trip. Doc said he was dehydrated or some shit but I don't believe it. Then again, I'm no doctor so what the fuck do I know?

"Hey, look at me." He's fidgety and I don't fucking like it.

My tone gets his attention right away and when I scan his eyes they seem clear, focused.

"Yeah?"

"You doin' okay?" I nod to his phone, which is another addiction all in itself.

"Yeah, waiting on a delivery for Sledge. Some tartan paint and a left-handed screwdriver for the garage."

Fucking Sledge and his Brit humor, as he calls it. I try hiding my grin but it's no use. Sledge tried the whole tartan thing on me once, but I'm not that fucking gullible—like yeah, let me just get some plaid paint for ya there.

"What?" He questions my small chuckle, but at this point, Python needs to figure the brothers out on his own. I can't explain it all to him, he's gotta learn the only way there is. Experience.

"Nothin', man. Make sure you sign for it." Hopping off the bike, I slap him on the shoulder and go inside, leaving him puzzled. It's clear he knows something's up, he just has no idea what that something is.

My best guess, Python's going to wait out here for a long time before he realizes he's been played. I mean, we could tell him but what's the fun in that?

Prez is at the bar with Bear, our treasurer, as they tally up the sales and receipts of the week. Sundays are fundays, I guess. As soon as Ninja sees my best friend, he's running down my arm, across the smooth surface of the bar and up onto Bear's shoulder.

"I need help." It's all I have to say to get their attention and from the corner of my eye I see a couple of other brothers stand from the couches and make their way over. It's what I love about being a part of this club. You may have personal shit happening but when you know you can't handle it on your own, they all come around for reinforcement. It's our way.

Ride, die, and bleed for speed.

"What's up?" Prez is the first to speak as silence blankets the rec room.

"Mackenzie wasn't at the station when I went to pick her up. She's back at her brother's trailer park." I'm staring at Prez, willing him to understand without me having to ask.

"You think she changed her mind?" Now, I know Crow, our road captain, means well and is trying to assess the situation, but that rage I've been keeping down and controlled bursts like a volcano that's been suppressed for centuries.

"No, asshole, I do not." With my teeth gritted and my lips curling into an animalistic snarl, I only calm down when Bear's hand lands on my shoulder, squeezing. Crow is a big guy with a heart like a marshmallow. Best part about him is the fact that he doesn't react. He observes, calculates, then strikes. It's the last part that's earned him his club name, Crow. The Reaper itself would cringe at what Crow is capable of doing. I guess being ex-Special Forces will do that to you.

Staring at me with his head cocked to the side, he just waits patiently.

"Sorry." It comes out as a mumble. Nobody likes apologizing for losing their shit. Especially when it has to do with our women. "I don't think so. I didn't hang around to hear the entire story but this has Jake's dirty paws all over it."

Everyone nods and, for a beat, there's only silence until Python comes back in.

"I put a tracker on her backpack."

Five pairs of eyes turn to Python, who's still staring at his phone, thumbs flying across the screen so fast they look fuzzy.

"You did what?" Now, this is a thin line and any respectable man would step back and allow his woman the privacy she deserves.

Unfortunately for Mackenzie, I left the respectful zone about the time I turned two.

"I figured she's your old lady and with her being a Rebel—"

"She's not a fucking Rebel." It's a moot point but I needed to put that out there.

"It was probably a good idea to keep tabs on her." He lifts his face from the screen and looks at me for once. Completely unfazed. "For her safety."

Holy shit. There's no holding my grin back. "Python, you may be of good use, after all."

The phone is shoved in my face, a red dot traveling on 17 heading west toward Stonebridge. It's that exact moment that I remember her bike is here. I dropped her off last night. There's a chance she's riding on some other douchebag's bike and that thought does nothing to calm me down.

"Time for a plan, Brother. Let's do this." Bear's words are the aloe that soothes the burning in my chest.

"Let's get your girl back." Crow grins and it's not supposed to be reassuring, it's scary as fuck.

We decide to ride out after dark, leaving Ninja in Vanessa's care, hoping that by the time we get there the Rebels will be too drunk or busy to suspect we're there. It took Prez, Bear, and Hoops to convince me that going in and shooting up the place without a safety net would only get someone hurt. Of course, Bear sealed the deal when he suggested that person could be Mackenzie. Motherfucker and his logic.

Instead of bringing the whole club, we go four-strong, deciding to bring Python and his tech wisdom with us.

The few times I've been here, I've noticed the path that leads into the woods on the side of the trailer park. I may have entertained the thought of fucking my girl against one of those trucks, hoping they could all hear her screaming my name every time I made her come on my dick.

We hide our bikes there, positioning them so they're ready to speed out when we get back. Pulling my hoodie up to keep me in the shadows, I lead the way along the fence until we reach the back of Mackenzie's trailer. It's late but not late enough, apparently. Their party trailer is in full party mode, music blaring loud enough to hide any noise we could be making.

Mackenzie's trailer is dark and we haven't seen any movement since we got here. I know Jake makes her work the bar so we wait until every single one of the Rebels stumbles out and the lights go out around the park.

It's when the party trailer light goes out and the skinny dude from yesterday locks up that it's clear Mackenzie has probably been asleep in her trailer this whole time. Thank fuck.

"Python, you stay here, whistle if you see anyone coming our way." With a nod, he pulls up his hoodie, hiding his normally light-brown eyes.

Bear and I slip through the hole in the fence, the same one I made last time I was here. I try the door but it's locked. Turning back to Bear, I tilt my head to the lock. Bear has skills and lock picking is one of them. Meanwhile, I slide against the side of the trailer, stepping on a chair so I can peek inside Mackenzie's window. The shades are pulled so it's wasted effort.

Python's discreet whistle has Bear and me freezing and listening. Slow, measured steps crunch against the gravel but still out of view. It could be skinny dude, Cameron, coming to warn Mackenzie about something, but my instincts are screaming at me that those steps sound pained, uneven. Heavy.

When I hear the click of the door, I know Bear has breached the entrance. On a whim, I decide that taking my girl home is the only priority and if killing a Rebel to get that done is on the agenda, well, so fucking be it.

Following Bear inside, I crouch down against the nearest wall and wait for whoever it is to either fuck right off or come inside.

The front door is unlocked right before it opens.

The light turns on, illuminating the front of the trailer and keeping us in the dark.

Shoes are the first things I see coming around the corner. Then long, toned legs. Jean shorts that reach the middle of her thighs followed by a red tank top.

No. Not red. Her tank top is white and covered in red. At first, my brain tries to convince me that it's paint. Red paint. Why would she be painting at this time of night? It makes no sense.

It's when my gaze reaches her face that everything clicks into place.

And that place is a dark, dangerous basement in the recesses of my fucked up mind.

Bear's huge hand on my bicep holds me back, his eyes intense and bearing no hint of humor.

"Be careful, Brother. Be very fucking careful with her." Clamping down on my molars to keep myself as calm as humanly possible, I rise out of my hiding spot and whisper.

"Mackenzie?"

My throat is so tight that I'm not even sure the sound traveled far enough for her to hear me. But her muscles freeze, her hands clench, and her spine straightens to the limit of her height. Yeah, she heard me all right, and it takes every single fiber of my being not to tackle her and protect her with my body.

"Get the fuck out, Aleko. There's nothing here for you." Her voice is broken, strained like she's been crying for decades.

"Yeah, not a goddamn chance of that happening, baby-doll."

Chapter Fourteen
Mackenzie

A few hours earlier

Something feels different tonight. There's tension swimming through the air as soon as I step out of the Uber outside the trailer park. A rock forms in the pit of my stomach and I almost turn around, ready to accept the consequences of never being able to see my mom again. Inhaling deeply, I squeeze my eyes shut and fist my hands before breathing out through my mouth and shaking myself off.

I can do this.

Making me work tonight at the Rebels' compound isn't the only punishment I'll be receiving, and even though a million other people would run a mile rather than accept their lot, I just can't do it. Call it the stupid in me, but I need to keep up appearances for just a little longer.

They've only broken bones once, and that was two of my toes and my pinky finger so I was still useful to them. It hurt like a motherfucker, but if that's what needs to happen tonight, so Mom can stay safe and Aleko can stay off their main radar because they think I'm loyal to them, I'm happy to be the focus of their ire.

If I knew a friend was in this situation, I'd tell them to run away and never look back, but it feels impossible to take my own advice and I'm aware of how fucking ridiculous that is.

Once inside my trailer, I pee for what feels like forever before taking a quick shower. I've whipped up a quick batch of cherry and chocolate chip cookies that are now baking in my tiny oven as I throw on some jean shorts and a white tank top. The sun set a little while ago, but it's still hot as Hell and I'm all about comfort when I have the choice. After blasting my thick blonde hair with the hairdryer, I throw it into a high messy bun to keep it off the back of my neck. It can get real hot inside the trailer bar and I'd rather not get sweatier than I need to before receiving today's bruises.

God, it feels fucking dumb to even think like this is normal. To be honest, I never really thought too much about it before now.

Closing my blinds, I pull the cookies from the oven and pop them into some tupperware. I've never been as obvious as this with my special variety of cookies, specifically bringing a batch to what I know will be a beating later. But I'm feeling particularly petulant today, like all the fucks I have to give are slowly running out. And soon, it won't matter anyway.

Yes, whoever decides to attend my punishment and use me as a punching bag will get the shits, they'll probably vomit quite a bit too, and if they're clever enough—which they're usually not—they'll put two and two together and come up with poisoned cookies.

I make sure the oven and all my lights are off before closing the door and heading toward the bar trailer. It seems busy this evening, with sluts and riders all over each other. Drinks are flowing, dicks are being sucked, and motorcycles are being mistreated by lunatics. Mona waves from behind the bar, the wide grin on her face fading as quickly as her hand lowers when I'm roughly grabbed by the arm.

"Come on, Kenz. Your brother is waiting." Brick's stubby fingers dig into my flesh as he pulls me along to one of the trailers used for sexy times with the club sluts.

Instead of struggling to get free, which would no doubt make things worse, I follow willingly, because this isn't the first time and it sure as fuck won't be the last. Maybe I break the rules on purpose, needing the pain from these beatings to remind me I'm still alive and I need to keep going.

Goblin is the first person I see when I'm practically dragged into the trailer, a large black cast taking up the majority of his arm. Inside, I'm smiling, because he deserved that—and more. He's sitting on the pull-out sofa bed, smoking a joint with his good hand, and the sneer on his face is pure evil. Next are my brother and the club Prez, Isaac.

They're both standing, a purple can in one hand, joints in the other. Isaac is grinning from ear to ear and my brother snarls at me, anger radiating from him like never before. It's making me feel tense because this isn't the same as other times. The uneasiness from before I even stepped foot on the property comes back tenfold and I'm beginning to think this was not the great problem-solving idea I thought it would be.

Take a beating, all is fine, keep my head down for a bit...no issues.

But no...this feels like more.

"Here, I brought y'all some cookies." Pretending I haven't noticed the weirdness of this situation, I'm hoping the cookies help lessen whatever kind of beating is coming my way. I hold them up and out toward Jake, forcing a timid smile onto my face before he snatches them from my hand, throwing the tupperware box onto the table beside him.

There's not a lot of room in here with the couch pulled out, so it feels a little like sardines in here right now. Jake and Isaac aren't exactly small men, they take up half the room with just their heads. Okay, I'm exaggerating, but being in this space with these four men makes me seem tiny in comparison.

"So, you think you can take matters into your own hands, do ya, girl? By saving the motherfucking enemy trying to kill our club members." Venom is practically spraying from Isaac's mouth as he speaks, and I accept it, as I do every time. Simply because the one and only time I did talk back was when the broken bones happened.

"You've been warned about what would happen if you betrayed us, *little sister*." Jake sneers, stepping forward from beside Isaac. "Did you really think you could hide your relationship with the SOK Enforcer?" The shock must be clear in my eyes because Jake laughs, pressing his nose against mine. "Dressing up like a slut on your birthday didn't hide you, Kenz. Next time you fuck someone, you shouldn't do it out in the open. Make sure nobody is watching."

I don't bother to ask who, because I couldn't give two fucks. It won't change the outcome of what's about to happen, so I remain silent, readying myself for the first punch to my gut.

But it doesn't come.

Not yet.

"We know why they took you on at Rocks Off, and it has nothing to do with your bar skills. We were happy to wait it out, see what happened and how we could use this. But you brought him here, fucked him on Toxic Rebel property, then let him loose with a mother fucking gun on our people. So, here's what's going to happen." Jake steps back, sipping from his can, toking on his joint, and his evil smile grows as his eyes narrow on me. Brick may as well be clapping his hands with excitement, I can see the giddiness dripping from him. "Prez is gonna rip your cunt open with his cock, Goblin is gonna destroy your ass, Brick is gonna watch, getting plenty of spank bank material to use for when he visits Mom next weekend, and I'm going to record it. So we can all watch it back, over and over. They're going to paint you with their cum, rub it into your cuts and bruises...of which I'm sure you've realized you have none yet." Jake tips his head to Brick, who's still behind me after closing the door when we came in.

Pain pierces through my cheek when Brick's fist connects and I struggle to remain standing from the sheer force of it. Jake's threats are scaring the fuck out of me too, because yeah, he's threatened all those things before, but they've never actually followed through.

What makes me believe this time is different is the fact that Isaac has already pulled his cock out and he's fisting it, watching Brick grab my bare arms and push me onto the pull-out bed next to Goblin. I slam onto the hard mattress face first, managing to put my hands out in time to soften the fall. It still hurts, pain shooting through my wrist where I've landed on it.

"Come on, Jake. You won't do this..." Turning onto my back, tentatively, I attempt to sit up until I'm pushed back down by Goblin's cast. His face is scrunched up in pain, but there's also glee in his eyes.

"I will, little sister. And you'll accept every last drop of cum they have to give your whore-self." Jake stubs out his joint on the wall and drops the butt on the floor before digging into his pocket. He pulls out his red switchblade, flipping it open and rushing toward me.

"Jake! What—Argh!"

He slices my cheek then grabs me by the throat and straddles me, the blade held above his head ready for another strike.

"Please, don't. I promise I won't see any of them again. I'll qui—"

Another cut to my other cheek this time, and pain lances through my body, his grip on my throat getting tighter. The edges of my vision are blurred as I claw at my brother's wrists, trying desperately to get him off me.

This really is the end. He's finally going to kill me.

When he relents, lifting the hand on my throat, I gasp for air, coughing and trying to catch my breath.

"Cover your mouth when you cough, you disgusting whore. Just like your goddamn mother."

I barely have time to register Jake's words before he rips open the top of my tank and slices through my bra, catching my skin in the process. It burns, and the tears now falling from my eyes are making the open wounds on my cheeks sting.

"Please...Jake...the club needs me, they—"

"The only thing we need from you now are your holes. We have backup plans for the race rankings because I knew you'd fuck up. I was waiting for the mother fucking day, dear sister." Jake undoes my jean shorts as Isaac moves forward, climbing onto the tiny bed and resting his knees on either side of my head.

Brick also comes over and grips one of my wrists, holding it out beside me while Goblin does the same with the other. Isaac pushes down on my chest, his dick held in one hand over my face as he pumps at it and squeezes my breast.

I don't want to open my mouth anymore because every word is met with vitriol. I'm outnumbered, outpowered, and out of fucking options.

How did I let it come to this? I thought I had it handled. I was wrong on so many levels.

I lost sight of my game plan, allowed myself to have a life, thinking that turning twenty-one would mean more freedom. It felt so good to have that. As much as I've been denying my real feelings toward a man I've known for mere days, I've loved every second spent arguing and being with him.

Aleko feels right. He fits.

And this is all kinds of wrong. I'm trying to separate myself from my body, from the torture my brother and his friends are inflicting. It's difficult, though, and I wince at the burning pain of another cut, this time across my abdomen. It's not deep, but it fucking stings. Then Isaac squeezes again, too hard, and I clench my teeth so tightly to hold back the scream. The movement hurts my cheeks, but I focus on that rather than what's really going on.

My wrists are still pinned, pain shooting up my arms from the tight grips on either side. My jean shorts and my panties are gone, my tank is ripped, I'm bleeding and bared.

"If you can whore yourself out to the SOK club, you can do it here." Jake's snarl is barely audible over Isaac's grunts and his knees squeezing the sides of my head.

I think of Aleko, the few short times we've spent together, the way he makes me feel. Light. Free. Sexy. Needed. Powerful. More tears spill from my closed eyes and a hand grips my throat again, squeezing tightly as I try to break free and gasp for breath. My arms and legs are being pushed down, held so tightly in place I fear the bones may break.

Opening my eyes, I try to plead for my life with a look, only to find my brother's face above me. His lips are curled up in a salacious smile, like he's enjoying every second of this and he was just waiting to watch the life leave my eyes.

My vision goes blurred again, dots flashing, pain lancing through me...

I wake up crying, wincing when pain burns all over my body. My cheeks, my chest, my wrists, my throat, my stomach, my…

They did it. They actually fucking did it.

Slowly sitting up, I'm glad to find that I'm alone and it sounds as though everything outside has died down. Which means I've been here a good couple of hours. Passed out while they did unspeakable things to my body. I look down, my tank and skin are covered in dried blood, along with what I know is cum.

Oh, God. My stomach rolls and I vomit beside me, onto the dirty-as-fuck mattress. Every wretch hurts, but I'm incapable of stopping until my stomach's empty.

This is all my fault. I allowed it to happen. I walked right into the situation I'm in with my eyes wide open, ignoring the danger because I thought I had a use. A place to call home. So Jake was a dick, but he was still my brother and it hasn't always been all bad. But he never hid who he was, never hid his intentions for me, and I thought I was fucking special.

I'm not.

I stand on wobbly legs and find my jean shorts on the floor. My panties are a ripped mess so I leave them where they are, carefully sliding my shorts on before adjusting my tank to at least cover my nipples. My Docs are still on my feet, looks like they couldn't be bothered with those.

If I can get to my trailer, I'll have a quick shower, change, then I'm taking my car to my storage unit and getting the hell out of here. There's nothing left for me to do.

Tonight has made all my plans obsolete because I can't stick around now. Not after that.

I love my mom, but she'll understand. She wouldn't want this for me and I'm fucking stupid for putting up with it for this long. I've been so fucking naïve, thinking I could carry out this big old plan to save us.

Fucking save us.

It's impossible.

My brother simply won't allow it and I don't know how I didn't see it before now.

All I am is nothing. I am nothing.

I have nothing.

My body is broken, but my mind is thankful that the violations happened while I was passed out because at least I didn't have to feel everything. That doesn't make it any less earth shattering though. How could I let myself get into this situation in the first place? What was I thinking? I'm nobody's hero.

Tears begin to roll down my face again, causing the now-dried cuts on my face to sting, but I welcome the pain. I deserve it for being a stupid bitch.

A whore is what they called me. The word reverberates around my head like a bouncy ball until I begin to believe it. I sniff up, using a clean part of my tank to try and dry my eyes.

Steeling my spine, I prepare myself to step back into the outside world. If they see me, I won't let them have the satisfaction of watching me break any more. I slowly make my way to my trailer, each step a reminder of what's been done to my body.

After unlocking my trailer door and heading inside, I flip the switch to turn the lights on so I don't walk into anything and hurt myself more. I freeze when I realize I'm not alone. Shame coursing through my veins at how I look and what I allowed to happen.

The men both have murderous looks on their faces, their breathing becoming ragged until Bear inhales deeply and rests one of his huge hands on Aleko's bicep.

"Be careful, brother. Be very fucking careful with her." Bear's deep voice is firm yet soothing all at the same time and I can imagine he gives a real good hug.

Which I definitely don't deserve right now.

Aleko moves a step closer and whispers, "Mackenzie?"

That one word, my name, spoken so carefully from his lips, makes me clench my fists and straighten my spine, holding my breath to contain the fountain of tears that want to escape. He deserves better than me. All I bring is trouble. I'll only make things worse for him and his club and I can't do that, especially after they were all so kind to me. He needs to go.

"Get the fuck out, Aleko. There's nothing here for you." My voice is broken, strained, my throat likely heavily bruised if the pain is anything to go by.

"Yeah, not a goddamn chance of that, babydoll." Aleko steps closer, carefully wrapping his arms around my shoulders and holding so gently, as though I could break at any moment.

Too late. I'm already broken.

I resist melting into him, because he can't be here. I'm the giant red flag in this scenario and he's better off without me. They all are.

"Go away. Go the fuck home." I try to step back, but he doesn't relent.

"Sweetheart, I'm about to shoot every motherfucker in this place so there'll be nothing left for you here. Bear, pack her bags, I have some walking dead men to hunt."

My eyes widen in horror and I wince again, inhaling sharply at the pain as I manage to step away from Aleko. He's going to get himself killed. Over me.

I'm not worth his life.

"Please don't. Just fuck off out of here. It's all a waste of your time because it's my own fault, I—"

"Don't you ever blame yourself for the actions of sadistic assholes, Cherry. None of this is your fucking fault. Now where the fuck are the ones who did this to you? Was it your fucking brother?" His voice is getting louder and he's pacing, looking as though he's trying to hold back from touching me again. I don't answer, unbidden tears streaking down my face and reminding me of the pain once more. "It was, wasn't it? I'm gonna fucking gut the bastard, make him watch as I burn this whole motherfucking place down. I'm gonna—"

"Psycho, dude, come on, man. Stop. Look at her." Bear gestures to me, standing here shivering, my arms wrapped around my body and tear stains on my cheeks. "Let's get her home, Brother. We'll reap vengeance with clear heads. I promise." Bear's hands are fisted by his sides and I can see he's fighting to maintain his own sense of calm.

"Come here." Aleko's features soften, though I know he's still struggling as he holds his arms open for me to come to him this time. "Please?" His eyes plead with mine, hurt swimming in the depths because he can't do a damn thing to take back what happened.

Something inside of me breaks and my façade crumbles. I don't want him to go away. I don't want to be alone. Just this once, I need saving. I need him to hold me and tell me everything's going to be okay.

So I step into him, wrapping my arms around his waist and holding on so tightly for fear of letting him go. His warm scent envelopes me, giving me that sense of safety he always brings, and I let the tears fall freely into his cut and black hoodie. Everything hurts, I feel pathetic and useless and like a used mess.

"Here." Bear hands Aleko his large black T-shirt, now only wearing his cut and pants.

"Nice thought, Brother, but the only man's clothes my old lady will be wearing are mine." With masterful precision, Aleko manages to pull off his cut and hoodie without jostling me too much or making me stop touching him in some way. I remain clinging on to him, as though he's my only lifeline in a sea of pain.

"Put your arms through here, darlin'." He slides it over my head and the hem falls just below my ass, covering most of the physical damage to my battered body.

I feel so unlike myself. Weak and timid. But every tender touch from this beautiful, headstrong man feels soothing somehow.

I allow Aleko to control me, needing now, more than ever, for him to tell me what to do and how to do it. The idea of thinking for myself makes me want to vomit because, well...my decisions, thus far, have led to my current situation.

They both pack some of my clothes into a duffel bag I had in my closet ready for escape day before Aleko lifts me, bridal style, and carries me out of the trailer door. Bear follows behind with my bag of clothes, all the while I'm silently watching, my arms glued around Aleko's neck. Through all of his darkness, he's somehow become my light.

The world passes by in a blur, then I'm gripping Aleko's waist as I ride bitch. Streetlights, trees, buildings all fade into nothing until we pull up into the SOK compound.

Turning off the engine, he climbs off before reaching for me and carrying me toward the entrance.

I let him because walking hurts. Everything does, really. My head, my face, my chest...my very soul is bleeding from the injustice of tonight.

"Thanks for the assist, guys. Head on home, I've got this."

"Brother, if a war is coming, I'm gonna be here for it. We need to keep your old lady and the compound safe, so you need numbers. Go on and take care of your woman." Bear's deep voice is soothing and I've decided I really like him.

It'll be a shame to be responsible for getting him killed. If the Rebels did this to *me*, what the fuck are they going to do to Aleko and his club?

Huge sobs begin wracking through my body, each one painful, but I'm unable to stop.

"Shh, darlin', I've got you now." Aleko whispers above my head, holding me carefully so as not to cause any more pain than I'm already feeling, before kissing me between the eyes and walking into the large building that I know was once a psychiatric hospital.

My tears don't relent, I'm powerless against my own body. The pain, the crying, it's all too much.

Aleko gently places me down onto the bed inside his room and I whimper at the loss of his touch, crying harder as he walks away from me into the bathroom. I barely hear the sound of running water before he's right next to me again, lifting me as though I'm the most precious thing in the world and carrying me through the door.

Slowly and carefully, he peels his hoodie off me, followed by the rest of my clothes and shoes until I'm naked in front of him. Next, he pushes down his jeans, leaving his boxers on, before removing his cut and T-shirt. He holds a palm out for me, which I take greedily, allowing him to lead me into the shower with him stepping in behind me.

It's not sexual in any way, but the way he touches me sets a fire beneath my skin. He gently washes me, rubbing slow, soothing circles all over my body, bending to his knees to do my legs and feet. He treats me like a queen, as though he's in awe of me, which is a fucking joke in itself.

The way he looks at me, as though I'm his entire world, breaks through the numb state I've once again found myself in, and here come more tears.

They slide down my face as Aleko stands, cupping my cheek lightly and kissing my eyelids, my cheeks, my nose, my chin, then my eyes again.

"You live here now, Cherry. Understood?"

Somehow, I manage to nod. At least, for now, it seems like the best idea. Not that I trust my own judgment anymore.

Aleko shampoos my hair, massaging my head after cleaning my body. He was careful not to scrub hard over the cuts, and I'm thankful for all the patience this man seems to have. When he's finished, he wraps me in a large fluffy blue towel before stripping out of his now-wet boxers. With his back to me, I can see some scars I hadn't noticed before, intertwined with the tattoos he has creeping up his spine. He pulls on some clean boxers from his chest of drawers, taking out another pair and walking toward me.

"Sit down, babydoll."

I do as he asks, sitting on the edge of the bed and allowing him to maneuver my feet into the boxers and slide them up my legs. He then pulls a black T-shirt from another drawer, and after patting my body dry and removing the towel, he slides it over my head.

Reaching across to the small fridge beneath the bedside table, he takes out a bottle of water, unscrews the lid, and encourages me to open my mouth by pushing his thumb between my lips. My whole body is too numb to register anything right now and I allow him to tip the water into my mouth. I swallow a few small sips at a time, the cool liquid soothing my sore throat while being painful at the same time.

Most of the cuts on my chest and abdomen were relatively superficial and they've scabbed over a little, much like the ones on my cheeks. Although, as my skin dries, the new scabs are drying out and every movement and wince of pain reminds me of my marred body, of how it became this way...

"Hey, come back to me, Cherry. Don't let them fucking win. You hear me?" He's cupping my cheek again, kneeling before me, gently wiping at the tears falling down my face once more. His touch is featherlight over my new cuts, careful not to hurt me.

I feel like I've been crying for a thousand years, the pain is never ending.

Aleko leans forward, closing his eyes and resting his forehead against mine.

"You're safe, I've got you."

CHAPTER FIFTEEN
ALEKO

"*You're safe, I've got you.*"

My words are on a constant loop in my mind as I slip out of bed the next morning. With the sleeping pill I had her take before bed, I'm not worried about waking her up as much as I am about stirring Ninja into his morning frenzy. Oddly enough, he doesn't move as he usually would. Instead, he pops open an eye, looks at me, then curls right back around Mackenzie's neck like a warm, purring necklace. It's as if he knows something is wrong and that only gets my body buzzing all the more.

I need an outlet—a wall to punch or a tree trunk to kick—so that I can be what Mackenzie needs from me. There's no doubt in my mind that if she could see me right now, she'd most likely be afraid. Hell, *I'm* afraid of what I'm capable of doing when I'm in this state. And that's saying something, considering my past.

It only takes me minutes to pull on a pair of shorts and sneakers so I can have a one-on-one with the punching bag down in the courtside garage.

"Psycho!"

Turning at the sound of my name, I bite back my frustration at being interrupted. Obviously, I won't be talking back to Vanessa, who's jogging her way to me as I turn and acknowledge her. Showing disrespect to the Prez's old lady is about the same thing as signing a death warrant. On most days, dying doesn't scare me one bit but now there's my Cherry Pie, and leaving her exposed to the fucking monster that is her brother is out of the fucking question.

"Mornin' V." My greeting is flat, my voice tight with pent up anger.

"I heard about Mac. How is she?" Shaking her head, she brings a hand to her mouth and rolls her eyes. "Sorry, that was stupid. Of course she's not okay."

"I get it but no, she's nowhere near okay." My hands on the top of my head, I release a breath that was nearly suffocating me.

"Do you mind if I go up there, take her some food?" One of her hands lands on my shoulder and she squeezes lightly. "Hey, this is not your fault." My eyes snap up to hers and the snarl almost—almost—lashes out.

"I know that. It's her fucking psychotic brother. I know it's my club name but holy shit, V, you didn't see her last night. I can't..." Taking one step back, I shake my head and steel my spine. "I gotta go. I need the punching bag." I soften my eyes because everything Vanessa tries to do is for the good of the club and here I am being a dick. "I'm sorry. I just..."

"Go. I'll take her some food." I nod at her words, knowing that no matter what I say, she'll do what she thinks is best. Honestly, I can't imagine Mackenzie will be eating...not today. I know I won't be, unless I want to hurl everything right back out. What I do want is to feel the pain, the exertion of all of this negative energy swirling inside me and ready to burst.

Seeing her last night was a whole new level of Hell. The blood, the bruises, the slashes on her face. So much fucking blood, so much destruction. My entire body shook with the need to rip Jake limb from limb. Even if it hadn't been him—which it fucking was in some capacity—I would have broken every bone in his body for letting this happen on his watch. His fucking sister. His blood.

Okay, so I'm not one to talk, but in my defense, my brother was a fucking demon spawn and the world is a better place without him in it. I don't regret that bullet all those years ago. I do not regret shooting the man responsible for child trafficking, let alone the whole list of other shit he was doing. I refused to associate myself with him on that level.

When I take my first punch, thoughts of Yiannis and Jake merge together, giving me the mental image of everything I hate in this world. My second fuels this rage inside like nothing else ever could. Every time my fist connects with the bag, I'm knocking out one of Jake's teeth, watching him spit it and a big ol' wad of blood right along with it.

The next thing I know, I'm barreling left, right, left, left into the bag until sweat runs down my spine and over my temples. Until my breath is so ragged that I can barely take in a gulp of air. Until my legs are so weak I have to hug the makeshift replacement for what I'd rather be punching...Jake's face.

With my hands resting against my knees, I heave in breath after breath and get all of my anger out in this very moment before I have to face Mackenzie and give her every ounce of strength that I have.

"Feeling better, Brother?"

Jumping at Bear's voice behind me, I scowl.

"What the fuck, man? Not a good idea sneaking up on a man ready to pummel." Christ, he knows better.

"Yeah, you look like you could lose a wrestling match with an ant." He positions himself on the other side of the bag and holds it firmly for me. "Get it all out, man. She's gonna need you clear headed up there."

Right, left, left.

"Don't you think I fucking know that? Why do you think I'm here?"

Left, right, right.

"Hmm, I think this is only making you angrier."

Duck, right, duck, left.

"So what do you suggest?"

Jab, jab, jab.

"You fucking plan." He steps away and stares at me, the murderous intent in his eyes is so fucking clear and I know it mirrors my own. "You plan their slow, painful, deaths. Then you deliver them to her and you let *her* decide how they die." I freeze at his words, our stares now matching glares at what he's suggesting.

"No fucking way I'm putting them in the same room. And fucking no, I'm not going to make her choose her brother's death. It'll fucking break her, man." I'm shaking my head, seriously contemplating Bear's mental state.

"Don't do that, Psycho."

"Don't do what?"

"Don't treat her like a fragile flower. She just went through Hell and walked right out of the flames. She deserves the choice and if you don't give her that, you don't fucking deserve her." Then the motherfucker walks away like he just dropped the fucking mic.

By the time I shower and have a bite to eat, Mackenzie has woken up twice and gone right back to sleep. My kisses on her forehead are gentle but my fingers wrapped around the headboard are tight, nearly cutting off the circulation.

"She deserves the choice and if you don't give her that, you don't fucking deserve her."

Bear's words bounce in my mind as I walk down to church, slowly starting to make sense but not enough for me to be convinced, yet. Sitting at the table, I try to imagine her face as she delivers the sentence on her brother. Then, I recoil at the idea that she might forgive him just because they're blood.

Now I'm fuming all over again.

The Prez's gavel slams against the circular wood and silence falls all around the room. We're all here. All the members and even the prospects. This isn't a regular church meeting, this is bigger.

"It's been a long time since we've had beef this serious with the Toxic Rebels. Or anyone else, for that matter. We do our business in our town, they do theirs in Stonebridge." Prez looks at me and raises his chin. "But our favorite Psycho has gone and fallen in love with the enemy's sister." There are a couple of chuckles but, by now, everyone has heard about what happened to Mackenzie so laughing seems inappropriate.

"Romeo and Juliet." My eyes search out who said that, landing on Python, whose smile is so fucking sincere it makes me roll my eyes.

"Shut the fuck up, Prospect," comes from a brother in the back.

"Although it's true, ennit?" Sledge is pointing his finger at Python, approving his analogy. "Reckon Shakespeare would love a bit of filthy biker gangs wagin' war for the damsel who falls in love. Fuckin' right." This time we all chuckle a little louder because Sledge is hard to ignore and his humor is always on point.

Until reality sets in.

They both die in the end and I won't fucking let that happen.

"All right, settle down. You can go read your classics when this shit is over." Sitting back on his chair, Prez rubs a palm over his bearded cheek and hums before he speaks again. "The safest thing to do is put our families, our close allies, on lockdown until this shit ends. We also call in our South Carolina charter in case we need back up." This gets everyone's attention, tenfold. "Wanna say something, Psycho?"

I nod. I've got a lot to fucking say but I'll keep it brief. Just as I'm about to speak, I look at Bear and all of a sudden his words make sense to me.

"You fucking plan."

"We're not going in gung-ho. This is my war, my old lady, and I won't ask you to sacrifice your lives for me. But until Jake Wilson is dead and fucking buried, I'll be putting all of my time and effort into doing this right so it doesn't fall back on the club."

"Ride, die, and bleed for speed," Bear calls out, voice booming across the table, one fist punching his heart.

"Ride, die, and bleed for speed," the rest of the room chants after him, their fists mimicking Bear's action.

The blood of the covenant is thicker than the water of the womb. This is my coven, my real family. And Mackenzie is now a part of it.

"It's settled. We go on lockdown and we go to war…together." We all look to Prez and try to digest the finality of his words.

Once the prospects file out the room, we get to club business. Boner's cousin is working out well, so far. Our first shipment was on time and nothing was missing. The parts are good quality, which means we're paying less for more. Can't fucking beat that.

"I spoke to Celia. The entire sheriff's department is worried. Something is out there killing college kids on our turf and it's seriously pissing me off." Prez is not a fan of the drug world. We may partake here and there, mostly pot and shrooms, sometimes a line or two of coke, but it ends there and we always know where the shit comes from. This shit, though, doesn't bode well for us. If anyone thinks we're the ones dealing, it'll destroy everything we've worked for here.

"Someone should talk to Python. Didn't he used to use back in the day? May have some contacts." We all nod to Hoops, who's right. After my conversation with Bash, I'm pretty sure Python has been clean for almost two months but he may still know people around who are buying or selling. Hopefully, his faceplant the other week was a coincidence.

"Boner, take care of it. Grinder, you go with him in case you need to beat answers out of someone." Grinder gives Prez his scary as fuck grin and nods.

"My pleasure, Boss." And we all groan, knowing the chances of a dealer walking away with all his teeth this week are zero to none.

"Anything else need handling?" Prez's gaze meets every single one of us before I raise my hand.

"Yeah, I need a favor." It's the first time I've called on the club for something this personal but the way I see it, if I solve this problem, I automatically make Jake Wilson yesterday's news in Mackenzie's world.

"Gotta do with your old lady?" I'm not surprised Prez has guessed it. To be fair, she's the only important thing in my life besides the club.

"Yeah. Well, actually her mother. She's the reason Mackenzie keeps going back to her brother and I need to stop that shit." All the brothers are staring at me, waiting for the whole story, so I tell them what I know. It isn't much, really, but enough to get them on board with a plan.

"You got an idea of how to break out a patient from the psych ward, Brother?" Bear can barely contain his amusement from this shit and I get it. It's kind of funny.

"Go in on the downlow, roll her out in a wheelchair. Kidnap her. Peel out. In that order. Simple as cherry fucking pie." There's a moment of silence when I finish my plan before everyone loses their shit.

"Yeah, simple. What the actual fuck could possibly go wrong?" At Bear's sarcasm, I do the only thing I can do. I flip him the bird.

By the time church is over, I'm biting at the bit to see my Cherry Pie.

"You wanna watch another movie or do you want to go back to sleep?" I've got Mackenzie tucked under my arm, her head lying on my chest and one of her bruised up legs bent over mine as her fingers clutch at my UNC T-shirt.

"Didn't take you for a college ball fan." Her lighthearted conversation starter takes me off guard. To be honest, I'm not sure why. What was I expecting? For her to only think dark thoughts and wallow in the horrific events of last night?

Fuck, I'm an asshole. My conversation with Bear comes back to bite me in the ass and I swallow down my need to envelop her in bubble wrap until the end of time.

"Hoops was a player for the Tarheels back in the day. Had a couple of boxes full of tees so we all got some and the rest he gave to Goodwill." The bobbing of her head against my chest tells me she's nodding. "Vanessa had a few National Lampoon's movies on DVD if you're down? Or we can just go to sleep." My fingers are massaging her scalp—almost the only place on her body that isn't battered—while Ninja wakes up, stretches, then scurries off to his food bowl to eat.

"Vanessa brought him some of the leftover cherries from the trees. He went a little mental over that." Her chuckle is the most beautiful sound in the world, giving me hope that she'll survive this. No, more than that, she'll fucking slay.

"Yeah, I may have given him my addiction. I've got sugar-free lollipops just for him. He can sit there for hours licking it until there's nothing left." Ninja stops eating, looks up at me, and I swear he mentally high-fives me for bringing home the ultimate cherry. Fucker thinks we're sharing. We are not.

"He's the cutest thing in the world, I swear."

Ninja, one. But I've got skills he'll never have.

"Oh yeah?" I flip us over so that she's on her back and I'm on top, holding myself up like I'm doing push-ups.

"Yeah." Fuck, her smile is life. Complete and total life.

"But is he cute enough to do this?" Reaching over to the bedside table, I swipe up the antibacterial cream and shake it in front of her.

Flashing her a winning grin when she groans to the ceiling, I kneel over her and slowly pull up her tank top.

"Is it okay if I lift it off completely?" Her smile is so generous and sincere, it spears me right through the heart.

"Yeah. I think it'll be harder for you than for me." When she turns her head to the side, I have no doubts it's some kind of misplaced shame dictating her. I grit my teeth with barely restrained frustration, the idea of her suffering makes me physically ill. My thumb and forefinger catch the tip of her chin so I can see her baby blues again.

"Hey, don't do that, okay? Don't look away from me. Don't shy away from this. I'm in, Mackenzie. I've been in since day one. This?" I look down to her battered body then fix her with a stare that would make grown men kneel. "This is mine. It's cut and bruised but it's still mine. They may have touched it but it's. Still. Mine. Do you understand what I'm saying?"

"I know, I do. It's just...a lot. And it hurts and more than anything, it pisses me off." Nodding, I lean closer and slide my lips, whisper soft, across hers before speaking into her mouth.

"Own that anger, Cherry Pie. Don't let it fester, give it an outlet. Give it a purpose." That spark that she's always had returns and I fucking thank all the Greek gods and even some of the Norse because we'll be okay.

"They're going to die, aren't they?" There's zero guilt or apprehension in her question, only the need for answers.

"Every single fucking one of them." And I plan to keep that promise if it's the last thing I do.

"Before y'all make plans, I have to tell you something." Raising a brow at her words, I hope she's not going to tell me something that's going to force me to lock her up so she doesn't go back there. Hell, if it were up to me, she'd never go anywhere outside of my bed. Except maybe to pee.

"I have a garden. My mother used to love gardening, it was something we did together. When shit started to go bad and the...the beatings began..."

I bite my tongue hard enough to make me flinch.

"Sorry."

"Go on, babydoll. Don't mind me." I'll just be over here making a list of all the offenses he's committed so I can tally them up on his body later.

"I planted some deadly plants. At first I thought I'd just make them sick, like vomit or have the shits for a while. It was like a tiny revenge without anyone knowing. Last night, though, I had a feeling something was up so I made cookies with enough poison that I'm pretty sure it would've killed them. At least, I think so." A frown mars her beautiful face as she thinks her plan through. "I mean, I don't know. I guess we'll see, right?"

"It doesn't matter, baby. They're not going to survive the end of summer." I've never been more honest than this moment.

"Good."

With my teeth biting down on my bottom lip, I smile before bending my head and kissing the tender flesh of her stomach, above, below, and on either side of where that fucker sliced her open. Our doctor saw her briefly, patched her up where the cuts were the deepest, this one the being the worst, the right cheek a close second.

Then, I soothe her wound with the cream before re-suming my onslaught of peppered kisses up and down her skin. Sometimes, they're soft, sometimes they make a tiny noise that has Ninja's ears perking up and his nose going a million miles a second. Sometimes, I nibble, but only where her skin is flawless.

I do this for every wound. For every cut. For every bruise until she's relaxed and breathing slowly and deeply.

I kiss every inch of her stomach and chest to replace the pain with better memories.

Memories of me. Of us. Of everything we will be when this nightmare is over.

Those assholes may have taken her for one moment in time but I'll have her for the rest of eternity while they rot in Hell.

Chapter Sixteen
Mackenzie

The bruises that cover my face and body are at their darkest. They're huge and ugly and, mixed with the aches in my bones, they're a reminder of what my brother and his friends did three days ago. Not that I'll ever forget, but it's almost like I'm still in the denial stage of what happened in that trailer, because I still can't quite believe it.

I've been content in the bubble Aleko has created for me inside his bedroom. There has been no contact with the outside world except for a couple of text messages from Spencer, checking in to see how I'm doing. I've explained a little, but I'd rather give him the details in person on our next shift. I've been able to push real life aside, pretending it doesn't exist. Today, though, I'm determined to pull on my big girl panties and push for that anger stage of grief to hit me. Because I can let what happened do one of two things to me: I can let it break me, allowing myself to morph into a shell of what I once was, or I can let it make me stronger, allowing myself to become who I was always supposed to be.

I may not be entirely sure who I'm supposed to be yet, and it's going to take time to get wherever that is, but I won't become my mother. I love her with all my heart, but if she had fought harder, our lives would've taken a very different route.

A lot of things could have been different. If I hadn't fucked a stranger in the bed of a truck at the last race night, would they have still...I can't even think the word. If Aleko had just left me alone, stayed away like I asked...

Ah fuck, I wished for it, and it shall appear. I think anger is kicking in. This situation isn't Aleko's fault or Mom's, or anyone else's. It's mine.

"Oh, God." The words slip out as I remember what Jake said Brick is going to do.

"Hey, what's up, my little Cherry Pie?" Aleko continues to gently massage my scalp as I lay on his bare chest. It's soothing, calming, but it doesn't change the fact that I've put a target on Mom's back. As well as every member of the Sons of Khaos. After Aleko came back from his meeting the other day, he informed me that the club is on lockdown, which means nobody goes home or leaves the compound unless the Prez gives the okay.

"Nothing." I can't put this on him too. Not after everything he's already done for me.

Honestly, I'm surprised he's sticking around at all. I haven't exactly been the best company, there's been no sex—I'm too sore and he hasn't even tried—and there are a million other girls this man could have that aren't traumatized or related to the enemy.

"Don't lie to me. We don't do that, remember? No secrets, no lies." Aleko uses his fingers to tilt my head up until I have no choice but to look at him, searching my eyes for answers I'm not sure I can share.

Ninja uses this moment to scurry onto the bed, poking Aleko's arm with his cute little nose before curling up against the back of my head on the pillow.

"Traitor." He huffs a low laugh and one side of his mouth tilts upward as he takes his eyes off me for a second to shake his head at Ninja. Then his multicolored eyes are back on mine, that same jaw-dropping half-smile in place. "Tell me what's on your mind or I'll make him sleep in his cage tonight."

The look of fake shock-horror on my face only makes Aleko's grin grow wider. "You wouldn't." It's not a question, because I know for a fact that he would never. Not to mention that Ninja's living quarters are more of a palace than some dinky metal cage all decked out with an entire amusement park for his entertainment. Plus, he roams free, most of the time, like a dog or a cat would. And don't get me started on his royal diet. That little thing eats better than I do, or at least more balanced meals including raw veggies for his gnawing pleasure.

"Okay, I wouldn't. But you will tell me."

I sigh, resigned to the fact that this man won't relent. On anything. Once he has set his sights on something, he doesn't hesitate.

"Jake told me he's sending Brick to..." I pause, needing to take a deep breath, composing myself. "He's sending Brick to take advantage of my mom."

"Oh, fuck." The massaging against my scalp stops and he closes his eyes, taking a deep breath of his own before gently kissing my forehead. "They're all going to die." His words are so quiet I almost don't hear them, it's as though his inner thoughts slipped out unbidden, and I don't hate it.

Picturing the deaths of the Rebels who abused me actually makes me feel a little giddy. I'm aware it's fucked up to have such a thought but, well, I'm done with lying to myself. I mean, why stop with one, right?

"Can I watch?"

Aleko raises a brow at my whispered request, a dangerous smile accentuating his strong jawline and high cheekbones. There's not a chance I would allow him to take the final blow from me now, but it's fun to imagine. That he wants it just as much as me is hot as fuck.

"Absofuckinglutely, Cherry. Abso*fucking*lutely."

A knock on the door interrupts our intense, sexy stare-off, followed by Vanessa calling through the wood. "Lunch is up, if you guys wanna join us. Sledge asked Sabrina and the Khunts to make what he calls bacon sarnies for everyone. Said they're shit if they get cold."

She's done this for every mealtime, and for each one, I've declined the invitation. Aleko has gone to get us a plate of something, bringing them back to his room so we can eat while watching the new cowboy TV series.

Aleko gets up, careful not to jostle me too much, and walks toward the door, opening it a crack as he always does to speak to Vanessa.

"I'll come get us some pla—"

"Wait." Sitting up, I wince a little, but I've decided to let the pain fuel me rather than break me. I think. "We can go for lunch, if you want?"

He turns to me, raising both his brows in surprise. "If I want?" He squints his beautiful eyes in my direction accusingly. It makes me squirm a little under his intense gaze, and now I'm doubting my decision. I knew decision making wasn't my thing, why did I even try? "Okay, baby." Understanding crosses his features and he nods before turning back to Vanessa. "We'll be right out, V."

I can't see her, but I hear her reaction and it's a happy one as she claps her hands together quietly. Aleko closes the door and heads toward the dresser, pulling out a sleeveless hoodie and putting it on. The way his muscles tense and the tattoos swirl around his biceps almost makes me forget the pain I'm still in. He is a work of art.

Next, he pulls out a black T-shirt and encourages me to sit on the edge of the bed.

"Arms up."

I do as he says, slowly because I don't want to stretch the cuts on my stomach and accidentally crack open the scabbing.

"You good?" He checks, and I nod before he begins pulling off the UNC T-shirt I stole yesterday when he left to get dinner. It smells like him and I wanted to be smothered. He then slides the fresh black T-shirt over my head, encouraging me to lower my arms once it's on.

Looking down, I smirk at the Sons of Khaos logo across the front. "Is this you branding me?"

His half grin sets my insides on fire. "Not yet, Cherry. But believe me, it's gonna happen. Shade's got a tattoo gun I can use." He wags his brows suggestively and I laugh. "I missed that laugh." Kneeling before me, he holds my face in his palms, careful not to brush against my cuts. The way he looks at me so reverently is breathtaking and I don't feel as though I deserve it.

Placing a soft kiss against my lips, he lingers before moving back, standing, and holding out a hand for me to take. He holds his other hand out toward the bed and Ninja runs across from the pillow, climbs up his arm, and makes himself comfortable in Aleko's hood.

"Let's go." Our fingers intertwine, like they were made to join together, and he leads me out of the room in the knee-length T-shirt, a rolled up pair of his sweats, and bare feet. Just as we reach the hangout room, I pause.

"I should cover myself up more. What if they stare at me? Ask me questions?" I can't help the words falling from my mouth, nerves and shame getting the better of me. The bruises are so clear on my face and bare arms...

"You look perfect, baby. And nobody is going to stare at you. You're my old lady and they know if they even try I'll shoot them in the nutsack." His gaze is so intense it's hard to deny him, but he's just placating me, telling me what I need to hear.

"So, perfect is scarred and bruised? Somehow, I don't believe you." I'm still choosing to ignore the whole "old lady" thing.

"Have I ever lied to you? Told you an untruth?" Gripping me by the chin, he pulls me closer toward him, backing himself up against the wall. I shake my head because, as far as I'm aware, he hasn't lied to me yet. "You could have blue horns protruding your forehead and I'd still think you were perfect, Cherry Pie. Do you know why?"

I shake my head again, a little speechless at his firm tone.

"Because what you may call flaws, I call life experience. They only have the power to make you feel 'less than' if you give it to them. Scars are memories and reminders, and it's up to you to make them mean something. To me, you will always be perfect, and to tell me I'm wrong says you don't trust me. Do you trust me, Cherry?"

Nodding, I blink away the threatening tears.

"Give me your words, baby." He leans in closer, his lips millimeters away from mine and our noses grazing.

"I trust you." And I really do. This man I've known for only a few weeks has worked his way into my life, becoming somewhat of a solid fixture, and while he probably shouldn't trust me, I realize that I do trust him.

"Good." Looking pleased with himself, Aleko licks the tip of my nose and grasps my hand again, pulling me through the doors to the large open space.

We head toward a large round table with a huge plate of sandwiches stacked up high in the center. Vanessa is sitting in her husband's lap—the Prez—while he feeds her, and Bear is mid-conversation with Hoops. At least, I think that's his name. He has a Vice President patch on his cut and I remember speaking to him briefly when Aleko first brought me here.

"Shit, what day is it?" I turn in Aleko's hold, where he's placed me on his lap, much the same as Vanessa and Prez. Thinking about coming here last time has prompted my question because if I'm right, I have to work tonight.

"Wednesday, the twenty-sixth." He doesn't ask why I want to know, and it's refreshing to not be bombarded with whys and hows.

"Okay, I have to work at eight tonight." I grimace, because the storm raging in his eyes tells me he doesn't like it.

"No. We're on lockdown." His voice is louder, so the rest of the table can hear, and I notice the other conversations stop.

"Lockdown or not, I still need to go to work." I have already lost so much of myself, I can't lose this too.

"Are you sure that's a good idea?" Hoops tilts his head curiously in my direction as he speaks, his blonde hair flopping over his eyes and concern causing tension in his mouth.

Bear snorts a laugh and the only thing I see in his gaze is respect. Respect I haven't earned so it makes me feel a little uneasy, but I try to return the confidence in my own small smile.

"Where do you work, sweetie?" Vanessa asks softly as she runs her fingers through Prez's hair.

"I'm an EMT. Twenty-four hour shifts every three days." Ignoring the tensed up Aleko beneath me, I give my full attention to the woman who has shown me nothing but kindness.

"I can imagine that's a tough job. Do you enjoy it?"

"Yeah, I love it. I'm hoping to train to be a full paramedic at some point. My partner, Spencer, has been helping." I thought coming out of Aleko's room would mean I'd be bombarded with questions on my mental and physical state, but I'm relieved to be having a relatively normal conversation.

There's no pressure for me to pretend I'm okay because these people have no expectations of me. They're not looking to see what I can do for them, and it's refreshing to say the least.

"Amazing, I bet your parents are proud of you. It's a very noble occupation." Her smile is so genuine, so sweet, and I mirror it with one of my own.

"My dad died six years ago in a motorcycle accident and my mom's in a psych facility an hour from here." I don't mean to be shocking, just truthful because it feels right, but the horror on Vanessa's face almost causes a laugh to break free.

"Oh, damn! Way to put your foot in your mouth, V." Grinder sits next to Prez and Vanessa, snickering into his sandwich.

Without hesitation, Prez slaps Grinder on the back of his head, causing more laughter around the table.

"I'm so sorry, Mackenzie. I didn't know. But if it helps, I'm in the dead dad club too. But mine wasn't a very nice man." She shrugs and it becomes a little clearer as to why she's not offering me the pathetic look of sympathy that usually comes with finding out my situation. Instead, it's just simple understanding.

Once the food is gone, we migrate to some comfortable sofas and Aleko doesn't give me an inch of space away from him. I actually don't hate it. It's like a constant comfort to my warring insides.

"Refills, ladies?" Python is hovering behind the couches with a pot of coffee in his trembling hands. I can't work out whether the tremble is because he's nervous after Hoops laid into him for letting our cups stay empty for more than a minute, or if there's something else going on with him. He's pale too, but I don't know him well enough to figure his quirks out.

The conversation between Vanessa and I flows as we sip at the delicious coffee, and it's like we've been friends for years. Aleko is sitting beneath me, talking with Bear and Sledge on the opposite couch as he draws careful patterns onto my thighs with his tattooed fingers.

Vanessa tells me about being a mature college student, where she's studying to become a psychiatrist. She wants to understand the way evil works after being subjected to it for so long before Prez literally saved her life. I can see the parallels between us because, in a way, Aleko is saving mine. I'm not sure I'd be coping as well as I am without his constant presence and support. Which feels ridiculous to even think, but he's becoming a lifeline I want to keep.

While I'm telling Vanessa about how my dad used to ride, some of the events he took part in, coming away with first place too many times to count, I suddenly realize the men have stopped talking. It's become super quiet and now I'm conscious that I was maybe talking too loud? I'm aware I can become a little animated when I'm excited about something, and talking about my dad always makes me happy.

"Sorry, too much?"

"Fuck, no. I love when you're having fun, Cherry. We're just interested in what you have to say. Those races are epic."

"You're shitting me. Don't tell me your dad is Chuck Wilson?" Sledge leans forward, resting his elbows on his knees, staring at me with wide, excited eyes.

"Okay, I won't tell you that. But I'd be lying." I shrug, aware that my dad was a big deal on the official racing circuit years ago.

"He was a fuckin' legend."

"Yeah, he really was." Hearing others speak about my dad like this is music to my ears. For so long, it's been a taboo subject, my brother reminding me his death was my fault every time he was mentioned, flooding me with guilt. Aleko squeezes gently on my thigh, the touch more comforting than I'd like to admit to myself.

"Is he the one who taught you to ride?" Bear's deep voice cuts through my thoughts and I smile, remembering the first time I was finally allowed to ride. Dad made me wait until I was big enough to reach the shifter and throttle at the same time, and I was so eager I made Mom measure me weekly against the doorframe of the kitchen.

"He is. I was thirteen and had been riding on the back with him since I was old enough to hold on."

"So you know your stuff then?" Sledge swigs from the beer one of the girls here brought over before she placed herself in his lap. She's yet to introduce herself, and if she's anything like the sluts over at the Rebels' place, she probably won't.

I'm telling myself that I'm respecting that decision by not striking up a conversation with her myself, but truthfully, she's a little intimidating.

Her hair is a dark blonde, falling around her face in beautiful thick waves, and she's shorter than me but cute as hell with her button nose and big brown eyes. I'm pretty sure she's not wearing any panties beneath her short, pleated skirt, either. Her confidence is through the roof, for good reason, and she's spent most of her time kissing Sledge's neck, no doubt leaving hickeys.

Sledge, on the other hand, is nonplussed, he's carrying on his conversations as though there isn't a beautiful woman grinding on his lap.

"I know some stuff, I suppose. I can hold my own." I smile, heat creeping up my chest because I hate talking about myself like this. There are much more interesting things to talk about than me. "How old were you when you first got on a motorcycle?"

I turn and look to Aleko, changing the subject smoothly, if I do say so myself, and also because I genuinely want to know more about this man who seems to have an obsession with me.

Honestly, I'm quickly becoming obsessed with him too, but I know how these things work. Obsessions can change at the drop of a hat. There will be a shiny new toy to play with soon enough, so I'm going to enjoy his attention while it lasts.

Having my heart broken by this man is far better than never knowing him at all.

"I started riding at thirteen too, although, not as organically as you. I stole a Yamaha MT-03 and crashed it within two minutes. My brother thought it was hilarious and told me I should never get on the back of a motorcycle again. Then he told our father, who whipped me with his belt a few times to show his disgust at my carelessness. Once my back had scabbed over, I tried again; lasted ten minutes that time. And the rest is history." He winks, pain flashing through his gaze briefly, and I wrap my arm around his neck.

"Glad you didn't give up?" His friends fade into nothing as our eyes connect.

"If you didn't know already, Cherry, I never give up on things I love."

I swear, my heart skips a beat at his admission. It almost makes me believe this could all be for real, which it obviously can't be because people don't fall this fast, do they?

"I should get ready for work." Swiftly changing the subject yet again, I move to stand. Only to be held down by a now-growling Aleko. "I can't sit on you all night, I really do have to go."

"You could sit on me forever and I'd die a happy man. Stay." The tug holding me in place makes me flinch a little at the pain, but somehow, with his arms wrapped around me, it's not all bad.

There's something wrong with me, there has to be. I'm a sucker for this man and all he has to give. Dangerous as that may be, I can't seem to find myself giving a shit.

"No. Spencer can check out my wounds and make sure they're healing okay, he may even need to pop a stitch into my cheek because the band-aids aren't cutting it." Hopefully, my explanation will encourage him to get onboard with me going to work.

"Call him and he can come here. Easy." Aleko's sexy as sin side grin implies he thinks he's winning this argument.

He's not.

"I'm going to work, and that's the end of it, Aleko." Raising my brows, I dare him to tell me no.

"Oooh, Psycho. She told you good." Sledge is now groping the woman all over him, laughing to himself without paying anyone else actual attention. "Ow, what the fuck, man?"

Bear chuckles after punching Sledge in the arm. "Better me than him, he would have knocked you the fuck out."

He tilts his head toward Aleko, who is still growling like an angry puppy beneath me.

Ninja chooses this moment to climb out of his hood, pausing on Aleko's shoulder to glare at him before jumping across to me and settling in my lap.

"Even Ninja wants you to stay." Aleko whispers into my ear as I stroke Ninja's tiny tummy.

"You can keep each other company while I'm gone." I smile and kiss him on the nose before giving my attention back to the fluffball in my lap.

"I don't like it, Cherry Pie. Jake or one of his fuckboys could show up, then what will you do?"

Sighing, I try to think of a way to make this easier, because he's not wrong. Jake literally showed up on my last shift. "Okay, how about this? You can take me, see me inside, where I'll let everyone know that if they see Jake, to not let him in. I promise not to leave early again, and you can pick me up when I'm finished at eight tomorrow night."

My car is still in Stonebridge anyway, so this actually works for me.

"Counter offer. Everything you just said, plus, Bash and Python will be watching the station during your shift and tailing you if you have to go out on a call."

"Deal."

It feels a little overboard, but he seems pretty pleased with himself. Arguing with him any further is going to be futile, I know it. So I exhale heavily and try again to raise one brow at him, the same way he does to me.

His light chuckle makes my nipples tingle, making me wince again at the pain from the bite marks scabbing over. I'm still skirting both denial and anger, but this afternoon with Aleko, Vanessa, and some of the club members has been therapeutic in a way. I'll be sad when I have to say goodbye.

"Good girl."

If I haven't melted into a puddle of lust yet, then I'm positive it's about to happen any second. That in itself is something I never thought I'd feel again, but Aleko keeps defying all the odds.

But I can't let him distract me from my plans. I have to follow through.

My brother can't and won't win. Not now. Not ever.

CHAPTER SEVENTEEN

MACKENZIE

"That concealer stash of yours is getting some good use at the moment then?" Spence's sarcastic tone makes me roll my eyes at him—which, of course, he calls me out on. "Don't roll those big blues at me, honey. That place is literally toxic, I'm just sad it had to come to this."

I chuckle at his reference, because he's not wrong. I've known it since the day Jake forced me out of my childhood home and shipped Mom away.

"I know. You're right." I sigh, pouring us both a coffee because we've got a long twenty-four hours ahead of us. Yeah, we can sleep in the rooms provided for these shifts, but it's difficult to fall into a deep sleep while remaining alert enough that we don't miss a call.

"Wanna say that again a little louder so I can record it? Steve would find it hilarious. I'd explain, but it's one of those jokes that's only funny to us." He shrugs and smiles as I hand him a steaming mug of black joy.

"Steve? As in, *Steve* Steve? What about Raheem?" I'm becoming a pro at this whole steering the subject away from myself thing.

"Bored me, so it's over. The fact that he didn't try and defend my honor when your new beau punched me in the face was strike one. Then he let me go to the doc alone for my X-ray. Strike two. And the other day, when we ordered take-out, he wanted to share my BBQ chicken wings. If he wanted chicken wings, he should have ordered them. Strike three. Told him it was over. Then, when I met up with Steve at one of the clubs down Bar Alley two nights ago, things just kind of...evolved." A wistful look spreads across his face; the serene smile, the sparkling eyes...

My best friend always falls hard and fast, but as soon as they do something he can find fault with, they're done for.

"Here, let me show you some pics."

I love the first stages of Spence's relationships, though there may be many, because his happiness is infectious. He never dwells on the bullshit and I admire the shit out of him for that.

"You have pics together already?" I laugh, because of course he does.

Sidling up beside him on one of the rec room couches, I grasp my own mug, sipping at my Heaven in liquid form while he begins searching for pics. "Here you go. This was last night at Crimson. Don't you think he looks a bit like your psycho in this one?" He shows me a picture of them both, he's holding a beer while Steve glares at the camera as if it wronged him somehow.

My Psycho...

This can't be a thing, we barely know each other. I know he keeps calling me his old lady, but the men in the Rebels would call whoever they were banging at the time their old lady. It holds no real significance so it's difficult to trust. The Sons of Khaos are definitely not the same breed of biker as the Rebels, though. In the end, it doesn't even matter. When this is all over, being his old lady or him being my Psycho will be the least of my worries.

"Nice, his jaw looks like it could cut a bitch." We both laugh and I note that Steve really is quite handsome. He definitely scrubs up well for a night out.

"What're we looking at?" Ryan comes up behind us, bending down to lean against the back of the couch with his head between ours.

"My new man." Spence locks his phone screen and gives me the look we both share when Ryan tries to insert himself into our downtime.

"Nice. Could I just have a second to speak to Mac?"

A please wouldn't go amiss, but either way, it's a no from me. Spence knows this. Since Ryan declared his feelings for me about a year ago, he's been trying to get me alone and ask me out after work at least three times a month. I thought it had died down a little but clearly, I was wrong.

"No can do, sorry. We have to go and do our vehicle checks." He's not lying, but we usually finish our coffee first.

"Come on, Mac, just for a minute." He stands fully and moves to perch on the couch opposite us. When his eyes roam over my face, his eyes widen. "What the fuck? Who did this to you? It was *him*, wasn't it?" He's practically spitting at this point.

"Calm your tits, Ryan. I'm fine. It's none of your business, but no. It wasn't Aleko." I remain calm, knowing that at least he can only really see the cuts on my face. The bruises around my eyes and neck are covered with concealer. I don't wanna imagine how he'd react if he knew how bad it really was.

"You need to call the police, Mac. That shit's not right. This is why you should stay away from those biker gangs. With a name like Psycho, things are only going to get worse."

It's like I don't exist as he continues his rant, regardless of the fact that I told him it wasn't Aleko.

"Ryan…"

He pauses and looks me in the eye, a little hope glinting in his irises. "Yeah?"

"Stay the fuck out of it." Standing, I finish off my coffee, almost scalding my mouth in the process. "Please and thank you." I nod, allowing a grimace of a smile in his direction before heading out to the vehicle with Spence close behind.

"You sure you're up for working tonight? I can get the chief to call someone in to cover you."

As lighthearted as Spencer is being about all this, I know, deep down, that he's just trying to protect me as best he can.

"Nah. I need to keep my mind occupied. Work is good for me."

Nodding, he pulls me into a light walking-side-hug, then swiftly releases me when we enter the main garage. Once our checks are complete, we head back to the rec room for more liquid gold, hoping and praying we don't have anyone needing to vomit tonight. It's something we always hope doesn't happen because it's a fucker to clean and sanitize in the back of the ambulance. Even with a bowl, they always miss. Always.

One DOA. Tonight, it was an elderly woman in her late nineties. Her husband called us in after discovering he couldn't wake her up. Devastating is what it was. Absolutely devastating.

Luckily, we had no seizing teenagers, which was nice. They've become a bit of a common call so to not have one was a relief. What's not a relief is the two motorcycles tailing me all fucking shift. At one point, I felt bad for them sitting outside the firehouse in ninety-degree weather. Although a heat stroke would be an easy way to get rid of them. Okay, that's mean...but still.

"Make sure you let that man of yours look after you over the next few days, Mac. Sounds like he's been doing a fine job so far, although I can't bring myself to trust someone who has a pet rat. What the fuck? That is not normal." I roll my eyes, pulling on my sneakers, the movement not helping the bruising and soreness all over my body.

"Ninja is the cutest thing ever. You'll understand when you get to know him." Tying my laces, I yawn, suddenly exhausted from...life.

"Yeah, that's not happening. I don't mingle with rodents, have you seen those teeth? No, ma'am." He side-eyes me, a grin planted firmly on his face. "We still on for race night?" I nod and Spence winks, slamming his locker shut dramatically. "I love you." After planting a careful kiss on my forehead, he leaves the room and I sigh, yet again. I feel like that's all I've done.

What if Aleko isn't outside waiting for me like he promised? I'd have to see if the local homeless shelter has a bed for me because there's no way I can go back to that trailer park. With my nerves all over the place, worry eating away at my insides, I close my own locker and head out.

I suppose I could stay in the storage unit I have, but if they found me they'd kick me out because apparently that's frowned upon. There was a very thorough speech about not sleeping in the units for any reason. One that I may have to ignore. Opening the door, I can't see Aleko's motorcycle, or him, and disappointment churns in my gut.

"There's my Cherry Pie." Aleko wraps himself around me, shoving his nose into my neck and sniffing, then his exhale is as though life has just been given to him. "Twenty-four hours is too long. Do they have a bring your man to work day?"

"Don't you mean, bring your psycho to work day?" I push all my sass and sarcasm into my words, but really, I'm feeling none of those things.

What I am feeling is overwhelmingly cherished, but I can't get too attached. I have shit I need to do and he can't be a part of my plans.

"You can call it whatever you want as long as I get to come to work with you." Pulling back slightly, he brings a hand up and grips my chin, controlling my head as he leans in to kiss me. Softly at first, then he's like a man starved, tasting every inch of my mouth with his pierced tongue, causing a fire to light within my veins. It's over almost as soon as it began, then he looks me in the eyes, raising that single sexy as fuck brow, and grins. "You're fucking pe—"

"I'm watching you, biker boy!"

Chapter Eighteen

Aleko

There are significant instances in your lifetime where you consciously know that you've grown, that something significant is happening. Some call them "ah-ha" moments, others say it's a "come to Jesus" moment. No matter what they're called, they're profound.

Like right now.

With my girl tucked in close enough for me to smell her sweet cherry scent, my best friend eager to nestle right into her cleavage, and my favorite bike just footsteps away, this warm summer night is fucking perfect.

Until, that is, that fucking douchebag ruins my exquisite Norman Rockwell setting. My first reaction is to break every fucking bone in his body and call it deserved, but one small squeeze from Mackenzie's hands on my forearms and a deep breath later, I let it go.

I. Let. It. Go.

If that's not me growing then I never will because holding back was one of the hardest fucking things I've ever done.

"He's not a bad guy, Aleko. He's just worried." Mackenzie's words do reassure me for a split second because it means her work colleagues have her back. "He thinks you're the one who beat me up."

Jesus fucking Christ, this whole growth thing is really fucking hard. It takes me a minute to feel just how tightly I'm squeezing my girl's waist in my fight against walking over to the guy and seeing how many punches I can throw before he's flat on his face.

"Did you correct him?" I'm speaking through clenched teeth, my eyes fixed on the guy who's just standing there watching us like he's about to be witness to a beat down.

"Yeah, but apparently he doesn't believe me. To be fair, a lot of the domestic abuse victims we intervene on are too afraid to accuse their partners, so I get it." I feel her shrug like all of this makes sense to her.

Fuck if it does.

I'd rather cut off my own dick than lay a hand on Mackenzie. Well, unless she's begging for more with her thighs spread and her cum calling my name. But never in anger. Fuck that.

Her next words, though, almost give me an aneurysm. "Poor guy's jealous."

"Cherry, baby, you need to stop talking or else that dude's gonna be in the back of an ambulance with multiple pieces of him needing reattachment." If looks could kill, he'd be a charred stain on the sidewalk.

"Aww, is the big, broody biker boy jealous of a hot fireman?" The only reason I'm still standing here is because with her cute little sing-song voice, Mackenzie turns in my arms to face me and brings her lips to mine, no doubt to placate me. It fucking works like voodoo magic. Her lips and tongue hypnotize me long enough to forget about firemen and jealous men, and hot men and...any men at all. But just in case douchecanoe is still there, I dig the fingers of one hand into her waist and wrap her ponytail around the other as I deepen the kiss and devour her whole.

Be jealous of that, asshole.

The next time I come up for air, he's gone. Good fucking riddance.

"Come on, my sweet Cherry Pie. Let's go home so I can take good care of you." She chuckles at my old-school eighties rock reference, shaking her head as we walk to my bike.

"I'm sure you could've come up with a less cheesy nick-name for me." She may not be able to raise one brow but her side-eye is on point.

"Why would I? You're hot, blonde, and smell like cherries. Warrant would be proud, baby." She groans at my words and all I want to do is swallow those sounds so they can feed my soul.

We take the long way back to the compound with Ninja secured in his pouch and Mackenzie's arms wrapped around my waist. It's fucking perfect, the way it should always be.

By the time we get to the compound, put Philia to rest after a gentle wipe-down and good night kisses, I take my woman to our suite, where I order dinner to be brought to us so I can get on with my nightly routine.

I'd like nothing more than to take her back to my one bedroom downtown but club lockdown is still in place for now.

"On your back, babydoll." While Ninja goes straight to his tiny bed in what looks more like a castle than a cage, Mackenzie complies by crawling up the bed and lying spread-eagle across my mattress. All I can do is stare at her, take in every inch as I wonder how the fuck I got so lucky.

Then I remember that luck had fuck all to do with it, I made this happen with sheer will and determination, knowing there wouldn't be a damn thing anyone could do to deter me or keep her away. Not even herself.

"Got all the ingredients I need to make you feel good." It hasn't even been a full week since Mackenzie's brother decided he wanted to die. Four days where I've put my priority on taking care of her while I follow Bear's advice and plan out Jake's last moments on this Earth. So every night, I use my hands and soothing oils all over her body so she associates my touch with love, to replace whatever memories she does have with memories of me making her better. At least as much as I can.

"How long are you going to keep this up, huh?"

I look up at her through my lashes, a cocky grin at the corner of my mouth.

"I have excellent stamina, babydoll. I can do this forever." Rubbing the oil between my hands, I heat it up before placing my palms on her feet and rubbing small circles up her ankles, her calves and shins, then her knees—front and back. It's when I reach her thighs that I keep my eyes solely on hers, making sure she's okay. Making sure this is consensual.

"I don't have any memories of it, Aleko. I promise. I'm sore and some of the bruises hurt when I move, but I wasn't conscious during the worst of it." It's that last part that always worries me. *During the worst of it.* It means she does remember some of it but thankfully not their morbid finale. Fuck, I can't wait to put them in the ground.

"Tell me to stop." I say this every time and just like every other night, she nods and says nothing. Tonight, however, she moans when my hands reach the inside of her thigh where I gently rub over one of the deepest of her bruises. It's almost black with purple and reds on the edges. I think it's a bite mark and the first time I saw it I fucking threw up from pure unleashed anger.

So attuned to her every sound and movement, I don't miss the way her legs spread just a tiny bit farther apart but I don't act on it. It's like I need to protect her from herself by being the adult in the room, which is fucking laughable since I'm the first to barrel through the rules of society and leave a gaping hole on the other side. But this is about Mackenzie, not me, and she will forever be my priority.

"More." Ah, fuck.

"Cherry baby, it's not what this is about." Determination. I have it in spades.

"If you don't give me an orgasm, I will get up, walk out of this suite, and find someone who can." I don't know how she manages to spew that kind of threat with a sweet, breathy voice like she's telling me I'm the love of her life. In fact, it takes me a heartbeat or four to register what she's saying. Instead of losing my ever loving shit, I give her a dose of her own medicine.

"You can try, babydoll," I coo, my lips whispering across her bruises but not touching her outright. "But don't feel guilty at the bloodbath that will cause."

"You wouldn't hurt your own brothers." She pauses, opens an eye as she raises her head from the pillow and looks at me before returning to her original position. "Too much."

"Mmmm." My tongue darts out, licking at print marks on her other thigh as visions of me dismembering those guilty fingers flash in my mind. "I think you forget who I am and what I'm called."

"I think you're right. Fuck it, I'll do it myself." Mackenzie's hand is suddenly sliding inside her panties, and with as much self-control as I possess, there's no fucking way I'm missing out on this. With careful movements, I slide the lace down her legs and sit back on my haunches, my hands still drawing careful, soft circles on her thighs while her middle finger goes round and round, playing with her clit. Her pussy lips are like a perfect orchid, petals spreading slowly as her fingers slide down the slit and two plunge inside her beautiful pink cunt.

Fuck my life, I want to be those fingers, own her body so her only memory is me.

"I'm not broken, Aleko. You still turn me on. Your touch makes me wet, makes my pussy all swollen with need. So if you won't touch me, then I'll do the job for you." She is actively trying to fucking kill me. Looking up, she stares straight at me as her fingers pull out of her cunt. "Taste me, baby. See what you're missing."

Fuck determination.

Fuck self-control.

Fuck those motherfuckers who thought they could break my girl. She's not even bent. Her spine is like a poisoned arrow with their names etched right on it.

No need to be told twice, I suck up her fingers and indulge on her sweet and tart cum like I've been starved for it. I lick up and down then in between, and when her fingers return to her pussy, my mouth follows until I'm feasting on her cunt, my tongue deep enough to get lost, my lips sucking on hers and my ears careful to pick up any cues that she's not okay.

All I hear are hums and moans. When her hand pushes the top of my head closer to her, I know exactly what she wants. So I give it to her.

Pushing myself between her spread thighs, I wrap my arms around them and pull her up so my mouth is fused to her cunt and my palms are spread across her ass cheeks. She's everywhere around me. The cherry scent mixed with her needy arousal, her smooth skin touching my hands, arms, legs, and chest. Her taste, my fucking God, her taste explodes on my tongue as I lap up every drop she has to give me. The only sounds in the room are those of me eating her out like I'm a starved animal with no patience for propriety.

Then she moans loud enough to break through my slurps and grunts, her calves wrapping around my back and her thighs squeezing the air from my neck. There's no better way to die than with my tongue buried deep in her pussy just as she's about to coat it with her juices.

The French call an orgasm "la petite mort" but instead of the little death, I'd call it the perfect one.

"Aleko, yes. Yes! Suck me harder, put your fingers in me, give me your cock. Oh, God!" Demands are hurdling out of her mouth as her body begins to tighten and her hips search me out faster and faster. At first, I'm careful not to leave her with more bruises than she already has, except it's impossible in this position. The only way to keep her pussy latched onto my mouth with all the thrusting her hips are doing, is for me to hold her in place. I do not have a death wish and I know for a fact that if I let her go just before she comes, she will stab me in the eye and call it collateral damage.

As her hands fly to the headboard, her fingers wrapping around the wooden slats against the wall, I release one thigh to sink my hand into my shorts and grab my hard, aching cock. It's already wet, precum leaking for the past ten minutes as I feasted on her. My pumps are in rhythm with my mouth and just before I come, I let myself go, keeping my shorts down and my dick ready to explode all over her swollen cunt.

All it takes are two fingers easily sliding inside her wet hole as I work her clit to the point of near pain for her to lose all the tension, all the stress, all the anger...even if for a little while. Even if for a second.

She screams with my name on her lips and her cum on mine. I open wide, my tongue pressed against her slit and drink her in. I fucking drink everything she has to give me, and just when she comes down from her high, I separate myself from her and grab my dick.

One stroke, then a second is all it takes to have my cock shooting cum all over her wet, red and puffy cunt. Best thing about it is that she watches. Her eyes are fixed on the head of my dick as it spurts string after string of pent-up need for her, coating her skin and adding to her own juices as it creates a brand new flavor made just for us.

My dick spent but still semi, I run it through her slit and bring the tip to her mouth.

"It's your turn to taste, babydoll." Without an ounce of hesitation, she opens wide and sucks, her tongue dipping into my own slit causing an aftershock to race down my spine. The vibrations of her moan almost make me come all over again but I'm still hungry so I pull out of her mouth and kiss her deep enough for a taste test myself.

"Aren't we delicious together?" Her voice sounds like she's just run a marathon. I fucking love that.

"We are exquisite, Cherry Pie. Just you and me."

The next morning, we grab the cooler Sabrina packed up for us with food and drinks for breakfast and lunch, an umbrella for shade, and a huge blanket before we head out to the beach. Normally, the beach is a day affair with the club, but sometimes I like to go with just Ninja to a place none of my brothers seem to know exists. With everything happening, I asked Prez if we could have a little time to ourselves even though we're on lockdown. Thankfully, the beach is so secluded that we all felt it was safe enough for an afternoon.

We take the truck, for obvious security reasons, but also because I know for a fact that last night's ride—although fun and liberating—was also on the side of painful for Mackenzie. She only admitted as much this morning and I want to punch myself in the throat for not thinking about that.

What would take ten, maybe fifteen minutes on a bike, takes us thirty-five in V's pickup. It's a weekday morning so college kids and working families are headed in for the day, but that's fine. We made it here and, as usual, my spot is deserted.

Ninja can sniff out the area. He knows exactly where we are because not too far is a mom and pop burger joint that serves cheese fries that are too good to be legal.

"Aren't you afraid he'll run away?" Mackenzie freaks out a little as Ninja runs down the length of my body into the sand, stopping right at the edge of the water line.

Whipping off my t-shirt, I raise my brow at her. "Are you kidding? He knows who feeds him. He's not going anywhere."

Not entirely convinced, she side-eyes me before returning her gaze to Ninja, who's playing with the lapping waves.

"Won't he drown if the waves catch him? Oh my God, Aleko, he can't drown." Turning, I take her cheeks in my palms and kiss her mouth. Hard. Then I pull her summer dress up and over her head so she's gracing me with her beautiful body. With barely a glance at her bruises, she gives back her attention.

"Cherry. Listen to me. If the water takes him, he'll float and love that shit until I go out there and grab him. We do this every week, so trust me, he always wins this game he's playing. When he really wants to go in the water, he'll run up to me and let me know." I kiss her again for good measure and because I can't keep my mouth off her.

Her tiny gasp into my mouth has me popping my lids open to see she's got her eyes nice and wide already and looking to the side. Pulling back, a little offended if I may say so, I follow her line of sight, landing on a happy Ninja jumping in and out of the water.

"You know, when you start having my babies, you'll have to get used to letting them learn lessons on their own." That gets her attention, and very fucking fast. Now, it's fixed solely on me, the way it always should be.

"First of all, who says I want kids?" One index finger pops up and I grin. This is our thing. "Second." There goes her middle finger. "Even if I did, twenty-one is not my number. I've got shit to do. Third." Her ring finger joins the others and again, I wonder how big I should go with the diamond. "Who the fuck says I'll have them with you?"

Oh, hell fucking no.

My arm shoots out, wrapping around her waist and bending her backward where I trap her long enough to kiss the lies from her lips.

"You, that's who. Your kisses, your moans, your orgasms. That's who tells me you're mine." When I pull her back up, she wobbles but harrumphs before shrugging and laying out the blanket, placing rocks and branches at the corners to keep it down when the wind kicks up. Her silence is a beautiful admission.

Once the umbrella is positioned just right, I sit down and pull her into my lap where she shuffles down between my legs, her back to my groin. It's not ideal since her touching me is pretty much a guarantee that I'm going to be hard within seconds but I have zero issues with that. I just don't want her to think she needs to act on it.

"What's your favorite childhood memory?"

I know she's reading a book, lying between my thighs with her back against my groin and her head using my abs as a pillow. Not sure how I feel about that, to be honest. Is she telling me I've gone soft?

"Really? You're playing 'let's get to know each other' in the middle of my chapter?" Her accompanying huff is cute as she slams the books shut and turns to face me.

Fuck. Her mouth is suddenly so close to my hardening dick that all she needs to do to suck it, is lean in just right.

"Well, you could suck my cock while I finish reading the chapter out loud to you." My smirk is confident because either way, I win. If she turns back around, I'll be able to breathe a sigh of relief and if she chooses to pull down my board shorts and swallow my cock, well...who am I to argue?

"Fine." Kneeling between my legs, she begins to turn as if she's getting back into her original position but only glances over at a happy Ninja. "But you don't need to read. I know what I'm doing."

I blink, a slow grin rising like my mouth registers her words before my brain can comprehend.

"You know I was kidding, right? You don't have to do this, babydoll." My hand is in her long, blonde locks, caressing her cheek with my pinky finger.

"I want to." Well...who can say no to that?

Just as her hand pulls the board shorts down and her mouth slides down the length of my shaft, I groan to my heart's content knowing not a soul is around to bear witness.

"Fuuuuuuck. Your mouth!" Her nose tickles my groin as she swallows me whole, the back of her throat massaging the tip of my cock. "Goddammit, Mackenzie, you feel so fucking good!" My eyes close with bliss and my head falls back and away from the shade of the umbrella, the burst of sun rays lighting up my retinas even behind my lids.

Nails dig into my abs, the sharp claws almost painful, but I'm too distracted by the warmth of her mouth to remove them.

Then all I feel is cool air.

All I hear is a gasp followed by a scream. "Oh my God!"

My eyes fly open, my body on high alert, wondering if I need to shoot someone then realizing I don't have a gun with me. Why didn't I bring my fucking gun?

But when I take in the scene, I don't even stop the burst of laughter that erupts from my chest.

"Well, I guess he's ready for that bath, then." Mackenzie's eyes snap up at me and I swear to fuck if her death glare didn't turn me on, it would scare the fuck out of me.

"He was watching me give you a blowjob," she whispers as if Ninja would understand her. Hell, maybe he could. I don't think rats know what a blowjob is. Hell, Ninja's never had sex...that I know of.

"He's a curious dude."

"Aleko! That's disturbing and I'm pretty sure he's now traumatized." As if on cue, Ninja turns and runs to my shoulder, practically pointing to the water with his tiny paws.

I kiss her open mouth, jaw slack from Ninja's betrayal. "Don't worry, baby. You can swallow my cum later tonight."

The rest of the day is spent talking, getting to know each other, cuddling with Ninja as she tells me about her dad and how much he loved riding. I know she rides, there was no mistaking her skill the day she saved my ass, but she never elaborates, only confirming her dad taught her.

Too soon, the sun begins to set and because we both left our phones in the truck to avoid any distractions, we have no idea what time it is but neither of us cares. This day was perfect. She's perfect.

Packing up our shit, I throw our waste into the trash can at the top of the dune before running back to her and kissing her hard on the mouth then grabbing her hand and pulling her behind me while Ninja travels in her hand, his tail wrapped around her forearm.

The drive back is quicker than the drive over so I turn and smirk. "We have unfinished business, babydoll."

"Yup, I see essential oils in my near future." I laugh because she's not wrong. I will make her feel so good but first, I'll feed her. And kiss her. And love her so thoroughly she'll wonde—

"What the hell?" Her words make my brain screech to a halt as the pickup continues down the driveway to the compound.

Red and blue lights are flashing, four patrol cars parked haphazardly with officers at the front door and brothers standing with their arms clearly visible.

"Did you check your phone?" I already know the answer but I'm hoping I missed something while I was daydreaming about her body.

"No."

"Well, I guess we're about to find out," I say just as we reach the cars and every single one of those officers turns their guns on us.

"Jesus Christ." Mackenzie automatically raises her hands in the air and I fucking hate the fear in her eyes. In fact, I want nothing more than to cut these bitches for their overzealous show of power. But again, I show control and place my hands on the wheel and stare fucking daggers at the officer rounding the truck to Mackenzie's side. I swear to fuck, if they touch her I won't be able to control myself.

"Aleko, whatever happens, please stay calm."

I scoff at her request.

"Fat fucking chance of that, baby."

The female officer opens the passenger-side door just as a male officer opens mine. My eyes stay on Mackenzie though. I don't give a fuck what they do to me as long as they're gentle with her.

"Ma'am, I need you to step out of the vehicle please."

"Is there a problem, officer?" Mackenzie's voice trembles as she asks her question but the officer only repeats her request.

"Go, Cherry. Do as they say."

Mackenzie looks at me, then the cop, before she nods.

"Sir, step out of your vehicle and face your car." Ninja starts to freak out so Mackenzie turns back around and grabs him, holding him close to her chest so he doesn't run after me. We lock eyes and I swear she says a thousand things in that second without uttering a single word and I wish more than anything that I could hear them all.

"Psycho, keep your mouth shut, we've got the lawyer on the phone." I don't look but I know it's Prez giving me an order.

Meanwhile, the cop Mirandarizes me and I know I'm fucked...for what though, I have no fucking clue.

"You have the right to remain silent. Anything you say can and will be used against you in a court of law. You have the right to an attorney. If you cannot afford an attorney, one will be provided for you. Do you understand these rights and want to tell me what happened?"

"Yeah, I want my attorney." One handcuff is slapped around my wrist but I don't care, my attention is on Mackenzie and I breathe easier when I see her being escorted to the side of the road, where the female cop stops to talk to her.

"What are the charges, Officer..." Looking down at his uniform, I add on his name. "Jones?" The guy looks like he's five years away from retiring but the way he's looking at me feels like he still cares about his job and I'm the piece of shit that stains his city.

"You're being charged with assault." I blink. Is this about the Rebel's elbow? I thought that shit was settled.

I mean, they've been eerily quiet this week but this doesn't feel like their type of retaliation.

When I look up at Mackenzie, she's frantically shaking her head and seeking me out. That's when the puzzle pieces come together.

Fucking hell, it's going to be a long night.

CHAPTER NINETEEN
MACKENZIE

Fucking Ryan and his big fucking mouth. Ugh! Why do men have to be such overprotective assholes?

I get it, he was trying to look out for me, but I can't help thinking that Ryan spoke to the police for a much more selfish reason. Allowing my brother and his club to treat me like dirt for the last six years hasn't made me naïve to the world around me. I don't believe that every man who presents as kind is only that one thing. I also don't believe the same of every evil man. In the year I've known Ryan, all his particular brand of kindness has done is piss me off.

When I say no, he challenges me to change my answer. When I push him away, he tries harder to get close to me—metaphorically. Everything about him makes my skin crawl. I mean, don't get me wrong, he's a good enough guy, but he's just not for me. One day, I'm sure some wonderful woman that isn't me will turn his head their way.

It's not the things he's doing though, because when Aleko challenges me, tries harder to get close to me, I crave it. I crave him in a way I really shouldn't. And now, not only is Aleko's whole club on lockdown and unable to go back to their homes because of me and my fucking brother, he's just been arrested because of me and my fucking work colleague.

"Ma'am, would you like to come to the station to answer a few questions?"

Shaking myself out of my stupor after watching as Aleko was driven away in the back of a cop car, I bring my attention back to Officer Hayes. Who, I'm pretty sure, has ignored everything I've said up to this point.

"No, I wouldn't like that at all, actually. I already told you, Aleko had nothing to do with these bruises."

Judgey Mcjudgerson purses her lips and nods slowly. "I understand. Maybe if we spoke in private." She raises her judging gaze and scans the crowd of bikers surrounding the front of the property before looking at me again. "It's okay. Really." Her tight smile is condescending, as though she knows better and this is all for my benefit. "Come on."

Gripping my elbow gently, she tries to lead me toward her vehicle, but I remain unmoving.

Ninja squeaks at her from my palm and she quickly removes her hand, looking down at him with disgust.

"I'll make my own way there, thank you." I know the cops in Rockford aren't the same as the ones that my brother has under his thumb in Stonebridge, but that doesn't mean I trust them any more. Plus, if Ninja doesn't like her, then I don't like her.

"I really must insist you come with me, Ma'am."

Closing my eyes, I take a deep breath. She's just doing her job. Women are in the position she believes me to be in daily. They lie, they protect their partners, and sometimes their friends are in on it too. There is nowhere for them to turn and telling the truth to the cops could get them killed. Worse, sometimes they've been gaslighted for so long they truly believe the fault is theirs and not the asshole using them as punching bags. I wish I could speak to every one of those women and remind them how fucking badass and strong they really are and help them get retribution against their abusers.

Fact is though, I'm not one of those women, I'm not lying to protect anyone—except maybe my brother and his friends because they're *my* problem.

"Bear, do you know where Python parked the motorcycle I rode in here on a couple of weeks ago?" Turning away from Officer Hayes, I give my best pleading face to Bear. I'd rather make my own way to the station, minus the caged police vehicle that makes me feel like a criminal.

I plan to avoid ever being in the back of a police car.

"Sure thing, darlin'. Go get some riding gear on, I'll set up Ninja's riding pouch on my motorcycle and we'll all meet you out here with the bikes in five minutes."

It's as though the whole club has had a silent conversation without me and they all begin walking over to the garages and parking area off to the side. The sight brings a lump to my throat because it's clear these men are not the same breed as the ones I've been living with for the last six years. Happy memories of Dad and his track friends walking toward their bikes before they spent an hour basically fucking around trying out new stunts and tricks make me smile and, suddenly, this place feels like home. These people feel like home.

The lump in my throat is joined by a prickling of tears behind my eyes and I push them back. Now is not the time.

"Are you sure you wouldn't rather come with us?" Officer Hayes looks worried and her hardass attitude from earlier is now more confusion, like she doesn't understand my decision here.

"I'm sure. Thank you, Officer." I give her a condescending smile of my own as she turns and walks away, shaking her head lightly with what I'm assuming is disappointment.

"Well done, Mac. Hoops has already called our club lawyer, she'll meet us there. I take it this is about those bruises your *brother* and his friends gave you?" Prez practically spits the word "brother", but his deep brown eyes are full of concern. He doesn't touch me, but I can see he wants to offer me some comfort and I appreciate the hell out of it.

"Of course it is. But those cops are fuckers. Any excuse to take one of these boys in, and they'll take it." Vanessa snakes her arm around Prez and snuggles into him. He looks down at her, hugging her back with a proud smile on his face.

"I'll leave a handful of men here with you and the girls, baby." He kisses the top of her head, throws me a quick wink, and heads toward the others, who are now walking their bikes out into the open front area.

"Stand your ground, sweetheart. We have friends at the station so don't worry too much. I'll have Sabrina and

Bash help me make something nice for when y'all get back." Vanessa hugs me lightly and leads me inside.

"Thank you." And I hope she knows how grateful I truly am because thank you doesn't feel like enough for what these people are giving me.

After changing into some jeans and one of Aleko's black hoodies, I handed Ninja over to Bear and am now sitting on my borrowed—from the Rebels—motorcycle in the middle of the Sons of Khaos. It's a sight to behold and I pull up my neck tube before sliding my gloves and helmet on.

Prez is up front, and Crow, the Road Captain, is staggered just behind him to his right. Shade, the Sergeant at Arms, is to his left, then Bear, Grinder, and Sledge are staggered behind me. Engines are revved, the sound beautiful, like music to my ears, and it helps me push aside the pain from the bruises on my thighs. Yeah, I could've asked someone to drive me in one of the trucks or vans on site, but I feel like I need this. After all the shit lately, I need to ride and get out of my own head.

Despite how it seems, I've never been questioned by the police before. Jake may be a grade-A criminal but he always kept me in the shadows when it came to the club. So to say having a red-faced Sheriff staring at me like I just ran over his favorite pet makes my hackles rise would be a gross understatement. Why is it that victims of sexual assault are somehow guilty of something? Who came up with that bullshit?

"Look, Miss Wilson," he starts, his tone exasperated because, sure...this is fun for me. *Asshole.* "We know the kinds of things the SOK are up to, you don't have to lie for them, we can protect you." Now, I've always been respectful of authority but my eyes have a mind of their own as they roll to the back of my head.

"I don't know what makes you think Aleko had anything to do with this," I point to my face since the evidence is right there in literal black and blue with some added red and yellow. "He'd rather fall off a cliff than hurt me." Well, unless I beg for it but I don't think the good old sheriff needs to know about that.

"Because he's a goddamned criminal. You girls are all the same, falling at their feet, thinking that spreading your legs will change them. Christ, it's sickening." Sheriff Hinshaw's words are practically spit at me as I jump out of my seat, ready to unleash some of my own fucking fury. Before I can tell him that it's men like him that propagate the rape culture in our country, Deputy Sheriff Shipman bursts into the small room and gives her boss a withering glare that I'm certain has brought many a criminal to their knees.

"Sheriff, I think we're good here." Waiting for Hinshaw to realize he's said enough, she steps to the side and allows him to walk out, huffing and muttering about the good old days when women did what they were told. "Sorry about that, Mackenzie. It's his last term and I think he wants to go out with a bang."

Maybe that's his problem...not getting banged enough. An involuntary shiver runs down my spine but I keep my cool and nod at Shipman.

"Like I keep saying to anyone who'll listen, Aleko has never laid an angry hand on me." At my words, Shipman nods like she has no doubts about that.

"Yeah, we got a call from a"—she looks up at the ceiling then back at me—"reliable source that Mr. Kastellanos has been physically abusing you. Somehow, that call made it all the way to the judge's desk, produced a warrant, and...here we are."

"It wasn't him," I repeat to drive the point home.

"I know." Shipman takes a seat, her elbows on the table, her hands clasped. "Care to tell me who it actually was?"

"No." My answer is way too quick and the narrowing of the deputy's eyes says she caught my eager denial. "I mean, I know who it is but I do not want to talk about it." It's not that I'm trying to protect my brother and his club, because fuck no, but I don't want to be linked to any official or unofficial reports by the cops with regards to the Rebels.

"I see." Tapping her short nails on the table top, Shipman seems lost in thought, probably trying to gather her arguments before dropping the proverbial bomb. "You wouldn't know anything about the drugs on the streets that are causing so many college kids to overdose, would you?"

Okay, I was expecting a lot more pushing about Aleko, but this shit? No.

Staring at the deputy, I size her up, assess just how sincere she is and if I can trust her. I know Aleko seemed comfortable with her at the strip club, so maybe she's one of the good ones. Except, the timing is completely off.

Leaning back in the chair, I eye the camera at the corner of the room before looking back at her.

"Am I being arrested for something or being charged or whatever?" I have no idea what the lingo is apart from watching FBI shows back at my mom's years ago.

"No, of course not. The sheriff just wanted some incriminating evidence so he could keep Aleko in lock-up." Wow, that was honest.

"Why would you think I know anything about that?" I do, but it's weird that she would ask me.

"Well, the way I see it," Shipman unclasps her fingers before tapping the side of her thumb on the table. "The only big enough players around here capable of running this much product are either the SOK or your brother."

I stiffen at her words but don't say a fucking word.

"Do you know anything about that?" Her gaze is so fucking penetrating I'm almost convinced that I'm losing gallons of sweat in mere minutes.

"I've only just met the SOK and my brother has never been open with me about...well, anything."

Deputy Shipman stares at me, her eyes roaming my face like she's reading the honesty on my features. With a curt nod, she pushes her chair back and stands. "Okay. You're both free to go."

A few hours after arriving, Aleko is escorted from the cells by Officer Hayes, and when his pale blue eyes find mine I swear my knees buckle. All my previous thoughts of being stupid and not good enough and a burden...they disappear in that brief moment as he raises his brow and gifts me with his half smile. Within seconds, he's in front of me, a palm at the back of my head, his fingers gripping my chin as he guides me into a kiss not safe for audiences.

Our tongues taste every inch of each other, and the feel of the stud in his against mine has my panties dampening with the memory of what else he can do with it. Every time Aleko touches me, it puts a warm blanket around all the shit, and while he may be a killer in his own right—from what I've heard about the SOK Enforcer and the way he went guns blazing in the Rebels' compound—I'm not okay with adding more to his death toll for my sake.

This is just one small reason I'm soaking up everything I can with him now because, soon, it will all change. I'll be the one behind those bars, and it won't be in the local sheriff's station.

"Need a hand, Brother?"

I don't immediately recognize the voice, and the low growl emitting from Aleko's chest causes whoever it is to laugh before I hear him being pulled away by who is unmistakably Bear.

"Come the fuck on, Grinder. We'll wait outside, Psycho." The bass in Bear's tone makes me smile because I think I'll miss it.

The whole situation makes me giggle into Aleko's chest and I feel his deep breaths as he tries to contain himself. Honestly, the jealousy is hot as fuck. A man has never acted this way with me before...I say man, I suppose they've all been boys barely in their twenties or late teens. My brother may have kept a tight leash on me, but I still went to high school and community college. Boys were a dime a dozen and I wanted to feel something other than pain and sadness.

That's not what this is with Aleko. It may have begun that way, but he makes me feel more than just "something other". With Aleko, I'm stronger, and that scares the hell out of me. I need to know I'm strong without a man to protect me. And I know for a fact that he will protect me to the ends of the Earth.

My own thoughts confuse even me right now.

"Vanessa wasn't wrong when she told me y'all had friends here. When they took me in for questioning I thought you'd be here for the next few days." The Rebels have the cops in Stonebridge in their pockets, but they still take every opportunity they can to lock them up. Something about keeping up appearances, though I suspect they just fucking hate them, like everyone else.

"Deputy Shipman doesn't fuck around." The quick wink almost makes my knees buckle. "Let's go home, Cherry. I missed you." Aleko whispers into my ear, his arms still banded around my waist. Wrapping my arms behind his neck, I jump up and straddle him, then I suck his bottom lip into my mouth and let it out with a pop.

"Mmm, cherry." He must have had one of his lollipops recently.

His grin, coupled with a light shake of his head before he kisses me, long and hard, sends shivers down my spine, and once again, this man has made me forget about the world.

Once we're all outside with helmets and gloves on, I assume Aleko will want to have me ride bitch on the way back so I stand aside and gesture for him to get on first.

"Baby, you ride like a badass, I'll be your bitch anytime." He winks, and his eyes are so expressive through the visor it reminds me of when he fucked me in my trailer with his neck tube over his face.

I know what a big deal it is for him to ride bitch with me, and I'm not entirely sure how I feel about it.

I smile laugh and lift my leg over, wincing a little as I get settled, but if Aleko's going to rub me all over again tonight then I'll take the pain. It feels odd to be so okay with sex again after what happened to me. Maybe I'm suppressing it or maybe my lack of memories is a blessing of some kind. That's not to say I haven't had brief and horrific flashbacks, but I guess we all deal with our pain in different ways.

And Aleko has been a key part of that.

He reminds me every day that I'm a powerful woman, that I belong, that I'm loved.

He climbs onto the back of the motorcycle and wraps one arm gently around my waist, the other hand on the back handles, stabilizing him, exactly as he did the first time—only without a gun and all the shooting.

The formation we ride back in is exactly the same as when we arrived, and I'm sure I laugh the whole time. Watching Grinder do stunts for a couple of kids in a car we pass, racing Sledge on the highway, and shaking his ass to a tune only he can hear was all fucking hilarious. They're all kind of crazy, but Grinder's a maniac and it's amazing the way they ride together.

It's late when we get back, but true to her word, Vanessa has prepared a treat for us all in the gardens behind the big old building. The whole scene is dominated by a huge bonfire, coolers and ice buckets filled with alcohol have been placed by the benches, and the whole square is lit up from what looks like old-fashioned street lights dotted around the area. The U-shaped building covers three sides, with the large pine trees surrounding the property lining the inside of the metal fencing. Benches and tables are strategically placed and planks of wood have been set up by the bonfire as make-shift seats, all of it creating a really great vibe.

None of them are being dicks on their motorcycles after drinking too much, not trying to start a fight with the prospects or anyone lower down the chain than them, they're laughing, talking, and I'm pretty sure that's Grinder dancing by the fire. They're like a real family. Old-school rock music sounds out around us, and I'm enjoying being held by Aleko and people-watching from his lap. He's been deep in conversation with Bear for the last fifteen minutes and I haven't been listening, simply enjoying the peace of the evening as the brothers celebrate. Not that Aleko was actually gone for more than a few hours, but you've gotta love the club's enthusiasm and unwavering support.

Ninja has been running around to get fussed by pretty much everyone so far, but he's spent most of his time nestled on my thighs, purring like a kitten every time I stroke his belly.

"Come here, Ninja." Bear holds his open palm out and Ninja immediately lifts his head. He twitches his nose a little before jumping across and nibbling on the square of cheese offered to him.

"I've shared you for long enough, Cherry. Let's go," Aleko whispers into my ear.

I squeal as he stands, lifting me up in a bridal carry and planting a kiss on my lips that promises pleasure. It causes a brick to drop inside my stomach because I want this. Like, I really want this, but I can't.

"Careful with her, Brother." Bear's deep timber tone is a warning, and I see the concern for me etched into his face; his furrowed brow, his tight mouth.

"I'm okay, Bear. Not a porcelain doll."

"I'd never hurt my sweet Cherry Pie."

We both speak at the same time and my smile toward Bear turns into another squeal as Aleko burrows his face into my neck and nips at the skin. It's a delicious tingle and I'm trying not to squirm in his hold, needing to put some distance between us because this shit is hard.

The trip to the beach today was wonderful, a great goodbye. Then seeing Aleko's face when he had been behind bars for a few hours was like a shock to my system. I had missed him. Missed his touch, his smile, his laughter, his possessive growling...all of it, and I hadn't expected the intense feelings to hit me like a Mac truck.

Inside his room, he gently places me down at the foot of the bed.

"Arms up." He encourages me to raise my arms as he grips the bottom of my tank top, ready to lift it up and over my head. Reluctantly, I comply with a heavy sigh. "What's up, Cherry?"

He stops and steps back, resting one hand on my hip and using the other to grip my chin so I'm looking him in the eye.

"Nothing. I'm fine." I smile, though it's probably more of a grimace because I'm aware I'm running hot and cold with him.

"Don't lie to me."

"Are you going to take my top off or can I put my arms down now?"

"Playing it like that, are you? Okay." He sighs and narrows his eyes, then pulls my tank up and over my head before grabbing my arms and bringing them back down to my sides.

Then he gets onto his knees, undoes my jeans, and fuck me, this man is trying to kill me. I know if I give in to what my body clearly wants then I'll just be making this whole thing harder than it needs to be. If he hates me or thinks I'm a bitch, not his sweet cherry pie, then that's okay. Today was a mistake and I will cherish those memories, but I can't continue this pretend fairytale anymore.

"Thanks." I step out of my jeans, ignoring his gentle touches across my skin, and climb on the bed, rolling onto my side and pulling the sheets up to my chin.

"I don't think so. You're not all healed up yet, Cherry." Following his low reprimand with a *tsk*, he shakes the bottle of oils at me as though reminding me of what needs to be done.

I ignore him, listening to him undress and using all my willpower not to look at his glorious and colorful tattooed chest.

Within a few minutes, he's climbing onto the bed beside me and sliding the sheet off my body. He begins his new nightly routine of rubbing essential oils into my skin, starting on my back, which is facing him.

His touch is soothing, a combination of soft and hard in all the right places, and I can't help it when a tear falls from my eye. When he's finished on my back, shoulders, and the arm he can reach, he moves to my ass, kneading the muscle in silence.

"Turn over, babydoll."

Every endearment is like a spear to my chest, but I do as he asks because I don't have the energy to argue with him. I keep my eyes closed, hoping that by not looking at him, I can save my heart, at least a little.

If Aleko notices the wet streak on my face, he doesn't say anything. Instead, he continues to rub oils into my skin, moving to my legs, my feet, all the while peppering soft kisses along the way. The same way he has every night since I left the trailer park.

I'm so close to just saying fuck it and giving in to what we both so desperately want when there's a banging on the door.

"Fuck off!" Aleko carries on rubbing at my feet, digging his thumbs in and I have to hold back a moan.

"Someone blew up Ronald's hardware store after we left the station. Prez just called Church."

Shit. The only people I know capable of doing that are the Rebels.

All thoughts of my fucked up feelings quickly flee and we both sit up.

"Be right there." Aleko doesn't get up straight away. Instead, he sighs heavily and holds my face, forcing me to look into his eyes. "We're not done here, Cherry. We talk about shit, okay? No secrets."

I nod slowly, holding my breath and trying to keep the tears from forming in my eyes.

Then he kisses me, hard and fast, as though he's trying to tell me everything all at once, and I hear him, responding with my own urgency. When it's over, he stands and throws on the clothes he was wearing earlier—jeans and a white T-shirt that Bear had thought to take with us to the station so he didn't have to ride back in his board shorts.

He leans over to me, kissing me again before heading toward the door and twisting the handle.

"I'll be back."

CHAPTER TWENTY

ALEKO

"I think it's pretty clear who's responsible for this shit." As always, I listen and watch as my brothers and I file into the old chapel for our meeting. Grinder is all worked up, bouncing up and down on the balls of his feet like he's holding himself back from going out there and creating havoc.

"It's almost been a week, we need to fucking take these assholes down for everything they've done." I feel every single pair of eyes on me at Grinder's ongoing tirade. I think he may have a tiny crush on my Cherry Pie. He's lucky I like him. Not to mention that I know for a fact he wouldn't even accidentally lay a finger on her for fear of losing it *and* all nine of its best friends.

Sucking in a breath through my teeth, I feel the weight of my black cloud resting on top of my shoulders, my mind going to places where psychopaths feel at home. Clinically, I'm no psycho. Love and guilt and regret all reside somewhere inside of me. I'd fucking rip my own heart out if it meant saving Mackenzie's life, but when hatred consumes me and shit needs to get done, I allow my monster to peek out. It's better to put my humanity on the back burner when dealing with scum.

"Jake is mine. If anyone finds him first, I want him brought to me." My voice is so low, the only reason anyone can even hear me is because the silence in here is absolute. "I want him brought to the Dahmer cell."

"Fuck yeah, that's what I'm talking about." Grinder is pumping an arm up and down like he's won the fucking lottery.

"You got it, Brother." Similar phrases ring out around me and it soothes my monster's appetite.

Prez bangs on the gavel, demanding our attention and getting it two seconds later.

"Ronald's wife called in tears, completely outta her mind." Prez pauses, gracing each of us with a pointed look. *Fuck.*

"Those motherfuckers." Bear's voice shakes as he speaks just under his breath.

"They didn't wait for him to close up. Arson was clear when they found all of the entryways chained from the outside." We all look to Prez as he chokes out the last few words. He, Shade, and Ronald all went to school together in Rockford Beach, grew up together from a very young age. When Prez and Shade joined the Marines, Ronald took over his father's hardware store and very quickly married Tori. "Vanessa is with the prospects now, on her way to pick up Tori." From the way he's grinding out his words, it's clear this decision was not his and Vanessa used every power she has to break the lockdown so she could get her friend here. I get it. I'd do the same.

"What's the police say? They got enough proof to ransack their trailer park?"

Shade shakes his head at Boner's question. "Nah, the fire erased any prints that could've been there and of course no witnesses. People ain't gonna talk if they see bikes, man."

We all nod at that. From a distance, it's not always easy to know which club is which when you don't belong to our world.

"Then we'll do their fucking jobs. I don't need witness reports to collect teeth, Prez. My clamps are equal opportunity torturers." On any other night, we would have ribbed Grinder about a dozen different things but tonight—hell, it's morning in an hour—we just don't have the heart for it.

"That reminds me!" Faces still drawn with anger, confusion, and most prominent, blood thirst, we give Prez our attention again. "Anyone seen Python? I went to his room but it was empty."

"I thought he was riding with Vanessa." Bear sits up straighter because shit has been weird with Python lately and my little Spidey senses tell me he's dived off the wagon head first.

"No, he wasn't in his room when I went up there to get 'em." Well, fuck. That's not good. "All right, we need to decide on retaliation and we need to decide now."

Popping a sucker in my mouth, I don't even pretend to suck on it. I bite hard and crunch that shit up into nothingness. "We go in, extract Jake and the two other motherfuckers who thought they could survive touching what's mine, then we blow that whole goddamn trailer park to fucking outer space."

"Hear, hear!"

"We'll watch them run around like fucking feral cats."

"Fuck those assholes, let 'em burn."

I have no idea who's saying what and it doesn't matter because all I hear is brotherhood.

"What about the women there?" Bear, the fucking voice of reason.

"What about 'em?" Grinder shrugs like killing innocent women doesn't affect him.

"They ain't got nothing to do with this, that's what." My head falls back on the chair when my Jiminy Cricket conscience comes tapping its foot on my shoulder. I don't want to fucking care but Mackenzie has made my heart regain some of its color red.

"They literally chose their beds, Brother. Now, they can lie on the burnt sheets." I point my stick to Grinder then turn to Bear.

"You can't fucking tell me none of those people in there knew what those assholes have been doing to my girl for years. Fucking years, Bear. You, of all people, know how fucked up that is."

Bear shakes his head, unwilling to sacrifice women who are basically pawns in that club. "Still ain't right, Psycho. Still ain't fucking right."

"Well, that's what club votes are for." Our VP chimes in just as Prez bangs the gavel.

"All for extracting Jake and the other rapists." Ayes ring out all around. I breathe easier knowing they've got my back.

"All for burning the trailer park to the ground."

"Aye." From me and Grinder right away, quickly joined by Boner, but in the end the "Nays" outvote us and that's fine. As long as I have Jake and his merry brothers of motherfuckers, my need for vengeance will be sated.

Because I will avenge my sweet Cherry Pie and bring home the trophy on a fucking spear for all the city to see.

"Tomorrow, we go in."

With the sound of the gavel echoing around the four walls, my monster retreats back into the shadows to bide his time.

Hours after I left Mackenzie in my bed, I walk back in with a hot plate of breakfast.

Church took another hour while we planned out the attack and made sure we had enough men to cover all the Rebels who would be there. Plus, we needed our prospects to clean out the Dahmer cell for Jake's final stay, not to mention covering our tracks so we're nowhere near the cops' radar.

I've debated telling Mackenzie but I've decided to prepare my surprise like a fucking proposal. It's not a secret if it's for the right reasons, right?

Right.

"Mmmm, it's too early for...anything." That throaty morning voice only gets my dick hard.

"It's never too early for bacon, Cherry baby. Our kids need to know this." I place the tray on the dresser as I prepare her plate and utensils.

"I think you got me confused with your baby mama fantasy." Her silly words are groaned as she puts in lots of dramatics, flopping from one side to the other and pulling the covers up over her head.

"Fantasies are for limp dicks, baby. I only deal in making dreams come true." I only brought one plate, no need for two. I'll feed her while she slowly wakes up. It's my job to heal her, get her back to some semblance of normality. It's my fucking honor to take care of everything for her. So, yeah, she can eat off my plate.

"Fuck off, Satan. I'm asleep."

Hmm, this won't do.

Placing the full plate of food on the nightstand, I reach back behind my head and pull off my T-shirt, letting it fall to the floor before sliding into bed and sitting up against the headboard.

"Sabrina made all this food just for you. Are you going to make me go down to the kitchen and explain that you're too tired to eat?" I have to bite my bottom lip in an effort to hold back my laughter.

"Fuck. Off. Satan. I'm not falling for your manipulations because I'm asleep." I can barely understand her with the covers muffling her words.

Plan B it is, then.

In one smooth move, I reach over to the side and scoop up my sleepy Cherry and curl her up on my lap, her legs close to her chest and her head on my shoulder.

"I hate you." There's absolutely no venom in her words, which makes me chuckle. "Also, that bacon smells really good and you don't play fair."

"Is that code for my cock? Are you saying you're hungry for my sausage, babydoll?" Just in case she's too sleep-deprived to understand, I flex my groin to let her know just how ready my meat is for her. Except instead of making her squirm, she just reaches down and squeezes my now steel-hard dick.

"Now who's not playing fair?" One hand goes to the top of her head, my fingers curling into the nest of blonde strands that look like they've been to war with the sheets, and pulls her back for better access. My other hand reaches out to the plate and I pinch a piece of bacon between my fore and middle fingers. "Open up, babydoll. Let me feed you."

Like a little bird, she closes her eyes and opens her mouth and all I want to do is devour her. Instead, I slide the bacon into her mouth and watch as she closes and starts to chew, a moan escaping her as she burrows impossibly closer to me. Fuck, I want her so close she's inside me, a part of me. Skin to skin, molecule to molecule.

"This is so fucking good." When she pops open her eyes, I grin. "Is there honey on it?"

"Yep." Then I kiss her, tasting cherries and bacon and honey and...her. Pure and unfiltered Mackenzie is now my favorite flavor that I can no longer live without.

"That's amazing."

It's only when the plate is finished that I let her go back to sleep with me curled up behind her, big spoon to little spoon, all the while my dick wishing for her hot, wet cunt to swallow him whole.

After spending all day in bed—which I'm never going to complain about when my sweet Cherry is beside me—we came down to the main bar room to be more social. Everyone is here, on lockdown, playing pool, shooting darts, talking and drinking and basically trying to get over the fact that Prez lost his close friend.

"I'm sorry for your loss." I tuck Mackenzie by my side after she shows her support to Tori, who's grateful for our open door.

"Thank you." Tori looks away, her eyes quickly filling with tears, but she fights the natural urge to let them fall down her cheeks.

Bowing my head to Tori, I lead Mackenzie over to the pool table as we watch a game between Bear and Bash when Shade comes up to the table.

"Y'all seen Python? He hasn't been here all day and I don't fucking like it." We all look at each other and shake our heads.

"I saw him late last night or...early this morning, I guess, when y'all were at Church." Looking down at my Cherry Pie, I furrow my brow.

"How did you see him? Did he come to our room?" Why the fuck would he need to come to our room?

"No, I went to the kitchen to grab something to drink and he was coming in from outside. I didn't hear him on a bike, though. I thought he was out there smoking or something since he smelled of cigarettes." We all look at each other with Mackenzie's new insight. "What?"

"Python doesn't smoke cigarettes. Or weed. At least, he's not supposed to." The disappointment in Shade's voice is palpable. Probably more so knowing Prez will be gutted.

"Oh. Well, shit. Maybe it wasn't cigarettes, though. It was late...or early. I could have been dreaming." Taking her chin between my thumb and forefinger, I squeeze until her mouth opens for me.

"Babydoll, this isn't on you, okay?" When our mouths come together, there's an actual crash in the room with gasps and "what the fucks" being thrown all over the place. It takes me a second to realize the commotion has nothing to do with the effect her kisses have on me.

"Oh my God!" One of the Khunts screams and we all turn to see Python stumbling from one table to another, pale and sweaty with eyes so red-rimmed they look translucent.

"Shit, let me go!" On instinct, instead of unhooking my arm from Mackenzie, it bands even tighter against her, like whatever is happening to Python could magically happen to my girl. "Aleko!" This time, her tone makes me act because this is bigger than me.

As soon as I let her go, Mackenzie is flying to where Python has just fallen to the floor without hitting it since Shade was there to break his fall.

"He's seizing, call nine-one-one and tell them what's going on. Aleko, hand me something soft and someone time the event NOW!" Without thought, I rip off my T-shirt and hand it to her, at the same time, Bear is kneeling at her side with his sleeveless hoodie for extra padding. She places it all under Python's shaking head, her hands prepped and ready to intervene by the way she's holding them out above him.

"Can't you do something? Make it stop?" Grinder has his fingers gripping his hair, eyes fixed on Python's ashy complexion.

"No, there's nothing to do except wait for the episode to stop and hope the ambulance is here sooner rather than later." Mackenzie answers without once looking up at Grinder.

We all breathe in a collective sigh of relief when the seizing ends and the shaking subsides. Except, as soon as that happens, my girl is checking his pulse on his wrist, then his neck, then her ear is at his chest, and before I know what the fuck is going on, she's straddling his chest and nearly breaking his ribs with every pump of her hands in a one-two-three-four-five rhythm. Then she's got her mouth latched to his, his nose pinched, and his neck at the optimal angle for air passage.

We all stand there, mouths open until I shake it off and position myself with my hands on his chest to relieve her.

The whole wait for the ambulance, we try to keep his heart beating, Mackenzie with mouth to mouth and me with compressions to his chest.

Crow, his sponsor, looks over, his eyes wide and full of pain. This isn't the first time a member has been lost to drugs, so we know what's coming, but Python is so fucking young. We all should've looked out for him more.

The seizing starts again and my woman takes charge, pushing me off him to do her thing.

I don't envy her job, I'm better at taking lives than I am at saving them.

Chapter Twenty-One
Mackenzie

"He's going to be okay, right?" Prez asks, his voice low, menacing, even.

The ambulance chooses that moment to arrive, the sirens cutting through the silence and tension like a rusty knife.

I don't want to be the bearer of bad news and I can't tell him what he wants to hear.

My heart is pounding against my chest, my head screaming at me that this is all wrong. I didn't exactly know Python well, but I do know that he is—was—loved here. Prospect or not, they're a giant fucked-up family and the looks on their faces as they all stand in a protective circle around us are full of sorrow. Vanessa is quietly sobbing into her husband's chest, Sabrina is comforting two of the Khunts, Grinder is on his haunches with his head in his hands, Bear is clenching his fists, and Aleko wastes no time in pulling me into him side-on, wrapping his arms around my shoulders as though I'm the one who needs comforting.

The seizing finally stops again and I check his pulse...I can't find it and a lump forms in my throat when I recognize Joshua and Katie, the paramedics, as they rush into the room with a stretcher and medical supplies. The club members all part like the red sea to let them through. Squeezing Aleko's hand, I unravel myself and put on my professional face.

I realize I know exactly nothing of relevance about Python at this point, so I'm unable to give them any useful information. I don't even know his real name.

"Hey, Mac. What's the situation?" Katie approaches first, crouching down beside me while Joshua prepares the stretcher.

"He's gone. About four minutes ago. He was acting strange, collapsed, then had a seizure." I keep my composure because this is my job, after all, but I also can't help thinking that this is another death connected to the ones we've been dealing with on my shifts a lot recently. All young males mostly, only a few females so far, and all seizures. Some have lived, some have died. It's becoming too common and I don't like it.

"Okay, thanks, Mac." She checks his vitals and airways anyway before looking at her watch. Immediately, she takes over, pumping at his chest to try and revive him. I sit back and allow Aleko to wrap his arms around my shoulders from behind me, selfishly accepting the comfort he so willingly gives.

Joshua is ready with the stretcher and they gently place Python on the bed before lifting it and rolling it out the door.

"Hoops, call Celia before this gets reported to someone else. Shade, come with me. Sledge, find out what you can about what happened. Get Bash to search his room if you have to." Prez kisses the top of Vanessa's head then whispers in her ear. She nods, determination on her face as he heads toward the door, following the paramedics out. But first, he stops with his palm against the wood and turns to me. "Thank you, Mac." Then he tilts his head ever so slightly in a gesture of respect and walks out.

I don't move from my kneeling position on the floor for what feels like hours, Aleko close beside me.

"You okay, Cherry?" He doesn't try to make me stand, content to stay exactly where I am, and his concern for me is just one more reason I hate this. He's the one who lost a brother today.

"Of course. Come on, let's get a drink." Shaking myself out of my own spiral, I turn to him and smile, quickly standing and holding my hand out for him.

As soon as we're up, Rea gets behind the bar and lines up as many shot glasses as she can before pouring a bottle of vodka across them to fill them up. Vanessa goes through to the kitchens with who I'm assuming is Sabrina, we have yet to be introduced so I can only guess, probably to make food because that's their love language, and most of the club members and Khunts surround the bar.

Aleko gives me that dangerous and sexy half-smile, though his eyes are cloaked in sadness as he takes my hand. Glasses are clinking, conversations are flowing again, and at a glance, the room would almost seem as though nothing happened. But the general atmosphere is more somber than before. Those glasses are toasting to what is now a memory, the conversations aren't as raucous as before, and this is how they're getting through this traumatic event. Together, as a family.

"What's your poison, Mac?" Bear hands a shot of what could be bourbon or rum to Aleko and I almost choke on air.

Aleko chuckles beside me because he knows all about my garden of poison that I was using to make the Rebels sick.

"He doesn't mean which one do you prefer to use against your enemies, babydoll." His grin is lackluster as he pulls me into a side hug, keeping his hand resting against my hip.

"Okay, now you're gonna have to explain that." Sledge sidles in beside Bear and grabs a shot of something from the bar.

"Let the woman get a drink first." Bear lightly taps him on the back of the head in jest.

"Tequila, please." The last time I had a real drink was my birthday. Which seems like a lifetime ago, yet it's only been about three weeks.

Bear hands me a shot glass full of tequila and raises one of his own. Aleko raises his glass, as does Sledge, and I raise mine.

"Down the hatch, up yours!" Sledge's British accent is difficult to understand at times, and this is one of them, but all three of them knock their shots back before slamming the glasses onto the bar. I shrug, when in Rome and all that, and drink my own shot, the delicious burn sliding down my throat. "I really thought he was off all that shit, ya know?"

"We all did." Bear casually gets Rea's attention and gestures for her to pour us another round. Others have gone off to tables with a bottle or two in hand to save them trips to the bar, I suppose.

"We need to find out where it's coming from, because nothing we deal packs that kinda punch."

Aleko's words surprise me, not that they deal in drugs, because that's pretty much part of the job description, but the way they seem to care about the quality.

"Celia might be able to shed some light. Hoops said she'll be here soon." Bear hands us all a fresh shot, which we don't toast with this time—although, I'm not sure what Sledge said can really be classed as a toast.

"Speak of the sexy devil and she shall appear. I'd chop my own dick off for a piece of that ass."

Bear slaps Sledge over the back of his head again, harder this time.

"You'd have to, Brother." Aleko laughs.

"Afternoon, boys." Celia approaches us at the bar. "Griffin around?"

"Nah, Prez and Shade went with Python so they can be there when his aunt shows up. Hoops is over in the corner," Bear looks over to said corner, where Hoops is currently getting a blowjob from one of the Khunts. "Scratch that. What do you know, Celia?"

I've noticed Aleko is one of the quiet ones in these situations, watching, waiting, plotting, assessing...but his arm remains firmly around me, his hand on my hip as we stand side by side.

"Luckily, I was already on my way after Hoops called, so Sheriff Hinshaw had no choice but to let me deal with it. Do you remember me asking what you know about those pills, the ones with the stupid smiley faces on the packets? Bottle of water, please." Celia switches from talking to us, to Rea, then her attention is back on us again in one smooth motion.

"What about the pills?" Short and sweet. That's my man. No...*fuck*, this is going to be hard.

"We know they're coming from a source outside of town, but we haven't figured out where yet." She barely hides the brief glance in my direction. "The college kids are sharing them around like they're fucking candy and none of them can 'remember' where they got them from. The seasoned drug users have been steering clear, but check your dealers to make sure nothing's going through them. For a lot of kids, when mixed with alcohol, they've been causing seizures and blackouts, and, too often, death. The parents are demanding answers we don't have, and not accepting responsibility for their kids taking drugs in the first place. It's a fucking mess." Celia lifts her brows and sighs, exasperated at the whole situation, before unscrewing the lid of her bottle and drinking down half the liquid.

I wish I had answers too. Hopefully, my plan goes off without a hitch and things can become clearer all round because this whole thing is messed up. It's gotten worse since I stopped running the packages with smiley faces and I can't help feeling responsible. If maybe I'd been a bit more subtle with the placebos or something.

My body stiffens and Aleko seems to notice because his gentle caresses of his fingers on my hip become firmer.

Obviously, I'm not saying anything in front of the deputy sheriff because I'm not that fucking stupid, and getting arrested for being a drug dealer so close to my end goal would not be okay.

Celia and Bear continue to talk about what they do or don't know so far, which isn't a lot of either, while Aleko does his listening thing. When she's exhausted her line of questions and answers, she excuses herself with an acknowledging head tilt in my direction before she leaves.

"I think I know who the pills are coming from. I don't know where they're sourced, but I have an idea of who's dealing them." I don't wait for Aleko to ask, because I do believe in his no secrets or lies statement, even though I'm choosing not to divulge everything. It's for his benefit.

Bear isn't listening to my whispered words, he's ordering more drinks, his back to us.

"Go on, Cherry. You can tell me." All I see is honesty in his pale blue eyes, never once has this man lied to me.

"The Toxic Rebels."

CHAPTER TWENTY-TWO

ALEKO

It's race night, and even though we should all be buzzing with amped up adrenaline for the events to come, the normal rush just isn't there. Python's death is taking a toll on all of us, with Prez taking the brunt of it.

Guilt is an emotional cancer infecting every honorable inch of us until all that's left is a tumorous version of who we used to be. There's no chemo for that, no amount of marijuana to take away the pain. All we have is time to learn to live with it.

The coroner hasn't released the body yet since it was a suspicious death directly connected to an ongoing investigation, therefore needing an extensive autopsy. This means the funeral will have to wait until the state releases Python into his aunt's care.

Goddammit. I fucking thought he was clean, and with all the shit going on, we should have checked on him more often to make sure he wasn't losing his shit.

Everything is ready for the race. The bikes are in prime condition, secured to the trucks and waiting to be hauled over to wherever the runway will be determined. We generally get a text message about an hour before the go-time to give those coming from outside of Rockford Beach enough leeway to get here.

The organizers have never fucked up this part of the drill. The messages are sent through an app and every person requesting access is vetted to within an inch of their privacy.

This gives me plenty of time to pick up Mackenzie at work and still make it back to the compound to gear up.

As usual, Ninja is in his pouch, his tiny pink nose going a million miles a second sniffing all around him. I promised my girl I wouldn't go inside the firehouse since killing Ryan would not go unnoticed. She knows me so well.

"Calm down, you little psycho rat." Ninja is turning in quick circles, losing his mind with excitement and I don't need to look up to know my Cherry Pie is walking down the large circular drive that accesses the firehouse.

Fuck, everything about her makes my body relax like she's a calm and soothing balm over my hyper-tensed nerves. It's fucking addictive, this serene feeling.

"Hey," she greets, quickly looking over her shoulder then back at me. "You ready?"

Ninja finally gets free, almost slipping in his haste to get to Mackenzie, but as soon as he's sniffing at her neck and purring when she starts scratching at his stomach, I grin at that little fucker.

"You okay?" I ignore her question because I don't like the way she's trying to hurry us out, being all twitchy and shit.

"Yeah, of course. I'm fine. Just excited about seeing you race." My eyes roam over her face and I notice her usual spark is dimmed under heavy lids and slightly downturned lips. She's tired, that much is to be expected after a twenty-four shift, but there's more, something underneath it all and I can't quite put my finger on it.

"Any stupid people blowing themselves up for the Fourth of July celebrations?" The news said there are specific days on the calendar when people show the limits to their mental capacities, Independence Day being one of them.

"One guy now has a permanent hole in his hand," she deadpans. Then her sad eyes meet mine and she whispers, "Another overdose. Same pills. It's fucking crazy, Aleko." I can't talk about this, it's too soon, only days since Python's death and the pain of his absence is like a stab to my chest. So, I bring her in and squeeze the fuck out of her before she takes a step back and away from me.

"Well, my little Cherry Pie, let's go make some memories." Before she can put on the helmet I brought for her, I dart out my hand and pull her to me. We're so close that my breaths are her breaths and my beating chest vibrates in her beating chest. "You're not telling me something, Cherry baby, but I'm choosing to let that go. For now. But I promise you this, babydoll, you will fucking tell me after the race when it's just you and me and nothing but time." And because I can't fucking help myself, I slam my lips to hers and demand entrance for a kiss so bruising it makes her moan into my mouth.

When we finally make it back to the compound, the excitement of the race is palpable. The dark cloud of Python's absence weighs on us but these races are what we live for, the reason we even exist. Sure, we delve into some illegal activities outside the street racing but really, it's all about feeding our hunger for speed. For that ultimate adrenaline rush. These races are our great wars and our grabs for power. They give us a place in the world and winning is like standing on the ultimate throne.

"This bike is incredible. Who did the fine tuning?" I watch her closely, take in every tick and every crease of her brows when something confuses her or fascinates her. There's no way anyone could mistake her for a Khunt, she's too invested in the mechanics of the machine, seconds away from literally getting her hands dirty.

"Sledge. Always Sledge. He's our official mechanic for our race bikes. We're too superstitious to change our rituals." Standing behind her, I wrap my arms around her waist and bring my lips to her neck. She stiffens at first, like her first reaction to my touch, or any touch, is to shy away. Every time she flinches, I bite down on my tongue to avoid telling her how I'm going to rip her brother from limb from fucking limb for what he's done. His list of crimes is long but the only one that matters is the one at the top: hurting Mackenzie.

"Magnesium wheels? Holy shit! Those are what they use for the MotoGP, they're insanely expensive." Squirming, she tries to free herself of my hold but fuck that, I just take a step closer to my second-favorite bike, Elektra, that I only use for racing.

"Only the best to win, baby."

"She's a beauty, that's for sure. But…" Turning to face me again, she narrows her eyes and pins me with a glare. "Serious question, Aleko. And this will determine if it'll even work between us." I scoff at the ridiculous notion that we're not forever. Crazy Cherry.

"Yeah, I don't think so. No matter what I say, you and me…we're not going anywhere. Hit me." Crossing my arms over my chest, I brace myself for the worst. I have no idea what she could ask me, the possibilities are endless and half of them would scare the shit out of her.

"Best MotoGP rider"—I'm about to throw out the only acceptable answer when she tacks on the last part of the question—"within the last ten years?" Little minx wants to make me work for it.

"The logical response here would be Marc Marquez but even at his worst, Valentino Rossi was the most impressive. The man is a legend. He built his entire brand, created a school for young riders, and basically made Yamaha what it is today." I shrug, confident in my answer.

"Valentino Rossi is, indeed, a legend but Casey Stoner was a true rider." I blink at Mackenzie's answer. She's not wrong as far as her assessment of the Australian rider, but…

"Stoner retired in twenty-twelve, he doesn't count. Ergo, I win." I raise a brow, knowing it frustrates her because she can't get that muscle to do what she wants.

"Oh, by one year. I didn't mean ten years on the dot, jeez. Anal much?" My grin is wide, taking up my whole face.

"Oh baby, I'm definitely anal and if we weren't waiting on a text message for a very important race, I'd show you just how anal I can be." Rolling her eyes, she pushes against my chest and I grab her wrist, bringing it to my mouth and kissing the inside where it meets the base of her thumb. "How do you know so much about bikes, baby girl?"

"My dad." The wistful way she speaks of her father makes me want to scoop her up and hide her in the proverbial tower so nothing and no one can ever hurt her again. But, she'd probably have my balls for that. "We watched all the races, sometimes getting up at all hours of the night so we didn't miss them. Would drive my mother crazy but...it was our thing." She's looking over my shoulder as though her father is standing right behind me, her lips ticking up as she smiles at the memory.

"Sounds like a cool dude."

"He really was." We stand there for a few minutes, absorbing the weight of this moment when my phone chirps and we both jump at the intrusion.

"It's on." I scroll down the list of racers and curse. "Fuck! Cain isn't racing tonight, which means I can't challenge him for first place." I look at Mackenzie and scowl. "Who is he?"

"Jake always hid all the important club business from me." She shrugs, taking my hand and leading me to our Philia where Ninja has been sleeping this whole time. "Let's go win a race, Koko."

I frown. Yeah, that's not going to be a thing.

"No. That nickname is ridiculous."

"Says the man who literally calls me by a hooker name." Raising both her eyebrows in challenge, I open my mouth to argue that it's more a stripper name but am graced with the good fortune of common sense and shut the fuck up, giving her the win. Koko may become a thing and I hate my life just a little for it.

The entire compound comes to life as everyone spills out of the main building, effervescence bubbling over on this cool summer night. We ride over as a team, bikes rumbling, wheelies galore all the way down Highway 17 to our isolated location. By the time we arrive, the whole area is already set up with barrels on the side, portable flood lights lined up along the wide stretch of road, and the track has been cleaned up from any debris nature or man could have left behind. The organizers never use the same location twice within the same two years and I know this place was used back when I first started racing. It's an ideal spot with woods for miles and an old barn where people can hang out while they wait for the next race.

Unlike the other races, this one is filled with a tension that has nothing to do with the winnings or the rivalry and everything to do with the need to kill these bastards. The fact that Cain isn't racing pisses me the fuck off. Good thing there are rules and he can't just stay at the top of the chart *ad vitam æternam;* nothing lasts forever in our world. Eventually, he'll have to show up so I can beat him, take the money and the glory, then shove the fucking trophy up Jake's ass...maybe even literally.

"I need you to keep Ninja with you and I don't want you moving, Mackenzie. I'm fucking serious, you stay with Bear. Where you go, he goes and vice versa. We good?" I narrow my eyes, knowing damn well that although my race is short, my girl is capable of wandering off without even realizing it as she admires all the pristine bikes showing off their big, loud engines. Is that a little drool at the corner of her mouth?

"Yes, sir, we are good." I don't miss the sarcasm dripping off her tongue. Then again, even if I were deaf, there's no mistaking the dramatic eye roll she just threw at me. With a sigh, I look to the most reasonable of us all and beg him with my eyes to keep her safe.

"If they even pretend to make their way here, fucking shoot them in the nuts." Bear flinches at my request but recovers quickly enough to fist bump me and flash me his signature grin.

"No one's getting close to your girl, Psycho. I promise." Relieved, I look over his shoulder as Bash rolls my Elektra off the bed of the truck and runs a sheepskin cloth over her beautiful body work.

After I win tonight, I'm going to celebrate with my girl and maybe, just maybe, I'll find the right words to make her mine permanently. She deserves to know that I'm hers no matter what, no matter how. Sooner, rather than later.

"Psycho, Brick. Get on your bikes and head to the start-ing line." The race chief, Barney, calls for us, using his small portable PA system attached to his hip. He held the top spot many years ago, but has never held loyalty to one particular club. This makes him ideal for the race chief position because he has no bias. It's all about the wheels on the blacktop for Barney.

The flood lights reflect off his jacket, making him visible to all around. If a rider wants to call someone out, they do it with the race chief as a witness. He attends every event and is respected by everyone except the Rebels because they respect fucking nobody.

My adrenaline is pumping like grade-A cocaine, making my entire body vibrate with unspent energy. I can feel it...tonight is going to change the rest of my life and I can't fucking wait.

"Look at me, Cherry baby. I'm going to win this race for you." The sounds that invade these races fade away completely as I look at my girl and will her to hear all the words I'm not saying until later. "Then I'm taking you home and making you mine. You got that?"

Mackenzie's smile is slow to rise, like she's processing my words and understanding the meaning behind them, but I don't have time to see if it reaches her eyes before Prez slaps me on the shoulder.

"Let's go, boy, time to show them how to race!" I grin at his words then wink at Cherry.

"Don't fucking move and, Cherry?"

"Yeah, Koko?" I cringe and she giggles, knowing Bear just heard that shit and I'm never going to fucking live that shit down...ever.

"I fucking love you, baby. This one's for you." Our mouths crash together in heat and relief and even if I don't give her the time, I can feel the love seep into me and give me that extra ingredient to win this race.

Pulling a sucker out of my jacket pocket, I unwrap it and push it between my woman's plump red lips. "When I win, you can swap that for my cock." I grab my crotch crudely and wink, wanting to bottle the laugh that escapes her.

Then I leave, jumping on Elektra and pushing the helmet over my head, clasping the chin strap tight, and make sure it's all secure. Engines are revving all around, people screaming and cheering for their favorite racer. When I look over at Brick, I fight the urge to fucking kill him with my bare hands, but the half-naked woman standing between us starts swinging the red cloth over her head so I turn my complete attention to the end of the runway, my eyes dictating to the bike where we need to go.

The rule is simple: the bike always follows the eye of the rider.

From the corner of my eye, I see the cloth drop and I'm off like a fucking bullet and heading straight to Hell.

Chapter Twenty-Three

Bear

"You don't have to babysit me, you know. I'll be fine." Psycho's old lady has her arms folded across her chest and a cute pout on her pink lips. Ninja is running around the flatbed having the time of his life.

"I made a promise to my brother. I'm going to keep it." The revving of engines brings my attention back to the race as Psycho and Brick set off. There's a barrel at the end for them to circle before returning to the finish line.

Brick called Psycho out to try and take the second spot on the rankings, but he's got no fucking chance. The differences between what the Rebels ride and what we ride are monumental, and it's obvious by the dull paintwork that they clearly have no time for the proper care and attention a motorcycle needs. It's surprising their bikes last the five minutes on the track at all.

I'm up for a cash race tonight against a rider called Nero from Surf City, no rankings involved. He's good, but he cuts his corners too tight and loses speed. Should be an easy win.

"Need to pee, I'll be right back."

Watching her jump off the back of the truck bed, I shake my head as she begins to wander off into the fray of people. It's like she doesn't care about her own safety but, luckily, there are a whole lot of bodies between our club and the Rebels. Toxic fucks.

She jumps when I put a hand on her shoulder to let her know I'm still here with her, following her every move, exactly as I promised.

"Go and watch the race, Bear." Pausing, she looks up at me, even with her heeled boots on, she's tiny compared to me. "Please. Go." Her blue eyes are begging me to listen to her, but I won't. I can't. My word is my honor and my life on the line.

"No. But where are you planning to pee, because every-where is outside? There are no bathrooms in the barn." Would I rather be watching the race? Yes, but am I happy to do this for my best friend? Also yes. He spent a lot of time fucking around and can certainly be unpredictable, but with his focus on his old lady, he hasn't been taking as many stupid risks on the road with Philia.

Sighing, she turns with her back to me and her shoulders drop, then she runs. Fucking runs in the direction of the Toxic Rebels, her hand beneath her light denim jacket before she pulls out a gun. Points it at her brother...

Time slows down and I'm unsure if this is real or some fucked up hallucination. My sole focus is my brother's Old Lady, her face contorted with rage, her mouth moving, yelling, but it's like I'm underwater. My legs won't move, watching this furious woman taking a stand against her abuser, which is exactly what didn't happen the first time I was in a similar situation. My heart is beating erratically in my chest, the pounding between my ears making me lose focus on what's in front of me. What's important right now.

"I fucking hate you!" Mac's screaming, pointing the gun at her scumbag brother, circling herself so she's on the outskirts of the crowd near the barn right before she pulls the trigger.

Time catches up to itself, speeding up and I barely have time to blink before I chase after her. Within seconds, the deafening sound of more gunshots rings out, and this could very quickly turn into a bloodbath.

Yells and shouts echo through the crowds. Engines start, tires screech, and for a brief second I lose sight of her. I watch her brother go down and sirens blare, as though they were just around the corner when this began.

This spells bad news for everyone, because not only is street racing illegal, but the fucking gunshots are a surefire way to get us all put behind bars. The scramble to get out of here is quick, weapons are put away because no one wants to get caught red handed by the cops, and the area empties relatively quickly.

Then I see her. On the ground. Blood pooling from her chest through her white T-shirt.

The world stops and I barely register anyone around me, my sole focus is on my brother's old lady, her eyes closed, her body unmoving.

On my knees, I pull her head into my lap and check her pulse. It's so faint, barely even a flicker. Quickly taking my hoodie off, I scrunch it up and hold it against her chest, putting pressure over the bleeding wound.

The crash of metal and a bloodcurdling scream make me look up, seeing my chosen brother throw his motorcycle to the ground and run toward me as if his whole world has just burned down.

"What the fuck happened?" Psycho's eyes are wild and unfocused, paying no attention to me as he positions himself beneath her. I move to the side, expecting nothing else from him right now. "Baby, no, open your eyes for me. Look at me, just...open your eyes, okay?"

The sirens are louder now and I see two ambulances parking up close to each other, the back doors opening and paramedics piling out.

"Wake up, baby. Come on." Psycho's voice breaks as he holds her close, repeating the same pleas over and over again, his arms wrapped so tightly around her I'm guessing he'll be covered in her blood soon enough.

"Sir, I need you to step away, please." A tall man with a paramedic uniform approaches slowly, pulling a stretcher behind him.

"I'm going with her." Psycho doesn't move his eyes from his old lady for even a second, but he does relent his hold a little so the paramedic can do his job.

It's impossible to see the paramedic's face with his cap pulled down over his eyes and my heart is pounding out of my chest, beating so hard it's difficult to breathe. The sucker Psycho gave his old lady earlier is lying on the ground, forgotten, next to a pool of blood. Watching the whole scene unfold with uncertainty is just a reminder of my own past, my anger and helplessness eating me alive.

Twenty feet away, another paramedic is loading Jake onto their ambulance. There are no other Toxic Rebels around to see their brother off. Fucking cowards through and through.

The cops haven't shown up yet, just the ambulances and two paramedics.

"Bear, get the fuck up and help!"

Prez and Hoops have their arms banded around Psycho as he tries to fight them to get into the ambulance with his old lady as the paramedic presses gauze onto her chest wound. Fuck, man. This isn't good.

"I swear to fuck, Prez, let me go. Let me go! Let me go!"

I stand quickly, taking Prez's place and holding Psycho from one side while Hoops has his other side.

"Let me go, she fucking needs me!" His voice is raw from the sheer force of his screams, every ounce of pain inside him filtering through those few words. Watching him break feels like shards of glass punching through my chest. Physically and emotionally, I can't look at him without my own memories bringing me to my knees. But I stand firm with my brother because he's going to need us and he's going to need us whole.

I watch every move the paramedic makes, forcing my body to stop trembling when it's clear. So fucking clear.

The paramedic pumps at her chest a few times, presses his mouth to hers...

"Stay with me, baby! I'm right here!"

Panic rises in all of us as time freezes and the paramedic checks her pulse, then shakes his head.

The roar that erupts from Psycho makes me want to throw up with the force of it. That sound will stay with me forever and I'm struggling to stay strong for my best friend. It's fucking hard. I don't know if I can do it.

The paramedic is quick to close the doors, then, as though time has sped up again, the ambulance is driving off, following the one with Jake inside.

Only Sons of Khaos brothers and a few stragglers remain, and I wish they'd all fuck off because nobody needs to see this. Nobody needs to see Psycho losing his ever-loving mind.

Psycho breaks free of our hold, not that we're really trying now that the ambulance has gone. The anger radiating off him is palpable, and we don't even know who to blame for this. I didn't see who shot Mac.

"I'm going to fucking kill them all! Argh!" He yells out again and storms toward his race bike, which is currently lying sideways on the ground where he dropped it to get to Mac.

It's definitely going to need a trip to the garage, but that's the last thing on anyone's mind right now as we watch him kick the fuck out of the motorcycle.

Suddenly, he turns to me, his normally handsome face contorted with anguish and a fire large enough to consume all of Hell's circles. That anger is now aimed straight at me. "And where the fuck were you, Brother? I told you to watch her!" He comes at me and I know what's next. It's okay, I deserve it.

Quick as a fucking cobra, his fist connects with my jaw but I don't fight back. My best friend needs this, it's the least I can do after letting him down.

"You were supposed to watch her." Yes, I was.

Prez and Hoops pull him off of me before he starts walking circles around his bike, his hands on his head almost ripping out his hair.

Every movement is accompanied by a scream of pain until eventually, Psycho crumbles to a heap on the ground, yelling out incoherent words to a God who's not listening.

My heart is breaking for my chosen brother and I don't know how to make this any better for him. What I do know is that I'm going to need to keep a close eye on him because if I thought he was a crazy motherfucker before, this is going to push him over the edge.

I kneel next to him, resting my arm across his back in some kind of comfort. He's trembling, his head in his hands, the noises near-deafening.

"What hospital did they say they were taking her to?" Prez, ever the practical man asks the question to no one in particular.

"They didn't. They just sped off." My words are mumbled because my attention is solely on my best friend's sickening screams.

Until they suddenly stop. He's still trembling, but he slowly lifts his head, his red-rimmed eyes full of determination.

"Where the fuck are my explosives?"

To be continued in Psycho Love, Book 2 of The Sons of Khaos Psycho Trilogy: https://geni.us/PsychoLove

The Blonde One

We've been dying to write this story since Aleko showed up in The Escort Series! We've been plotting and planning for over a year and finally, FINALLY we have book 1 done, words on pages, all the things. There are things that we were always going to do with this trilogy, and things we changed our minds on halfway through writing the book :)

The characters, as always, have their own voices, their own wants and needs, and sometimes the way we plotted it is not the way they wanted it to go. So, of course, we've accommodated for our characters because that's what they wanted!

Writing with Brunette is one of my fave things in the world. Do you wanna know why? Because she's a freaking queen. We bounce off each other, feed each other ideas, generally force each other to write better because neither of us will accept anything less than our best! We both spend hours, days even, researching even the smallest details, because we want everything to be just right.

I even made myself watch the newest Fast and Furious movie—had nothing to do with Jason Mamoa who, by the way, is one of the best villains I've ever seen and would absolutely let him do bad things to me. And yeah, okay, it was completely irrelevant because they don't even friggin' race anymore!

Anyway, I digress... Thank you to all our amazing readers who take the time to message us, make posts about us, recommend us, all the things, because I swear, these things give us life!

Also, thank you to our amazing Betas, Alphas, general cheerleaders. You are ALL Royalty to us! <3

So... onto book 2...

Where oh where could we be taking this story now...? ;)

THE BRUNETTE ONE

I swear doing this after Blondie is a challenge because she says it all and says it so well.

Aleko, Aleko, Aleko…

As Blondie mentioned, this book had some preliminary ideas all mapped out but dayum, Aleko was all… "Nah, I'm not down with that shit." Obviously, we changed it. Like… completely rewrote the first five chapters.

But I'm okay with that because writing with Blondie means forging the perfect story for our characters. It's such an honor to write with someone who takes as much pride and self-discipline when it comes to her writing. At this point, she's not allowed to leave me.

Now, I know a LOT of you have questions concerning the ending. In fact, as I write this I'm anticipating the DMs with lots of growling and threats. But y'all…you know us by now, this shouldn't even be on the top ten of the shocking shit we do in books.

We do apologize for that cliffy, it's brutal, we know. However, we pride ourselves on putting out books quick enough to keep you satisfied...we hope. Do not fret, the answers will come relatively quickly in book 2.

Writing can be a lonely process but publishing can be hard and time-consuming. As of February 1st, that work-load has been alleviated with the support of Hudson Indie Ink. We now have Blake, Claire, and Libby to help us focus on our writing and less on our marketing. Thank you for taking a chance on us, we hope to make you proud.

As always, we thank you, the readers, for giving our stories a try. Some of you have been with us since the very beginning. You have no idea how much that means to us. We may not say it every day but YOU have made a difference in our lives and one day we'll find a way to thank you.

So, yeah...keep reading, keep reviewing, keep sharing the love and we'll keep writing and entertaining you with our funny author pseudo-drama!

A special shout out to Hilary, Zoe, and Sarah for taking apart our words so we could put them back together...better.

Sam O'Neill, our saving grace, thank you for making sure we don't screw it all up to hell. Seriously, I don't know where we'd be without you. Oh wait, that's right...in a fetal position.

Candi Kane PR...not sure where we'd be without you, thank you for all your help, beyond your job description. You saved us!

Mandy from Bookish Girls...your support is everything, thank you for forcing our books onto your friends (hopefully they still love you for it!), we truly appreciate every single thing you do for us!

And David? We love your face.

Stalk Us

Website & Newsletter: www.author-no-one.com
Facebook: https://geni.us/Facebookauthor
Facebook Group: https://geni.us/FierceReaders
Instagram: https://geni.us/Instagramauthor
Goodreads: https://geni.us/Goodreadsauthor
Bookbub: https://www.bookbub.com/profile/n-o-one
YouTube Channel: N.O One @darkromanceauthor htt
ps://geni.us/YouTubeAuthor
Pinterest: https://geni.us/Pinterestauthor
TikTok: https://geni.us/TikTokauthor
Linktree: https://linktr.ee/n.o.one

MORE BOOKS BY N.O. ONE

Dark Romance

The Escort Series (MF)

The Rich One ~https://geni.us/TheRichOne

The Kinky One ~https://geni.us/TheKinkyOne

The Filthy One ~https://geni.us/TheFithyOne

The Broken One ~https://geni.us/TheBrokenOne

The Almost One ~https://geni.us/TheAlmostOne

The Forever One ~https://geni.us/TheForeverOne

KOK (RH)

Kings of Kink ~https://geni.us/KingsOfKink

The Reapers Mafia Crew Duet (MF)

One Kill ~https://geni.us/TheReapers1
One Love ~https://geni.us/TheReapers2

Sons Of Khaos

The Psycho Trilogy (MF)

Psycho Hate ~ https://geni.us/PsychoHate
Psycho Love ~ https://geni.us/PsychoLove
Psycho Reign ~ https://geni.us/PsychoReign

A Night To Remember Auction - Shared World (MF)

Once Upon A Sale ~ https://geni.us/OnceUponASale
Books in the Auction Shared world by other authors ~
https://www.amazon.com/dp/B0CLKVXLXJ

Sons Of Khaos

The Standalones

Bear Hunt (MF) ~ https://geni.us/SOKBearHunt

Molly Shelby

Dark Romance

Date with the Devil (MF) ~ https://geni.us/DWTD

EVA LENOIR

Contemporary

The UCC SAGA

Disheveled ~http://amzn.to/2arpbXp

Disarmed ~http://amzn.to/2myvxNn

Discarded ~https://amzn.to/2vWTRPf

UCC Boxset ~https://amzn.to/3ljvepE

Contemporary Standalone

The Wish ~https://amzn.to/2FTiKQB

Supernatural

Soul Guardians Series

Reprise ~https://bit.ly/3cT9nPe

Other Hudson Indie Ink Authors

Paranormal Romance/Urban Fantasy

Stephanie Hudson

Tatum Rayne

Xen Randell

Sorcha Dawn

Georgia Seren Mills

Crime/Action

Blake Hudson

Jack Walker

Contemporary Romance

Gemma Weir

Nikki Ashton

Nicky Priest

Jax Knight

N.O. One